The Valkyrie Profiles

K. S. Daniels

Open Field
Mobile

Edited by Heather Wilkins
And Susan Basham
Cover Art by Ana Cruz

ISBN-10: 0615751199
ISBN-13: 978-0615751191

ACKNOWLEDGMENTS

I'd like to send out a wholehearted thank you to the many people who supported and encouraged me through the long, tedious process of writing this novel. First, of course, my family for putting up with me and giving me the time and space I so desperately required to work. Heather Wilkins, for being a gracious and wonderful editor. Ana Cruz, for lending her artistic talents to the creation of a book cover that truly is a work of art. Dr. Larry Beason, Dr. Annmarie Guzy, Dr. Cristopher Hollingsworth, and Carolyn Haines for the much needed direction in the early stages of this novel. Dr. Kent Clark for making sure my physics was actually physics. My father, Robert Skinner, and my Grandfather, James Skinner Jr., for introducing me to the masters of Science Fiction so I could learn from the best of the best.

CONTENTS

The Valkyrie Profiles

1

EPILOGUE TO A FUNERAL

It had been a private execution and Vladia Robespierre tried hard to be grateful for it. She tried even harder to be grateful she'd not been condemned to join her mother in death.

As the black funeral auto glided down the crowded streets of St. Petersburg, turning buildings into blurs of brick and mortar, Vladia, a girl of no more than eleven, sat motionless in the back seat with crossed ankles that didn't quite reach the floor and gloved hands folded over her lap. This city had once been an epicenter of fine architecture, but the entire continent had been literally burnt to the ground almost a hundred years ago. In her school books there had been tell of cathedrals and castles long gone. There were no holos, only some crude, two-dimensional representations remained. But Vladia could imagine and that's just what she did. Looking out the window, she replaced the stoic, grey skyscrapers with lavish structures that rolled like country hills–stained glass on every one. This city was her home now and she could feel it suffocating the life from her. If she'd been more vocal during her confinement, she'd be making this trip in a coffin; maybe that would have been for the best, she thought.

Brushing a blonde, frizzy curl from her face, she dared a glance at the lean man beside her. She wanted to hate his kind. The anger she harbored ached for an outlet. She needed to hate someone. Everyone already hated him so it was convenient if nothing else.

The man's eyes shifted to meet hers as he asked, "Is there anything you need, Miss Vladia?"

He had dark, brown eyes, large and deep like a dog's, and rust colored hair. His eternally youthful countenance was expressionless, but seemed to mask a quality of innocence not even children possessed anymore. She didn't answer. Instead, looking back down at her lap, she remained silent, fingering the onyx lace that trimmed the bottom of her dress. She focused on the movements of her hands, crinkling then straightening the hem as the man continued to examine her. She knew she couldn't hate those eyes. They were much too loyal.

"Miss Vladia, your blood pressure is slightly elevated, as is your pulse. These are unhealthy signs for a girl your age." He waited for a response, but when none came he continued. "If you wish to seek medical assistance before we arrive you must tell me, as I am responsible for your well-being until we have reached your father's estate."

Vladia winced at the word 'father'. She knew it was a strange term; one might even go as far as to call it vulgar. Most children never heard it, let alone used it. The Government Rearing Facilities had long since taken the place of mothers and fathers for all but the most wealthy of the aristocracy. She'd been raised by her mother, but even she'd never called her by that. Now she was being shuffled away to a father. It was the first time in her life she almost wished for the normalcy of a proper childhood. To be raised by qualified strangers certified in child rearing. To have a State Nanny she would share with a group of other children, instead of a blood mother who had been wonderfully intelligent and loving, but utterly careless. If her mother had been state trained, Vladia was certain she'd not be in her current predicament.

Vladia looked again to the man sitting stiffly by her side. She remembered this face; it was one of her models. All models from a particular series had the same shell so it was a difficult task to tell specific units apart. This one was a Gen D model. Their uniforms differentiated them by rank and purpose, but even the robot was dressed in black today.

"What's your name?" she asked, finally.

"My designation number is HCV-1178, division B, formerly under the command of Dr. Robespierre," he replied.

Vladia nodded in approval. "You are a Gen D then."

"Affirmative."

"That's a good model," Vladia commented absently. She felt tears welling up in her eyes again. The only other person she'd ever seen cry was Maria so there was a strange comfort in them.

It had all happened in less than a week. The facility was raided, tipped off by a disgruntled employee perhaps, the new models confiscated, and her mother taken into custody. That was just day one. There was no trial; no need for that. Maria Robespierre had broken the law and the evidence was in every new model she'd installed the modified nanobots in. They were progressive nanos capable of adaptation, not just comprehension and repairs.

It would allow the new models to evolve, like humans. That made them a threat and her mother a criminal. So the Terran Government punished her, first by destroying all the research documents, and then Maria Robespierre was executed.

Dr. Robespierre had been brilliant. Even her enemies, and she'd acquired quite a few over the years, attested to that. A first-rate roboticist and a pretty good pilot as well. Even though her research kept her busy, Vladia didn't mind; she had always been proud of Maria's work. But once she was gone, it wasn't her brilliance Vladia thought of. It was Maria's smile and soft hugs, her dark brown hair that always smelled faintly of spiced ginger and vanilla, nothing at all like Vladia's golden locks. And her kindnesses, not just to her, but everyone she worked with, even the robots.

Vladia also remembered her frailness. The woman had always seemed so small compared to the world around her. Maria had been a rule breaker and a boundary pusher, but that behavior had taken its toll and the last few years it was evident even to Vladia. It was as if the harshness of Earth had finally broken her and all Maria could do was shrink away from it.

Vladia couldn't understand why she'd done it, and she'd be lying if she said she wasn't mad at Maria. It was selfish of her, Vladia felt. Maria had to have known what would happen to her, and to Vladia, after she was caught. The girl hated to think Maria had wanted to get caught, but that seemed the only logical explanation. Getting caught would put an end to it all. Maybe the woman had reached her limit.

Robotics was Maria's life's work, and her strange fondness of robots had hastened her end. Yet, it was more than work; it was an obsession. Vladia believed her mother truly loved robots, maybe even more than she loved people–maybe even more than she loved her own daughter. They were at least equal in Maria Robespierre's heart, Vladia felt, for she and the robots were all her children in one way or another. It was as if she felt a kinship to them that she did not share with her human counterparts.

As anti-robot legislation grew stronger, roboticists were subjected to harsh criticism and sanctions. It was a profession that was becoming dangerous and soon the robots, along with their creators, would be gone forever. Perhaps Maria wanted at least some robots to have a fighting chance? At any rate, that was a theory Vladia could live with.

She turned her attention back to HCV-1178. "What will happen to them, the new models I mean?"

"They will be destroyed," the robot answered, matter-of-fact.

"But why? Why can't they just remove the nanos?"

"The Generation F models are contaminated. They must be completely destroyed to avoid further contamination to other robots and computer systems."

"And what about you and all the other robots that worked at the facility? Will they destroy you as well?"

"It is a possibility. Once screened for contaminants, we may be integrated into other areas of the government based on need. The remaining robots will be destroyed," he explained.

"That doesn't bother you?" The robot's calmness about his own destruction made her uneasy. He was the willing prey and it felt all wrong.

"No. If I no longer have a function to fulfill then the

continuation of my existence would be meaningless."

"Just because the government doesn't have a place for you doesn't mean your existence is meaningless," Vladia snapped. She didn't know why she was pressing the point. It wasn't as if the robot had any say in the situation. Even if she managed to convince him, it wouldn't matter in the end.

But still, she pressed on. "We should start with a name. HCV-1178 just won't do. It's much too long. But I couldn't give you one. You're not a pet or a painting, you're a person so you must think of your own."

"Negative. I am not a person. I am a machine."

Vladia sighed and began tapping her black heels against the seat. "Well of course you are, if you go around talking like that."

"Your reasoning is illogical. Just because a person calls himself by another name does not mean they are anything other than what they have always been."

"You're impossible."

"Negative. I am following the guidelines of logic as intended. It is you who imagine the impossible, which is normal behavior for a young girl."

Vladia stopped her repetitive heel tapping, and the two rode in silence. She didn't know what else to say to HCV-1178. The talking had helped, even if it was nonsense.

Vladia reached down the front of her black dress and pulled out the large oval locket she'd tucked away before the funeral. She'd been careful to hide it lest it too become subject to confiscation. Unclasping it, she took the locket off and opened it, revealing a tiny holograph of Maria's warm, happy face.

Vladia peeked up at her companion who was once again staring ahead. "Do you miss her?" She knew her question was foolish, but asked anyway.

It took the robot a few moments to respond. "My logic pathways are limited for efficiency, not allowing me to express the emotion you are referring to. Sadness, longing, fear, happiness: none of these would be useful in my processes. In fact, they would be a hindrance." He paused, and then seemed to soften his tone. "But if you are asking if I notice the effects of Maria Robespierre's absence, then yes. Many have suffered in her absence and science will be at a loss without her further contribution."

"I miss her. It hurts. But that's okay because it should hurt when someone you love dies. I think you should miss her too."

HCV-1178 again took a few moments to answer. "People, and myself, would benefit from the continuation of her existence. In that regard, I am able to mourn Dr. Robespierre in my own way."

The auto came to a smooth halt. Vladia made no move to get out. She suddenly found herself with so much she wanted to say. "Will you come with me?"

"I cannot. Robots are not allowed on residential properties inside the metropolitan limits," HCV-1178 replied.

Vladia stifled a sob. Chin quivering, she couldn't even bring herself to respond. He was the last thing in the world that bound her to her old life. She wasn't ready to see this tie break.

The robot pressed the release panel on the side of the door; it glided out, then up and a gush of cool wind swept around them. Vladia's curls danced wildly around her face.

Without thinking, she leapt towards him, wrapping her pale, little arms around the machine's neck. HCV-1178 was stiff in her embrace. He made no attempt to return the affection, but neither did he pull away.

"HCV-1178, I order you not to let yourself be destroyed!" Vladia's sudden outburst seemed to have no impact on the robot.

She shut her eyes and tightened her hold on him. "You have not been reassigned yet and as Dr. Robespierre's daughter you are my property now. No matter what happens you are not to disobey my orders. Do you understand?"

To her surprise the robot answered, "Yes, Miss Vladia. I understand."

Vladia clung to the robot steadfast, too fearful to let him go. Everything, her entire life, felt as if it was slipping away from her. Despite it all, he made no motion to remove her.

Finally, she loosened her grip, and then slowly freed him.

Struggling against the tears, she took his hand and pressed the locket into his palm. "I want you to hold on to this for me. Just until you don't need it anymore."

HCV-1178 nodded and closed his hand around the gift.

Vladia climbed out of the auto and brushed the creases out of her dress. She smiled weakly.

Choking out a final goodbye, she waved as the door locked back into place and the auto drove off.

HCV-1178 unclasped his hand, revealing the little girl's locket. Without opening it, he tucked it into his jacket pocket. "Goodbye, Vladia Robespierre."

∞

The early autumn wind picked up again. Vladia stood rigid in front of the iron gates blocking the path to her father's estate. Although Vladia had never met the man, she did know a lot about his professional life. United Terran Admiral Urada Nikola Malthus, now officially retired, was a well-known figure in both the political and military realms of Earth. His military career encompassed the tail end of the Eurasia Civil War in 2215 to the beginning of last year. It was a time of peace–a fact he openly resented. He was reportedly a hot-tempered man, often engaging in conflicts with those he worked with. His skill was at waging war, they said, and a thousand years ago, he would have been worshipped like a god.

Vladia wasn't looking forward to their meeting.

She sucked in a gulp of cool air to calm her nerves. She wished HCV-1178 could have stayed, at least until she was safely settled inside the house. Wiping away the last of her tears, she walked up to the entry panel on the right of the iron gate. She placed her right hand on the sensory pad and pressed the scan button.

"11 dash 4 3 1 8 8 dash H B D dash 1 0 7 8," she recited her temporary entry code assigned to her just yesterday. She would receive her personalized code, complete with voice recognition and full body scan later in the week.

"Access granted. Welcome home, Vladia Robespierre," the interface chirped as the large gate panels receded into the walls.

Vladia let out a quiet gasp. What appeared before her was nothing like what she had seen looking through the gate bars. A labyrinth of exotic trees and vegetation greeted her. There must have been a holograph embedded on the gateway to keep the thieves away. Growth such as this was a rarity and people would pay big money to get their hands on a sapling. It was a sign of status to have a plant or animal in your home; her mother had only a small atrium of fruit trees. This was probably common for the aristocracy, but the idea that the fiercely stringent Urada Malthus would keep such a bountiful garden baffled her. She wondered in tepid excitement if there was also a dog or cat on the premises. Her mother had a dog when Vladia was very small, but it had died when she was six. Vladia had never seen a live cat before.

A red light blinked on the control panel, signaling that the gates were about to close. Vladia walked in but lingered near the entrance as the gate shut with a shrill creak. She squinted her eyes and, shielding them from the sun, could just make out the top of the house looming in the distance.

Her momentary enthusiasm had now faded. She wasn't ready for this. This was not her home.

Vladia was supposed to meet the Admiral at dinner, but it was still mid-afternoon so she saw no reason why she shouldn't explore the garden before going in. Besides, assuming the garden would be the only part of this experience she would enjoy, she might as well get a head start. She tried to push her anxiety aside and focus on the task of scouting out an animal.

Vladia skirted around the edge of the estate first, noting many strange hybrid species of both trees and plants. Removing her gloves, she touched the velvety petals of a group of black poinsettias. There were also a few familiar ones such as clusters of pink Japanese snowballs and plum trees. These were plants her mother had kept in the enclosed atrium near her office at the research facility. When the plums were ripe, her mother would let her pick a few to eat. Vladia decided to have a look at the plums to see if there were any left.

As she drew closer, she noticed a large cluster of brilliant blue maples to her left. In the middle was a stone table and benches. Forgetting the plums, she headed over to have a look at the maples.

"Hey!" a voice shouted from nowhere. Vladia froze.

"I said hey!" the voice shouted again. Vladia looked around. Seeing no one, she looked up at the treetops. Hanging above her head was a dark-haired boy perched on a thick branch, one leg at his chest and the other dangling down.

"Are you a maid?" he asked.

"What?" Vladia exclaimed, obviously offended.

"A cook perhaps? You look a little young to be a cook though."

Vladia didn't know how to respond.

The boy continued, "If you're either, you shouldn't be wandering about the gardens. It's not permitted."

She felt her cheeks going red. "I'm Vladia Robespierre. I've come to live here," she announced loudly, with more than a touch of pride.

The boy laughed. "Oh, I see." He shifted his weight on the branch causing star-shaped blue leaves to flutter down around her.

"Well, you are in all black, like a servant or something. Maybe you should update your wardrobe," he explained.

Vladia batted the leaves from her face and waited for the boy to introduce himself. But he just sat there studying her intently. "Well do *you* have a name?" she demanded.

"Do you want to play a game?"

"No, I want to know your name, boy." Vladia refused to be evaded. He'd already insulted her, and now he was ignoring her.

"I'll tell you what. Let's play a game, and if you win I will tell you my name and give you a prize," he negotiated.

She knew what he was doing; it was a play for seniority. Clearly, there was no point in arguing. This one was used to getting his way. "And if I lose?"

"Nothing."

"Nothing? Then what's the point if you don't get anything in return?"

"It's not that I don't get anything," the boy began. "If I win, then that means you lose, and *that,* as it just so happens, is all I need."

Shielding her eyes from sun, she tried to get a better look at the boy's face but he was too high up for her to see much more than an outline against the light. She knew how to get him down though. With a sigh, she answered, "Okay."

The boy began his descent from the tree. He was nimble and climbed down with relative ease. Vladia thought he was about her age, but once they were face to face it was apparent he was a few years older. He was tall and thin, dressed in burgundy slacks and a black shirt as dark as his hair. His eyes were blue like hers, but had an odd sternness to them, and she'd been around enough adults to know they were much too stern for a boy. Those eyes belonged to a soldier.

With a slight grin, he sauntered over to the table and pulled a compact game board from his back pocket. Sitting down on one of the benches, he motioned for Vladia to take the seat across from him. As she sat, the boy manipulated the tiny controls on the side until the board was full size, and the game pieces materialized on the surface. "Chess?" she asked.

The boy nodded.

She frowned. "I don't know how to play chess."

"That's not true. Everyone knows how to play chess."

"Well, I've only played it once or twice, so I'm not very good and–"

"Well of course not! How presumptuous that would be of you." The boy shook his head in firm disapproval.

Vladia couldn't believe how serious he took this childish game. This boy was a waste of time. Yelling at her, making her feel incompetent and adolescent, all over a game!

Her mother was dead and he was yelling about a game!

"How dare you scold me like a child when you can't be more than a year or two older," she shouted, standing up with a jerk.

The boy was unmoved, calm. He sat expressionless, watching her fight back tears. He was mocking her, and she knew it. She refused to let this continue. She squelched her anger and, locking eyes with him, sat back down.

"Pawn to G-3," she huffed with renewed determination. She had to win.

The boy looked pleased. Casually leaning his elbows on the table, he made his first move, which was quickly followed fourteen moves later by his last. "Checkmate."

Vladia blinked twice, studying the board again and again. There was nowhere to progress. Was it already over? Had she really lost that quickly? She wanted to contest her defeat, but there was no reason. He'd won fairly.

The boy stood. Vladia still stared down at the board. "You lost, Vladia Robespierre. You should reflect on this for next time."

"Are you that proud to have beaten someone who

doesn't know the game?" she grimaced, looking up at him with a burning glare.

"A win is a win, and a loss is a loss. After the end is determined, the means and circumstances no longer matter. If your life is ripped away, does it really matter how? Dead is dead," he explained.

"Of course it matters!" Vladia stood up, pressing her palms heavily on the smooth stone table. "If you play someone unskilled, the win is obviously less important."

The boy shook his head. "Dead is dead." He paused just half a second before adding, "Like Maria."

Vladia smacked him across the face. She turned her head hastily as tears rimmed the edge of her eyes. She rubbed them away, refusing to let this boy see them again.

When Vladia looked back at him she expected anger. Instead he appeared surprised, yet curious. He touched the pinkness on his cheek lightly as if examining a new sensation.

She hadn't really meant to hit him, but she was glad she had.

"You haven't got the slightest bit of self-control, have you?" He smiled as he spoke. "How disappointing."

The boy pocketed his hands and strolled towards the large house in the distance.

"Even though you didn't win," he called back to her, "I'll still tell you my name. It'd be a nuisance to keep it from you until you beat me. The name's Tolen Malthus."

Vladia looked up. Eyes wide, momentarily forgetting her anger, "Malthus?" she whispered faintly.

"Nice to meet you," Tolen said with a curt wave. She watched him until his figure disappeared into the trees as if he had never been there at all.

Vladia sat down, staring again at her defeat. "Reset

game, single player, difficulty level three." The pieces vanished then reappeared at their opening positions. "Next time," Vladia swore aloud, "I'll win for sure!"

∞

She stayed outside at the stone table until a maid came to fetch her. She was human.

Vladia, surrounded by robots all her life, simply assumed the servants wouldn't be human and she felt a twinge of sadness when she realized there would be no robots here at all. But when she thought about it, the robots that taught her lessons weren't servants and it certainly wasn't their intended roles. It had been her mother's way of negotiating around the Robot Regulatory Laws. There was a specific ratio of robots to humans for every home, business, and government organization. Maria Robespierre was allotted the maximum amount because she designed them. But she also found sneaky ways to circumvent the strict ratios, like using her older models as nannies and cooks instead of disposing of them to make room for new models and prototypes.

The maid, who was indeed dressed much like her, closed down the game board and tucked it away in her front skirt pocket. With gloved hands, the woman grabbed Vladia by the elbow and tugged her out of her seat and towards the house.

"You should have come in an hour ago. Dinner is on the table and Admiral Malthus is furious!" she exclaimed, releasing her grip on Vladia.

"I didn't know," Vladia stammered, taking large, hurried steps to keep up.

"Not knowing is certainly no excuse. Not in this house

anyway."

With her last statement the maid's voice had softened, but only slightly. Maybe she felt sorry for the girl who had been so suddenly displaced. Vladia would never know.

They reached the back door and the maid stood still for her scan, confirming her identity. The door clicked in confirmation; the older woman stepped in, but as Vladia tried to follow her she was stopped by a firm hand in front of her face.

"What d'you think you're doing? You've got to be scanned too."

With a gentle push, the maid forced Vladia back over the threshold and the door glided back shut. Vladia rattled off her temporary entry code and the door clicked and slid open for her.

"Now then," the maid pulled her through the doorway. "You've no time to change; let me look at you." She bent down to scan Vladia quickly. With a trained eye, she spun her around inspecting her like a doll before purchase.

"At least you kept yourself clean. The dining hall is out that door to your right. Go down the hallway and go through the fourth door to your left. Remember your manners. If you've got any, now is the time to be using them, girl."

"Wait–," Vladia began, stretching out her hand to stop the maid.

The woman saw her reaching and slapped her arm away, eyeing her bare hand in terror.

Vladia felt her heart sink. This was how it would be then. They really were scared of them. She had never known Maria to hold such fear, and of course the robots of her childhood could not fear anything. With a record low population caused by war, disease, and low birth rates, the people of Earth were frightened to death of contagions. Vladia expected the maid was further frightened of her since she was blood-born. It was a common belief that children raised out of the system were riddled with germs. For all she knew it was true, but that didn't make her feelings any less hurt.

The maid backed away slowly.

Vladia retrieved her gloves from her pocket and pulled them on.

After a nervous clearing of the throat, the woman gave Vladia a firm nod then went back to her duties, disappearing behind a far door to her left.

It was then that Vladia noticed she was in a large room that appeared to be a pantry. The walls were covered with white cabinetry with bright bronze touchpads. Curiosity got the best of her, as she typed in her temp code into the nearest cabinet. The panel flashed red. Apparently the Admiral didn't trust anyone, she decided. She wondered if Tolen was allowed any other access codes besides the exterior doors.

Vladia followed the maid's instructions and made her way to the dining hall. The corridors were dimly lit, the light coming from nowhere in particular. It seemed to just be there. She touched the bare walls and found them oddly textured. Even though they appeared to be just blue painted walls, the light came from there, that much she was certain. She felt ignorant in this house. Her mother, though immersed in technology, spent her resources on her robots, not her home. It had been simple, primitive even, in comparison to this one. She supposed the aristocracy, even her beast of a father, was expected to maintain things at a certain level of opulence.

Vladia ran her fingers over the walls, letting her nails

scrape just slightly over the texture as if to slow her approach to the dining hall. She didn't want to eat dinner here with these strangers. This would be her first meal outside of Maria's compound. For her, breaking bread with these people truly signaled the end of her current life. Any second she could stall that was precious indeed.

She could see the fourth door now and before Vladia realized, she was facing the ingress with hands pressed against the panels to push it open. Yet she hesitated.

"Come in!" a deep voice boomed from the other side.

Vladia reacted on command and found herself standing stiffly on the inside of the dining hall facing a long mahogany table with twelve chairs, places set at each.

At the head of the table sat a bear of a man. He was in an admiral's dress uniform, but that did nothing to hide his grizzly persona. His face was thickly bearded, salt and pepper trimmed neatly, and gray hair parted sharply on the left.

The large man threw his navy napkin on the table and cleared his throat. "Take a seat. Third on the right, across from Tolen. That is your seat, and it is where you are to always sit when we eat."

Vladia walked to her assigned chair and sat down. Tolen ignored her presence and continued to eat. All was quiet as she was served an adequate portion of smashed potatoes, salad and roasted chicken.

She picked up her fork tentatively and sampled each item. They were quite good, but she only intended to eat just enough to keep up appearances and be excused.

The Admiral finished his last few bites and wiped his beard vigorously. "Now then," he began. "There are rules in this house. You memorize them and do not break them.

"First, knowing Maria, I am sure she had no structure

for you. She probably let you run barefoot all over the place doing as you please. She was a genius but had no control of it, and likewise I imagine had no control over you. That will not be the case here. There are designated areas you are allowed in, and you will be provided appropriate codes for those areas. As you progress in your studies and training you will have the opportunity to earn the right to visit other areas of the house. Take Tolen here. He is allowed in the library; you are not. He has earned it; you have not."

He paused his soliloquy as he stood and, pulling on a pair of thick, silver gloves, walked towards Vladia. His aura seemed to encompass the whole room as his heavy footsteps knocked on the marbled floor beneath. The Admiral was broad shouldered and his frame large, but solid. Vladia felt herself grow smaller as he drew near. Tolen, head down and eating slowly, remained unimpressed and quiet. His dark hair hung just enough to cover his eyes.

"Second, you will have strict lessons from seven to sixteen hundred hours. You will have a private tutor for each subject, ranging from math and history to combat training and etiquette. Third, I don't want to hear you, I don't want to see you, I don't want to know you are even breathing unless I summon you."

The Admiral now stood behind her. Placing his great hands on her shoulders, which she now fought desperately to keep from trembling, he continued, "Fourth, I will weed out those bad habits I know have sunk in from being exposed to Maria. I couldn't fix her, but I will fix you, girl. The state should never have let that woman raise a child," he sneered.

The Admiral leaned in close; the musty odor of his

uniform was overwhelming. "Just because you are above the statute cut off for state rearing, don't think I do not have the power to send you there regardless."

Vladia flinched at the mention of the state rearing facilities. It's one thing to be born into one, but to be transported in at her age–the mere thought was terrifying. She'd felt the love of a real, blood mother, not many could attest to that, and that made her different, and frightening. Vladia knew she would integrate poorly. The other children would tease her, call her names like 'Blood Baby'. She'd heard this talk before the handful of times she had traveled to the labs with her mother. The workers whispered and leered at her like she was a failed experiment, Maria too absorbed in her work to notice.

A stiff squeeze on her shoulders brought her back to the present threat. "If you show no progress I will be rid of you. I will shrug you off as if I know you not. You can be a meaningless cog in the wheel of society or you can stay here and be a part of greatness."

His release was abrupt as the Admiral backed away, and Vladia let out a breath she hadn't realized she was holding. She remained frozen, looking intently at her nearly full plate of food, as she now felt both the Admiral's and Tolen's eyes on her.

"Tolen, after dinner you may use the library until bed," the Admiral bellowed as he pulled the dining hall door open.

"Thank you, Admiral," Tolen acknowledged respectfully.

The man nodded tightly then closed the door, leaving the two children to finish dinner alone.

Once the Admiral's footsteps were out of earshot, Tolen wasted no time in altering his demeanor. "Wow, you did really well! I thought for sure you were going to cry!" he laughed heartily.

Vladia, shocked by this quick transformation, scowled at the boy and resumed her meal.

"I hate to admit this," he continued, "but I'm impressed. After that little display in the garden I thought you'd break-down without a doubt. I guess you have a bit more self-control than I initially thought."

"Like I care what you think," Vladia huffed. This boy was annoying. His self-assured attitude, his overconfidence, his changing of faces. Is this the result of a father's rearing?

"I'm finished," she proclaimed, pushing her chair back from the table to stand. "Goodnight, Tolen Malthus."

"Wait. Don't you want to see the library?"

There it was again. That change in tone. What was he doing? Trying to get her in trouble already?

"I'm not trying to get you in trouble," he reassured her, as if perceiving the reason for her reluctance. "The old man's study is far from the library and not once has he ever popped in on me there. I just thought you'd like to see it."

"Why are you being so nice now? What do you want from me?"

"I told you earlier I don't want anything from you. It might be nice to have someone to talk to around here for a change. And since we're going to be under the same roof for a while there's no reason not to be civil. We may even be able to help each other out a little," he explained.

"I doubt that," she said, though that had been her hope all along. She wanted them to be friends since they were blood, but he was hard to like. Maybe that would change in time but for now she didn't trust him; he was as good as an enemy.

"Fine. Go on to bed then," Tolen took the last swallow of his drink then rose from his seat.

He hesitated for a moment. Vladia wondered if he was waiting for her to protest.

When Vladia made no move to stop him, Tolen pushed his chair under the table and moved towards the door.

"Wait," she whispered. After all she'd been through today, the last thing she wanted was to be alone in this house. He was aggravating, but he was the only one not afraid of her. They were born of the same circumstance and Vladia felt it was important for them to stick together.

The boy stopped and smiled. "Come on then."

∞

Tolen entered the library first, followed closely by Vladia. "Help yourself. We've got books on just about everything. Lots of old ones too, with pictures even."

He watched the girl's face light up. He'd guessed correctly that Maria didn't keep a proper library. Her mother had money, but she wasn't an aristocrat like the Admiral.

As Vladia explored, he plopped down on the floor and let his head rest on a plush, red pillow that was half as big as he was. He favored this room more than any other in the house. Circular in design, the kingwood bookcases built into the walls stretched all the way to the domed ceiling, which was decorated with sky, moon, and stars. The pattern changed with the time of day, mimicking the real sky in a sort of storybook rendition style. It was a rare thing to have a library with bound books, even for the aristocracy. But this house was older than most, dating back almost three and a half centuries, and when the Admiral purchased the building it became part of his job to manage the place. Luckily for Tolen, this included preserving and expanding the library.

He inhaled the sweet musk of decaying paper and closed his eyes. Maybe he'd just sleep here tonight. He had done so many times in the past, though never on purpose. Tolen liked to read real, bound books and sometimes the hours passed so fast. More than a dozen times he'd awoken here on the floor with a large book pressed over his face, his nose numb from its weight.

He reached above his head and dragged his half-finished copy of *The Invisible Man* across the rug until it rested on his chest. Removing the ribbon place marker, he began where he'd left off the night before.

Tolen must have read the same page three times before giving in to distraction and setting the book down. Out of the corner of his eye, he watched Vladia scanning the shelves. She already had two books tucked under her arm as she reached for a third.

Being of the same blood, he had expected her to favor his appearance more, like a smaller version of himself. Maybe it was just the stark contrast of their hair, but she seemed wholly different from him. Never had he seen hair the color of sunshine before. There was a maid that had blonde hair, but it was ruddy and thin. Vladia's was sleek from the centered part to about an inch above her ears. From there it curled in large loops that rested on her lithe shoulders. She was like a storybook character he'd read when his tastes were less evolved. Goldie something or other.

He'd never told anyone, not even when the servants pestered him about it, but he had been excited to have the girl move in. Not that being alone bothered him especially, but this was to be a new adventure. They would be comrades and he was certain, being blood related, that Vladia would be much like himself. It was true that she'd been a great disappointment earlier in the garden, but she did so well at dinner his confidence in her had been renewed. He tried to rationalize her intense reactions based on what he knew of people from his books and limited observations.

She was younger, so neither her mind nor her emotions were fully developed. She was a girl, which given his inade-quate experience with the opposite sex told him little, save that Vladia would likely be more sensitive and physically weaker. She'd apparently been raised by a madwoman and there was no guessing how that had damaged her. But, he decided, he could forgive her all those faults if she was willing to learn from him.

Soon after he'd become aware of Vladia's imminent arrival, Tolen remembered he'd spied the name Robe-spierre somewhere in the library before, so, he'd gone on the hunt. It took him a short three hours to locate the book on the poorly organized, traditional style shelves.

Essays and Research on the Robot Psyche: Progress and Implications by Maria Robespierre. It wasn't one he'd read as non-fiction held little to no interest for him, unless it was historical in nature and at that point it just as well might have been fiction. And this was about robotics of all things.

Tolen had never even seen a robot before. From what little information he siphoned from the maids' gossip, people seemed to hate them though, mainly because of their extensive use in the Anglo-Eastern War. And since the robots in stories were much too fantastical for him to take seriously, that was where his knowledge on the subject ended. He imagined that if he delved into the non-fiction section he was sure to come across a bountiful selection regarding honest-to-goodness robots.

Tolen had heard Dr. Robespierre's research had been all but destroyed. This copy had been a gift to the Admiral, according to the inscription in the front anyway, from the woman herself, and it was probably the only copy to actually be printed on real paper. In fact, Tolen imagined Robespierre must have had the thing printed privately, leaving no record of its production. Otherwise, the state would have come to collect it for disposal.

He planned to give this to Vladia so she could read it, maybe even tonight as a sort of welcome gift.

Vladia approached with five books in her arms now. Gently, she stacked the books on the floor and sat down beside him.

Tolen pressed up on an elbow and leaned over to view her selections.

"They're all fiction. Maria didn't have anything but research books and academic journals, and none of them were bound," Vladia explained.

"We've got those too."

"Thank you for letting me come here. I hope you don't get in trouble," she said earnestly.

Tolen shrugged. "It's fine. The Admiral is a collector of oddities, but once he has them he's quick to lose interest. I've the faintest notion he's not been in this room for years."

Picking up the top book from her stack, Vladia cautiously opened the cover. Her eyebrows scrunched together fearfully as if the book would disintegrate between her palms.

He had planned to let her be and read, but Tolen found himself longing for conversation. The sensation was so odd it made him feel a bit fidgety. "You know," he began, "the maids talk a lot when they think I'm not listening. I'm pretty stealthy and I like to procure information."

Vladia looked up and waited for him to continue.

"I'm just saying if there's anything you need to know that isn't in these books I can help," he offered, prodding her to question him. It could be trivial or nonsense or top secret. It didn't matter.

"Okay." Considering his proposal, she closed the book and placed the relic atop her book pile. "How old are you?"

"I'm almost fourteen."

"And you have been living here all your life?"

"Yes."

"So you lived here when Maria was contracted to the Admiral."

Tolen sat up and scooted closer to her. "Do you want me to tell you what I know about her?"

She was hesitant to accept the offer. It'd been her intention to get to this point he was sure; yet he imagined she now found herself afraid of what he had to say.

She finally nodded in consent.

"I told you the Admiral is a collector of oddities. To him, Maria was not any different than these bound books. She was a peculiarity, and he chased her down until he had her. It took three years before she consented. My own mother, Anjou, expired just after childbirth, and he was pursuing Maria as she lay dying in this very house. Anjou had her name drawn in the lottery, so she'd no choice but to conceive. I think the Admiral found it all rather disguising and would have cut all ties with her as soon as possible if she'd not died so conveniently.

"Anyway, Maria gave in and they made a contract together. It only lasted until he found out she was pregnant, about ten months. Maria was notoriously forgetful I've been told, and she'd missed a few of her injections. Having a child because your number is up is one thing, but having a child on purpose, or accident in this case, is unheard of. When she refused to abort, he had their contract dissolved and Maria left. I was almost three by then."

Vladia didn't seem all that surprised by this. She probably knew Maria well enough to expect that kind of behavior from her. But she couldn't hide her distress over the information as she pressed her lips together until they were nothing more than a pale, thin line. She drew her knees up to her chin and asked a sensible question. "Do you remember her at all?"

Tolen shrugged. "Not really. What I do recall is vague. I remember her giving me candy once. Of course it was confiscated as soon as the maids found out. I cried when they took it away, but it was rather foolish to give such a small child candy."

"She used to give me candy," Vladia reminisced. "Usually Martian. A lot of her colleagues immigrated to Mars and they'd send her packages. They wanted her to leave Earth, but she always refused. Maria couldn't leave her robots behind."

"That was stupid. She should have gone."

"She couldn't. She'd have died without them."

"She died anyway," he rightly pointed out, "At least on Mars it wouldn't have been in disgrace."

Vladia stood up with a jerk, toppling her stack of books as she did.

"The only thing disgraceful about Maria's death was the injustice of it! She was trying to save her robots from a tyrannical government that–"

Before she could say more, Tolen leapt up and tackled her, roughly pressing her mouth shut with his hand. She struggled against him, but he had all his weight on her. And three years made a big difference at their age.

"You are a fool to speak so freely," he whispered in her ear as she uselessly tried wringing her body free. Vladia struck at him with flailing arms, but she succeeded only in creating a mild annoyance for him.

"There are eyes and ears everywhere and I'm not talking about the Admiral's," he spoke a soft, final warning before releasing her.

Vladia's eyes were wild with rage as she pushed away from him. "You're the fool, Tolen Malthus!"

He remained silent. She was angry and irrational. There was no point in further discussion with her.

Vladia got off the floor; her hair and dress were disoriented from the tussle. She marched out of the library in a fury, not bothering to close the door on her way out.

Tolen waited until he could no longer hear her footsteps before gently shutting the library door, though in his mind he'd slammed it with a furious shout. In his mind, he'd also said a lot of choice words to that stupid girl. He was trying to stop her from irreversible damage. She'd get herself killed just like Maria if she continued down this path of careless disregard.

But he wasn't ready to give up on her just yet. Vladia was young still and Maria's death was probably making her extra irrational.

Tolen ambled over to a decorative, leather armchair on the far side of the room. Reaching behind the large pillow occupying the seat, he plucked a heavy, brown book from behind it. Flipping through the pages, he sat down in the chair to consider the situation.

Vladia didn't need this book. She would use it only to further feed her sick sentimentality. The book would hinder her, but not him. He harbored no emotional attachment to the book or Maria and it could prove useful at a later date.

He walked back to his spot on the floor, accidentally kicking his unfinished novel in the process. It skidded under a nearby chair, but Tolen paid it no mind as he settled back down and opened the book intended for Vladia.

2

CASE IN POINT

Vladia didn't set foot in the library until two years and seven months later when she earned the access code to it on her own. In that time she began to think of Tolen more and more as both a rival and an objective she must meet. They studied most academic subjects separately, but physical training was shared. They did relay courses, sparring, and piloting simulations mostly. Vladia pushed herself to keep up with the older boy, but was never able to come even close. He always earned better times on the courses; he always beat her at fencing; and he always took down more enemy targets during simulations.

Yet, Vladia learned to be less angered by this, or at least less apparent about it. That was the one thing she learned from Tolen: control over her emotions. Although often she still raged inside, she tried, though often failing, to never let anyone see her frustration. She admired this control of his yet it bothered her as well. He always kept her at arm's length, and she felt like she didn't really understand him at all. That time in the library was the closest he'd ever let her get. Neither of them ever mentioned the incident, but Vladia couldn't help but feel she had somehow spoiled something important between them.

The Admiral kept his word and was scarcely seen by either of them. He was like the boogie man: ever present, possibly behind the next door or watching through a nearby window. They were summoned twice a year to his study, once together and once separate. He reviewed their progress, explained where they should strive to improve, and conducted a sort of interview to gage their opinions, values and beliefs. It was nerve-racking. Vladia was fifteen, yet the man still made chills tear down her spine. She would never forget her first impression of him. Though he had aged, graying more and less solid in his build, he was still the same beast of a man who had once whispered threats of sending her to the state's facility with the rest of the population's youth.

Vladia and Tolen, now fifteen and eighteen respectively, sat in adjacent chairs outside the large, bronze double doors of the Admiral's study waiting for their last interview together. Tolen was leaving the next morning and she wouldn't see him again for some time.

Tolen sat quiet as usual, legs crossed and slouching slightly. He looked bored. His standard military cadet uniform was pressed to perfection. The dark blue material was crisp with newness. It was the first time she had seen him in it and felt a twinge of jealousy knowing it would still be three years before she would have the honor of wearing one. She was dressed in her usual garb: tan high-waisted trousers and a fitted black blouse. His uniform made her feel awkward in her normally comfortable attire.

Tolen had let his hair grow out over the years but had always kept it neatly tied back at the nape of his neck. Vladia thought it looked too much like all the other aristocratic snobs, but Tolen did it just for that reason. He gave them what they wanted at every level. Today was different though. It was his last day here and in preparation of the academy he'd cut his hair completely. Now it was trimmed short, neatly parted to one side.

Absently, Vladia tugged at one of her curls. She'd let her hair grow long as well. Her bright, sunflower curls were large and fell halfway down her back. They were a nuisance in the morning, she wouldn't pretend otherwise, but her mother had always kept her hair long and curled. Though they weren't dark like Maria's, it was just about the only physical feature Vladia appeared to inherit from her. So she kept them, despite the bothersome morning ritual of arranging them, as a remembrance. She too would have to shear her extensive locks before entering the academy.

She actually resembled Tolen more than she liked to admit. Their bone structure, build, and pale coloring were altogether similar. Tolen was slender like her, giving him a delicate, almost feminine quality. It made him nimble in combat and proved that brute strength, a quality greatly admired by the Admiral, was not necessary to win. Vladia, also quite agile, still lagged behind. The three year gap between them was something it seemed she could not close no matter how hard she tried.

"What time do you leave in the morning?" Vladia whispered, breaking the silence. She had a habit of doing that when she thought the Admiral might be in close proximity.

Tolen showed no such concern and spoke normally. "Five. Why? Were you planning to see me off?"

"Maybe. I thought someone should anyway," she said, raising her voice as much as she dared.

Tolen smiled. "You're still so sentimental. You'll miss

me then?"

"No. It'll just be strange. I've never had to stay in the big place with just me and him." Her eyes darted to the door with slight suspicion.

"So you're scared then? That's even worse. You should have just said you'd miss me."

Vladia should've expected that. She sighed and tried to relax. The wait this time felt longer than ever before.

Just then, the bronze doors glided open and a low voice called them from the interior.

The two stood and walked in, Vladia delayed a moment letting Tolen take the lead.

The space between the entrance and the Admiral's desk was great. It was a large room, about thirty meters long, and the pair had to walk the entire length of it to reach their destination. Their footsteps clicked out of sync and despite herself, Vladia adjusted her stride to line up with Tolen's.

They each took a chair. The massive walnut desk was all that separated them from the Admiral.

He didn't speak and continued to tap away at his datapad for several minutes. This was usual. Yet, Vladia still felt herself growing more and more anxious. Tolen, calm as ever, simply waited. Vladia watched the Admiral's brown eyes squint, quickly proofed whatever he'd been typing. The skin around his eyes wrinkled as he did so, making him look even more worn and ill-tempered.

"Well then," the Admiral finally began, still gripping the datapad in one hand. "Today is a special day. Tolen, this will be the last I see of you I imagine. The military will keep you quite busy, but I can read all about that and your accomplishments to come in the monthly reports. I expect you'll exceed most, if not all, in your class. Yes, you'll make a fine solider indeed. One of my own creation, modeled to perfection. I wished I'd had a hundred of you under me when I was still in command."

This was all meant as the pinnacle of compliments, and Tolen bowed his head in grateful acceptance.

"And Vladia, well, we've still got three years yet to get you ready. I expect you'll fare well when your time comes." This too was a compliment, barely. But regardless, she quickly lowered her head with respect.

The Admiral cleared his throat, making an under-the-breath sort of growl. "There will be no interview today. There'll be just one task before you go. Think of it as a reward for all your hard work." He motioned for his study attendant who brought forth a small, square table with a checkerboard pattern on it and a wooden box about the size of a bread loaf.

"Vladia. Open the box and set up the game."

She hesitated before complying. This was no reward, not for her anyway. Playing this game in front of the Admiral would be torture. Vladia had played chess against Tolen many times since their initial encounter and she had continuously lost, though never as gloriously as the first time. She had most certainly improved and could probably beat most other contenders, but Tolen was still beyond her. He was too clever at prediction and set-ups. A game could last close to an hour, but the end was inevitable. Vladia would lose. Going in knowing she had next to no chance was hard enough, but to do so with Tolen and the Admiral also knowing she couldn't win was painfully demoralizing.

She set up the pieces slowly, buying herself time to think. How could she pull this off? How could she not lose? She always studied his playing style, always watched his expression and eyes for clues that would give his secrets away. But he was straight-faced, looking completely uninterested when they played. He was impossible to read.

Vladia placed the final piece on the table and handed the box to the waiting attendant.

"Why don't you begin, Vladia?" the Admiral offered as if he was doing her a favor. Going first was horrible. It gave Tolen the opportunity to begin analyzing her strategy first, leaving her step after step behind.

She made her move and found it unusual to actually move real pieces by hand. She had never played on anything but the hologame boards where all movements were handled verbally. Chess had been a purely visual experience until now. The pieces were cold to the touch and clacked roughly on the table.

Tolen made his first move and appeared to feel no different about playing the game this way. It was probably not his first time playing with real chess pieces. Again, Vladia felt disadvantaged.

The game was well into the first hour, maybe the longest they'd played yet, when Vladia began to notice something subtle. Something, it appeared, Tolen did not. The pace of the game and Tolen's expression remained constant, but the sounds the pieces made when he placed them on the table had changed. They were heavier. Vladia realized that although more than half the pieces remained on the board and both queens seemingly well protected, Tolen was going in for the kill. Yet knowing this alone was not enough to stop him. She needed more.

So she let things continue and with each new piece he moved, the clack on the board was just slightly sharper.

He was counting down the moves to victory. The only way to stop him would be to alter her strategy drastically just before his final moves. But that would be difficult to pinpoint since the end could come at almost any moment.

Vladia bided her time, studied the board, and listened. After two more turns, there it was, she decided. The board was in a position so it appeared both parties were close to winning. Vladia knew she could win in five moves, but so did Tolen. So she made her next move and deviated from her plan entirely. It was an erratic move, designed not necessarily to gain or lose any ground, but instead aimed to confound her opponent into thinking he missed something. Tolen always won by predicting her moves, not just her next move, but her next ten moves. Well, he'd have a hard time predicting something that she did at random.

Tolen was already in the process of reaching for his next piece when Vladia made her move. His hand froze, hovering over the board in hesitation. The Admiral caught wind of Tolen's sudden loss of certainty and shifted in his chair. The leather made an uneasy chirr as he did so, interrupting the silence that had until now pervaded the room.

Vladia fought a smile. It was a rare thing to see Tolen like this, his absolute fortitude disrupted. For a brief moment anger blazed across his face.

At this point Vladia no longer cared for winning the game, for she had won at something far greater now. She'd broken his mask. She'd broken it in front of the Admiral.

All of this lasted no more than seven seconds. But those seconds were the longest in the world for all three of them. Tolen recovered and moved.

"Check," he said, anger not entirely absent from his voice.

There was nowhere for Vladia to progress that could counter this. Her unpredictable move had cost her the game, but all that really meant was now she was going to lose in one move instead of three. Vladia shifted an arbitrary piece and let Tolen take her queen. The game was over. Vladia had lost, but couldn't help feeling like she'd won nonetheless.

The Admiral congratulated Tolen, wishing him well at the academy, but with less vigor than expected, and then dismissed them.

The two walked to the exit in silence and once the door closed behind them they stood silently side by side, neither making a move to leave.

"Do you need his approval so badly as to aim to humiliate me in front of him before I leave?" Tolen asked, his voice was normal now: confident and devoid of anger.

"That's funny. I'm pretty sure that whole charade was set up to do just the opposite. Should I apologize for fighting back?" Vladia questioned, crossing her arms over her chest defiantly.

"If that is how you fight back I'm sorry for that. Fighting back should involve winning or you're not doing it right."

Tolen turned to her, making eye contact for the first time since before they'd entered the Admiral's office. "You should have saved that little trick of yours for something more important than a stupid game. Now, I've learned something new about myself and about you as well. I'll be much more careful from now on and don't think you'll be able to do that again."

"What's wrong with you? You act as if I'm out to get

you. Don't worry, I won't steal the Admiral's favor in your absence."

"You're so ignorant, Vladia." It was a rare thing for him to address her by name. This entire day was full of rarities, yet now it seemed to be taking a terrible turn for the worst.

"Haven't you noticed yet?" he asked.

Vladia shook her head.

"What the hell do you think all this training and preparation has been about? Do you think that warmonger is pushing us towards greatness?"

"Well, he said–" she began.

"He says! Ha!" Tolen was getting agitated again. "You lack perspective. Sure, he is pushing us toward his idea of greatness. You know what that is? Perfect, obedient soldiers. We're his test subjects, his guinea pigs. The soldiers he always wanted to command. Nothing more."

"You're wrong." It's all she could say. Despite the fear she held for man, Vladia had always believed the Admiral had their best interests at heart. He pushed them so hard and expected so much to prepare them for leadership. To think all this effort was for nothing more than to be a soldier, even a superior one, was insane. Children from the state facilities were soldiers. She and Tolen should be destined for more. If they were all the same then what was the point?

"You think I'm entering the academy under special provisions? Going into some advanced unit or special forces? No, I'm entering on equal grounds with all the rest of the eighteen year olds from the state. How else could he gain accurate results other than to place us with the regular cadets? If the Admiral has it his way, I'll become the finest cog in the wheel," Tolen clenched his fists.

"If you knew all this, why did you play along?" Vladia asked.

"What else would you have me do? Rebel and get sent to the state facility? I have my own plans for after I get to the academy. I've remained in the old man's good graces and have done all he's asked of me. One day he'll be dead, and his wealth will fall to me. So, he has given me an advantage after all." Tolen seemed to be relaxing now. The edge of anger had left his voice, his mask firmly back in place.

"Besides, I don't need any help on my way to the top. You on the other hand–I don't even think you'll make a fine soldier. I had hoped one day we would become great allies," he began, casually tucking a hand in his trouser pocket. "Yet you continue to disappoint me with things like that little stunt in there. You've barely changed at all, you know. You're more skilled in many areas, but you still lack control and let your emotions make the decisions."

He paused a moment, turning his back to her. "In a word: reckless. Just like her, you'll end up dead by your own foolish actions."

Those last, few words registered slowly in Vladia's brain. They crashed into her mind like heavy drops from a slow, leaky faucet. With the last drop, she reacted, taking a powerful swing at the back of his head.

In one swift motion, Tolen caught her fist, spun her around and shoved her face first into the wall, pinning her there with his weight. His left hand gripped her fist and pressed it into the base of her spine while his right forearm rested neatly at the nape of her neck. She tried to shake free but stopped as Tolen applied more pressure to her neck.

"Case in point," he whispered in her ear. "All I have to

do is press harder."

It was true. He could kill her right now and for a few moments, Vladia wasn't entirely sure he wouldn't.

The seconds felt like minutes. He released her slowly, letting her body slide to the floor as she coughed painfully. He stepped back from her as she pulled herself off the floor.

Before she had recovered enough to speak, Tolen walked away.

"Next time we meet, you won't be calling me by my first name. Despite everything, I expect due respect from you and a complete disregard of the familiarity between us. I'll not have our unfortunate upbringing alter my plans," he called back to her before he disappeared around the corner.

∞

Vladia's room lights came on at four thirty a.m. She had no intention of seeing him off anymore, but had purposefully neglected to change her alarm. She lay in bed watching the clock tick closer to five.

She was angry with him, but with herself just as much. She'd no good reason to be mad with him since everything he said was true, but she couldn't help it. She didn't want him to be right about her. She hated how poorly she'd responded to his words. If she could just make herself stop and think before she reacted. Her thoughts drifted to the robot that had escorted her to this house so many years ago and wished in vain she could be more like him. He couldn't have emotionally reacted to yesterday's situation. He didn't have the capacity for it and Vladia didn't have the capacity for anything but that.

At a quarter to five she sat up in bed and rubbed her eyes gently. She stared at her window that looked out at the front gate. She couldn't actually see anything since the windows were still set to blackout, but she knew that if she could, she would be able to catch sight of Tolen standing at the gate waiting for his shuttle.

She got out of bed and moved towards the window. Pressing her palms firmly on the window sill, she stared at the blackness. Her face was so close the tip of her nose touched the cool visoglass panel.

At five till five she let her hand move slowly towards the settings panel beside the window. Her hand lingered over the controls, not quite touching them. Vladia bit her lower lip and backed away.

No, she decided. She would not see him off in any form or fashion. Not because she was still mad at him. Nor was she being petty or childish. She decided then and there that she wasn't going to lay eyes on him until she was stronger.

She watched her clock count down to five a.m. then crawled back into bed, pulling the covers up to her chin. She had three years to prepare and was going to make the most of it. He was wrong about her and she would prove it. The next time Vladia would see Tolen Malthus, she would be ready.

3

VALKYRIE

Lieutenant Vladia Robespierre dashed down the corridor that led to launch pad C of The Kazan United Terran Military Base, maneuvering around other officers as she pulled her blonde curls into a lopsided ponytail. She yanked her gloves from the front of her maroon and black flight suit and jerked them on. After zipping her suit to her neck, Vladia quickened her pace. She was well on her way to being late for her first flight out since being officially instated into the Valkyrie Squadron, a position sought by almost every rising cadet, though only attained by a select few.

Vladia rounded the corner, narrowly avoiding a face-first collision with a lanky warrant officer. "Sorry!" she shouted as she picked up her pace again.

Ahead, two research assistants precariously held one end of a large specimen tray. She didn't have time to slow down. The assistants froze when they realized she was barreling toward them full speed. The one on the right let out a shriek and slammed her eyes shut as the other shouted for Vladia to stop.

Vladia dropped to the floor, slid under the tray, and did a forward roll back onto her feet. Breaking her stride to avoid the crash cost her only a few seconds. Straight ahead on her left was the hangar door.

She gripped the doorframe, slowing but not stopping, and skidded into the hangar bay. Lieutenant Commander Abel Duren, leaning against his Valkyrie, tossed Vladia her ignition key. "You're late, Lieutenant."

"I noticed." She caught the key and sped past him, towards her Valkyrie, *Freya*.

She'd met Abel during her first two years of cadet training when he was scouting for potential pilots. Not just anybody could pilot a Valkyrie. In fact, less than ten percent of the military could even sync-up with the machine, let alone pilot it effectively. This meant that scouting out new members was a year-round task. Abel was ten years her senior and had been a Valkyrie pilot almost as long. He administered both her career ladder test and her pilot test.

Her scores bumped her to the top of the Valkyrie candidate list, but even still she had to be wait-listed for four years and stationed in the Komodo Squad, a basic jet-style flight unit, until a spot opened up. This left her on the leadership ladder, which would eventually land her a commanding position on a dreadnought or destroyer if a spot on the squad didn't open up within a decade. Either way she would do well, but she wanted to be a Valkyrie, a position Tolen had held now for seven years.

In the end, it was Abel's partner that made a way for Vladia to enter the squad. Women in the military had always been exempt from the birth lottery. But after the wars, the migrations, and the phobias, Earth's population continued to dwindle. So the military exemption was revoked and Abel's partner pilot was the first military woman to be drawn from the lottery, allowing a coveted position in the Valkyrie squadron to open up. This placed Vladia one step closer to surpassing her brother.

"Doesn't matter much to me if you're late," Abel called after her, suppressing a yawn as he climbed the ladder towards the helm. "*Him* on the other hand..." he continued, glancing towards the Captain's Valkyrie, *Sigrún*.

Vladia climbed up the ladder and dropped into the cockpit. She took a moment to catch her breath, and then inserted her commlink into her right ear after switching it on. "Lieutenant Robespierre reporting in."

"Good morning, Lieutenant Robespierre. Glad you could join us today," Squad Captain Tolen Malthus buzzed in her ear.

Vladia felt her face flush. She began to apologize, but Malthus interrupted. "All right, sync up and begin ignition phase," he addressed everyone.

A rush of noise enveloped the hangar as nine Valkyries powered up. It was overwhelming, all of them standing together like colossal golems of metal and circuitry. Twenty-two meters high and six meters wide, each was unique in appearance but all were equal in massiveness. An offspring of the Bipedal Mechanical Engineering Division, the Valkyrie class was the most advanced means of hand-to-hand combat in both the sky and space. No other fighter of this size could match them.

Valkyrie class fighters were divided into teams of two: one Gunslinger and one Defender. The Gunslingers were heavily armed, a light-weight blaster mounted on each forearm, shoulder, and palms, plus back-up weapons attached to the backs of the crafts. Yet they were much lighter and more agile than their Defender counterparts. Because of their speed and maneuverability, Gunslingers could engage numerous enemies at one time. They were the offense, using hand-to-hand and short-range combat to the fullest.

The Defender units were thickly shielded and though capable of the same hand-to-hand techniques as Gunslingers, relied mainly on long-range attacks. Precision was key for a Defender. Instead of multiple weapons, the Defender had only two shoulder canons and a long-range blaster canon used to pick off enemy vessels so the Gunslinger could focus on offense alone.

Once synced, Valkyrie and pilot become one, essentially; it was Vladia's consciousness that controlled the Valkyrie and while the two were connected her body remained the anchor of her human consciousness. Since the human consciousness is not a separate entity from the brain, rather it is an accumulation of many different things (emotional responses, memories, learned habits, genetic tendencies, sensory decoding, etc.), it was quite impossible to take an individual consciousness and put it into something else. If this could be done, the death count in a war would be drastically reduced. Say the machine holding the human consciousness was destroyed. It could be transmitted back to the human body then sent back out in another machine with nothing lost but the machine.

But even if one was able to transfer a consciousness, and it was done successfully at one time, it was no longer the same person. The 'thing' became a new person; new as an infant. Language was lost, memories, whatever it is that makes you *you* was lost in transmission. So, the anchor remained.

Vladia sealed her hatch, cutting off all sound but that of

her own breath. She eased into her seat and strapped in. Inserting her ignition key, she gave it a quick turn to join the roar and clamor of the other Valkyries. *Freya* had received a thorough cleaning and a fresh black and red paint job at Vladia's request. This ship felt like hers now, every inch of it.

From the slim recess of her headrest, Vladia pulled out the cerebral connectors and gingerly applied the four sticky disks to the nape of her neck. Once her helmet was secured, she closed her eyes and after a moment of queasiness, Vladia and *Freya* linked as one. Her eyes were now *Freya's* as was everything else. Vladia could see a clear, wider view of the hangar through *Freya's* eyes. Lining the bottom of her new eyes were the stats of all her systems. There was no need to manually control a thing now, though she could if needed. All she had to do was tell, or think rather, what she wanted and *Freya* would make it so, if possible.

To an onlooker, it would appear Vladia was on the brink of unconsciousness. And in fact, her human body was very much in a state similar to sleep as her mind now controlled *Freya*'s massive body instead. But Vladia wasn't asleep and could still make her body move. It was the equivalent of thinking about one thing and doing something else. Vladia's 'thinking' controlled *Freya,* but she could still perform other tasks with her own body; not easily or fast, but she could do it.

Given the right equipment, Vladia could sync up with *Freya* from just about anywhere. But that would do little good in any situation other than training simulations; in a real fight any transmission could eventually be interrupted by an enemy. Physically being in the ship had other advantages as well. In a pinch if, say, a Valkyrie was hit and lost navigation systems or another critical components, the pilot was in the ship and could try to fix the damage or at the least use manual mode to get to safety.

"Good Afternoon, Lt. Robespierre," *Freya's* central computer cordial greeting resounded in her head.

"Afternoon, *Freya*. Ready to show these guys what we can do?"

"Always, Lt. Robespierre. Ignition sequence will complete in ninety seconds."

Vladia rotated her mechanical avatar's arms to get used to the oddness she felt at moving a body that was not her own. In her peripheral vision, Vladia spied a blue light flashing to her right, signaling that her private commlink was being engaged. She opened the channel.

"That wasn't so bad. He didn't seem angry at all," Abel's warm voice filled the cockpit.

"Yeah, well he never seems angry," she sighed.

"Ha, that's true. Nervous?"

"It's just a formation drill, Abel," she reassured him, and herself.

The ceiling panels opened slowly revealing the blue, almost cloudless sky. It was good weather for a flight, Vladia thought with satisfaction.

"Well, even if it is just a formation drill, it's still your first as part of team Delta. So, keep up and don't make me and *Gunnr* look bad. We've got a reputation to maintain," Abel said, referring to his Valkyrie as if it were a person.

Vladia laughed. "Roger that. I wouldn't want to see *Gunnr* embarrassed by my amateurness."

"For a big guy he's very sensitive, you know."

"All right, all right. See you two in the skies," she said, closing the channel.

"All pilots report in," Malthus boomed over the general

channel.

"Team Alpha Gunslinger, *Alruna* standing by," the sound off began as Vladia continued to work *Freya's* limbs about in preparation for take-off.

"Team Alpha Defender, *Sváfa* standing by."

"Team Beta, Defender *Geirdriful* standing by."

"Team Beta Gunslinger, *Alvitr* standing by."

"Team Gamma Gunslinger, *Reginleif* standing by."

"Team Gamma Defender, *Sigrdrífa* standing by."

"Team Delta Gunslinger, *Gunnr* standing by."

"Team Delta Defender, *Freya* standing by," Vladia chimed in last before the Captain's team.

"Team Omega Defender, *Hildr* standing by."

"Team Omega, Gunslinger *Sigrún* standing by," Malthus concluded. "Rehel, are you ready?"

"Positive," replied the robot monitoring the drill data inside the hangar control room.

"Beginning formation: Falcon's Reach. All teams, initiate launch," commanded Captain Malthus.

"Yes, Sir!" roared the pilots in unison as the Valkyries' feet and side thrusters fired, blasting them out of the hangar and into the crisp, clean sky. They continued to soar until reaching a flight level of seven thousand meters before entering the first formation.

"Hold at forty percent thrust," Captain Malthus' voice crackled over the open channel. "Switch formation to Odin's Spear."

Valkyrie teams Alpha and Gamma adjusted their positions accordingly. Vladia's team was positioned southwest of team Omega as they held this formation for several minutes.

"Begin ascension formation and prepare for atmospheric adjustments. Increase speed to sixty percent."

Freya's speed climbed as Vladia modified her position. Other than simulations and her test flights, this was the first time she had flown a Valkyrie as part of a group. It would also be the first time she would break the atmosphere and pilot in space.

"Oi! Keep up, newbie, or we'll leave your ass behind!" roared Lt. Takashi Gammarow, pilot of the Team Beta Defender, *Geirdriful*.

"You trying to provoke me already, Gammarow?" Vladia snapped. Gammarow was notorious at inciting conflict and had been singling Vladia out ever since she'd begun running simulations with the squad. But Vladia was well past getting angered by those kinds of childish remarks. It took a lot more than that to get her fired up these days. She begrudgingly thanked Tolen for that.

Gammarow laughed heartily, "Oh? The ice princess is super cold today! But we'll see how well you really pilot once we break the atmosphere!"

"Enough. Keep the general channel clear," Malthus interrupted.

"Yes, Captain," Gammarow acknowledged unwillingly.

"Atmospheric adjustments completed," *Freya* reported as the Valkyries powered their way through the Earth's atmosphere until the vacuum of space surrounded them.

Vladia suppressed a gasp. Stars dotted the blackness around her, as if little glittering holes had been punched through a cosmic blanket. She had been in space before, most people had. But that had been on a crowded space liner making the rounds from Earth to Luna. Being synced with a Valkyrie, it was as if you were in space completely–no barriers between you and the black. The vastness was frighteningly penetrating, yet amazing; it was a whole new experience.

"Captain," Rehel's voice charged in, interrupting her thoughts, "Several vessels are rapidly approaching your position from Sector twelve."

"How many?"

"Sixteen. They will reach your position in approx.-imately three minutes."

"Can you open a channel?"

"Negative. There is no response. Judging by speed and formation, it appears to be the Forerunner squadron. Probability: seventy-eight percent."

"Forerunner squadron?" exclaimed Lt. Commander Isobel Falis, Team Omega's Defender.

"Captain Malthus!" a voice barked over the general channel. "I hear you've a greenhorn you need broken in."

"Captain Gavril, I didn't know your squad was scheduled for drills today," said Malthus.

"Oh? You keep tabs on us Lunar squads as well? Really, Malthus, I didn't know you cared so much!"

"I keep tabs on everything."

Captain Gavril snickered. "Just thought we'd lend a hand. After all, it's been a long time since the Valkyrie squad received a new pilot."

"True."

"So what do you say? Instead of a bunch of lame ass formations, let's have a good ol' dog fight?" Captain Gavril proposed happily. "Besides, my boys could use some fun. It isn't every day we get to smack the Valkyries around."

Malthus laughed. "We'll see about that."

"How 'bout it? Let's have a hands-off battle. I don't want any scratches on my shiny toys. I'll even drop shields to fifty percent as compensation for your handicap."

"I won't go easy on you," warned Malthus.

"I wouldn't want you to," Gavril replied.

After encrypting the general channel, Captain Malthus shouted, "Valkyries! Prepare to engage Forerunner squad on my mark!"

The Valkyrie pilots cheered. A real skirmish was a rare thing. The simulators were top notch, but there was still no substitute for the rush of actual combat.

Vladia watched as the other squadron finally came into sensor range, appearing as little green blips on her tracking screen. She was as glad to be rid of the formation drill as the rest. This would be her chance to shine.

Not organized by teams, Forerunners worked independently for the most part, making their combat style completely different from Valkyries. The Forerunners consisted of sixteen traditional-style fighters, which were smaller than Valkyries, but slightly faster. Valkyries relied on hand-to-hand techniques and long-range sniping, while the Forerunner's strong suit was speed and maneuverability. Though not as advanced as the Valkyrie class, in a hands-off battle the Forerunners were formidable opponents.

"Teams Alpha and Beta," Malthus began, "engage targets F1 thru F6. Gamma and Delta, take F7 thru F12. Leave the rest to my team. Go!"

"Yes, Sir!" the pilots shouted as they shot towards the enemy at full power.

"Stay back and pick them off slow. We wanna have a little fun first," Abel relayed to Vladia as he sped ahead of her.

"Acknowledged," she answered. Abel swooped between F7 and F8, luring them away from her. They chased after him, but despite their advantage in speed, could not keep up.

"*Freya,* set view to negative three zoom," Vladia ordered. The computer adjusted the external sensors, widening her vision to encompass a larger area.

Although they were firing training rounds, the lasers still maintained a charge and if hit in a vital area, the ships would short out momentarily, cutting all power systems except life support and communication. Vladia fired her blaster canon at F7, but only grazed him. As she prepared to take her next shot, *Freya's* right leg was struck. The electricity from the blank penetrated her hull and sent a sharp tingle up her legs.

F10 zoomed towards her.

Vladia only had time to dodge his next attacks. She dove down at full power, but F10 was quickly gaining. The fighter let off another volley that Vladia easily avoided. But she couldn't run forever, and Abel was still being pursued. She needed to end this quickly and get back in position.

"*Freya,* lock on and fire shoulder canons!"

Freya responded with a barrage of shots, forcing her target to maneuver around them, slowing his pursuit.

F10 swooped under her and fired a grappling hook and Vladia cursed as the hook slammed into *Freya's* chest plate. The Forerunner set off a charge, sending a current down the cord. The shock made Vladia's targeting system short out. With the Defender's thick shields, it'd take more than that to knock her out of the fight.

Her view screen flickered then vanished, leaving Vladia in darkness. She disengaged from *Freya,* trying to overcome the queasiness as quick as possible.

She kept her thrusters at full, dragging her captor along for the ride. Maneuverability was limited but she did as best she could while tethered to the enemy. At this range, standing still was the worst she could do.

F10 continued to fire; the grappling hook had improved his accuracy a hundred fold.

With nothing to go on but a limited view through the window in her cockpit, she flipped the ship around to lay eyes on her attacker. Using the manual controls and her own eyes to line up the shot, she fired point blank just as her nav system started to phase out.

Singling out his thrusters and weapons, her wave of fire locked him out of the fight.

"*Freya*?"

There was no response. Vladia diverted auxiliary power to her targeting and nav systems.

"*Freya*?" she tried again. "You all right?"

"Affirmative. Thank you, Lt. Robespierre," its voice wavered in pitch.

Re-syncing with her ship, Vladia yanked the hook from *Freya's* chest. It left some deep surface marks, but didn't appear to completely penetrate the hull.

Vladia rushed back to Abel's aid. He didn't seem to be struggling much, he'd already taken out one himself, but she picked off the last one quickly, just in case.

"Thanks. Was hoping you might come back," Abel joked as he flew up beside her. "That's a nasty little gash you got there. I thought this was hands-off?"

"Apparently that only goes for us."

"Tsk, we'll see about that."

"Delta," Captain Malthus' voice interrupted. "Alpha is down. Move to assist Beta."

"Yes, Sir," Abel answered as the two flew to aid their comrades.

Teams Alpha and Beta had managed to disable F2 and

F6, but with Alpha down *Geirdriful* and *Alvitr* were struggling with the remaining targets. Abel immediately flew into the fray, drawing F1 away from the other vessels.

"Thought you could use a hand," Abel said over the general channel.

"Like hell I do," responded Gammarow as he shot down F3.

Vladia lined up her shot and took out F4.

"Team Gamma is down! Watch for incoming!" the captain warned.

Vladia watched as *Gunnr* grabbed hold of F1 by the wings and fired dead on.

"Oops, I think I bent it," Abel quipped.

"Now that's what I'm talkin' about, Duren!" Gammarow cheered.

A fighter plunged between her and Abel. Vladia pulled up, dodging a volley of blasts from the new target, F12.

Abel fired, drawing F12 away from Vladia. It was evident F12 was not in the same class as the other Forerunners; Abel barely managed to keep *Gunnr* unscathed as he whirled and evaded the other ship's blasts.

Geirdriful joined the chase while *Alvitr* hung back with *Freya* to try and pick the fighter from a distance. Both Abel and Gammarow swooped around the target firing wildly, yet F12 evaded their fire with ease.

Vladia tried to line up a clear shot, but her opponent was quick and his movements too erratic for her damaged targeting system. She swore under her breath.

F12 looped around and shot at her and *Alvitr*, catching them off guard. Two shots grazed *Freya's* left arm and one scored a critical hit on *Alvitr*. Then without losing more than a moment, continued his chase of *Gunnr*.

"Damn it," Cornelia, *Alvitr's* pilot, cursed as all power

but life support and communications shut down.

"Take the shot!" hollered Gammarow.

Vladia fired. The shot scorched past F12, missing the bottom of the hull by what must have been centimeters, and hit *Gunnr's* left shoulder cannon.

It wasn't critical, but the impact threw Abel off course, allowing F12 to gain a significant advantage.

A shot fired above her and hit F12 directly on its left thruster. Vladia checked her sensors; it was *Sigrún* and *Hildr*. "Captain," she called out.

Abel's voice crackled over the channel. "Thank you, Captain, I was getting dizzy," he said, making light of the situation.

"Captain Gavril," Malthus began, "can be a tough target to nail. Rehel, what's the final tally?"

"Five Valkyries remain operational. However, three of these five received non-critical hits."

"So, Captain Gavril," Malthus addressed both squads once the general channel was no longer jammed. "You owe me, let's say, two drinks, since three of my remaining Valkyries carelessly let themselves get hit."

"All right. Two it is then," Gavril acknowledged, "but you must admit, I almost had you that time. If you'd been just a minute later I would've had those down as well."

"Yes, but you would never have gotten me down," Malthus laughed.

"Who knows," the other captain pondered. "Well, we had a fun go of it. Next time you're on Luna, don't forget to cash in on those drinks!"

Everyone's vessels had fully recovered by now.

Although glad of the win, Vladia was furious at her own carelessness. She shouldn't have taken that shot. Before she fired, she knew she couldn't make it. She had shot down her own comrade and Tolen had made the shot she couldn't. She was still in his shadow, fumbling around like a damn fool.

∞

Freya's hatch door opened, and cool air rushed inside the helm. Vladia removed her helmet and tucked it under the seat. She stared down into her lap, pressing her fingers against each other as she waited for the ladder to emerge from the floor panels.

"You okay in there?" a gentle voice called from her commlink. It was Abel. Vladia lifted her head and spied him standing in his open cockpit, arms crossed, as he leaned on the edge.

"I shouldn't have been so quick to fire." She tilted her head back down. He didn't need to see her so disappointed with herself.

"It was a tough call and a tough shot," Abel assured her.

"You would have made it."

"Probably," he laughed.

"I shouldn't have taken the shot. If this had been a real battle–"

"But it wasn't, and you won't let it happen again."

"You're right about that. It won't ever happen again." That was a shot she should have been able to make and if she had to train until her mind and body fell apart, she'd make it next time.

"You've got great potential, Vladia. One day I expect you to surpass me." Vladia looked up at him with a meager smile. "So don't keep me waiting! I'm getting too old for this!" he yelled with a thumbs-up. His voice resounded across the hangar, but everyone was so used to his antics no one even looked up.

"You have no shame," she scolded lightly.

"Not an ounce."

Vladia pulled herself up and out of her Valkyrie, and grabbing hold of the ladder, she slid down.

She scanned around for Tolen until she noticed him speaking with Lt. Commander Falis in the control room. Malthus commanded such a presence that he was never hard to spot, unless he didn't want to be spotted that is. He'd kept his black hair relatively short, though it wasn't expected of anyone other than the cadets. His flight suit, a dark shade of indigo with a double stripe of gold down each side of his chest to mimic the color scheme of his Valkyrie, also set him apart from the other pilots.

"You waiting around for punishment or something?" Abel asked, approaching from behind.

Vladia glanced back at him but said nothing. Almost everyone else had left to attend to other duties.

Abel leaned against the leg of Vladia's Valkyrie. "You know," he began, "running laps around the hangar isn't going to help you improve and it certainly won't change what happened. If I were you, I would run some extra simulations on your own time. I've heard that practice makes perfect." He gave her a quick wink and flashed her a goofy smile.

Rehel was walking their way clad in a black officer's uniform with a single red stripe off-centered down the front of his jacket. His uniform was specifically designated for a Valkyrie Squad robot, and it was the only feature that separated him from the rest of the squad.

He was the perfect build with ideal human statistics. Rust colored hair, dark eyes, and creamy skin. All Gen D

Series Nine robots looked the same, but he was one of a mere handful of robots remaining on the base and the only Gen D-9. It was one of her mother's designs and Vladia had grown up with many of them during her early childhood. Whenever she saw Rehel, she always thought fondly of her mother.

Yet anti-robot legislation had grown stronger in the last decade, and many models deemed unnecessary were disassembled. It was exactly what her mother had predicted and tried to prevent at the cost of her life. This also crept into her thoughts every time she saw Rehel.

Anti-technology sentiments in general had been on the rise for decades. There had always been strong support against the overuse and abuse of technology since the disastrous Anglo-Eastern War in 2162, and it was no longer just the extremists who were anti-robot. Robots had been used extensively during that war and now the radicals wanted them out of the military altogether. They looked for any excuse to dismantle them and because the robots were so limited in what they were allowed to do, more and more were destroyed because they no longer served a purpose. They had no access to weapons of any sort, nor could they pilot any armed craft or crafts large enough to be weapons in their own right. Being three laws safe wasn't enough to keep many from fearing and hating them.

Rehel, for example, would make a far superior pilot than even the most skilled human. His reaction time wasn't bogged down by human nuances. Yet, his function was to monitor and review fight footage, and create programs to aid the pilot with any difficulties. That was it. He was locked into doing menial tasks and the only advantage was that he could study footage and create simulations faster and more accurately than a human. This, of course, had its value, but compared to his potential, his function was laughable.

Vladia couldn't help but feel sympathy for the robot. He was a class toppling towards extinction at the cruel hands of its creator.

Abel pushed his lean body off the Valkyrie and spun around to face Vladia. Lost in her thoughts, she hadn't realized Abel had still been talking. She tried to look attentive, but he'd already noticed her vacant stare.

"Sorry."

"I said: a few of us are going to make a run to town tonight. You should come."

"I don't think so."

"Don't be like that. This is a team if you haven't noticed and there's something to be said about camaraderie and whatnot," he said with a wave of his hand. "What you need to do is clear your head. Have a drink, and a little fun, then go at your goal of perfection with a fresh spirit," Abel pressed gently.

Vladia thought he might have a point, but she hated to give in so easily. It felt like losing somehow, although she knew it wasn't like that with him. He wasn't Tolen; Abel's intentions were not based on any sort of self-gain.

"I'll consider it," she compromised.

"Great. We're leaving at 20:00. I'll swing by your quarters."

"Fine."

"You still insist on sticking around for your bout of punishment?"

Vladia nodded curtly.

Abel rolled his blue eyes and shrugged. "Well, you do what you want," he continued, walking towards Rehel. "If being a masochist is your thing, by all means proceed."

The two exited together and with a short huff Vladia turned her attention back to Tolen.

4

TO KNOW YOUR ENEMY

"So, how did the stats look for today?" Abel asked, unzipping the front of his flight suit halfway and tying the arms of it around his waist as he and Rehel walked out of Hangar C.

"Individual deviation was minimal; however, the overall results differed significantly due to the inclusion of Lieutenant Vladia Robespierre," Rehel responded in his usual indifferent monotone.

"And her marks?"

"I still believe she has the potential to become the ideal pilot, but because of the friendly fire incident her marks were naturally lower than expected. I have recommended appropriate simulations to correct the problem."

Abel nodded. "She'll do them and extra. She won't let it happen again."

"I assume no mention has been made of her relationship to Captain Malthus? That was one of your primary concerns."

Abel inadvertently shushed him. There was no one around, but still. Talk of such things made him nervous.

"Of course not. I wouldn't have known if you hadn't dug up those records I requested. This is good though, her not relying on him. It's a good sign," Abel said just above a whisper, more to himself than to Rehel. Although he'd scouted Vladia out himself, when Rehel uncovered her records it was an unexpected shock to say the least. It wasn't merely the fact that she'd been raised outside the traditional state facilities, although that was a concern, but it was the fact that she'd been raised alongside her half-brother who just happened to be Tolen Malthus.

Abel didn't trust Malthus; hadn't for a long time now.

"In other words, she can be depended upon?" Rehel interrupted his thoughts.

Abel considered this before answering, "I wouldn't go that far yet. Either way it's clear she doesn't have any useful information regarding that particular incident, but her capacity to match Malthus in certain areas is there. That is even more important I'd say."

"I see you still believe she is the best possible choice."

Abel scratched his head thoughtfully, mussing up his short brown hair. "It's not that I think she's the best possible choice. But if it comes to that she's our only option."

"If your theory is correct, and I am not entirely sure that it is, then there is a high probability that you are correct about her potential as well."

Abel stopped and Rehel followed suit. He looked hard into the robot's empty, brown eyes, wondering what thoughts lingered behind those dark mirrors. All he could see was his own reflection. "I'm not entirely sure either. That's why I need your help. All we've got to go on so far is an uneasy feeling and that just isn't enough, I know. But by the time we find the truth, any countermeasures we try to take I fear will be too late."

"Expect the best, but prepare for the worst."

"Exactly," Abel concurred as he stuffed his hands in his pockets. "Unfortunately in my experience, the worst is usually what you get. Both of them are high risk factors. Being raised by that warlord rather than coming up in the System like normal kids, it's a wonder they can function in society at all."

"Neither has displayed any irregularities in behavior," Rehel added.

"That's what bothers me. There should be some irregularities. People raised that way just don't think like the rest of us. Anyway, she's nothing like Malthus, and as long as it stays that way we're good as gold."

"She looks up to him, though. Even I can see that."

With a sigh, Abel walked towards his quarters, pretending not to hear Rehel's last words of caution. "You should get going. It's your month to transcribe the senior officers' meeting, and it won't do for you to be late."

Rehel nodded in acknowledgement and headed toward the secondary conference room.

"Oh, and we're going into town tonight."

Rehel stopped and turned, but made no response.

"I need you to come."

"That is a bad idea, Abel."

"I'll make an excuse. Don't you worry about it," he assured, pointing an accusing finger. Of course the robot wasn't actually capable of worrying. "Be ready at 19:30."

Without further delay, Rehel left in silence, but Abel knew he'd consented. It was a risk–he'd been developing a bad habit for risk-taking lately–but it was necessary. Tonight he'd find out what this girl was made of.

∞

Captain Malthus dismissed his co-pilot but showed no signs of acknowledging Vladia's presence as he continued scrolling through the day's stats. Vladia suddenly felt as if she was waiting outside the Admiral's door again. But he was not the Admiral and she refused to wait at his leisure. She entered the control room, standing rigid at attention until Malthus put away his datapad.

"Yes, Lieutenant Robespierre?"

"Captain, requesting appropriate action be taken for my careless maneuvers during today's exercise."

"This is not the academy. I do not dole out punishment for those kinds of mistakes," Malthus explained, folding his hands behind his back. "Rehel has already processed the information from today's exercise and has assigned everyone, including myself, specific simulation runs based on that data. Check the simulation schedule for your punishment."

The formality in his voice was severe. Even with her, his own flesh and blood, Tolen Malthus maintained this rigid distance. In truth, it was something she had grown to respect about him more and more. He maintained such control and poise under any circumstance. As children, only once did she ever recall him being upset or angry. With simple, calm determination, he solved every problem and overcame any obstacle. She was the reckless one, though she had improved over the last several years.

Vladia moved to dismiss herself when Malthus spoke again. "Simulations alone are not going to help you make that kind of shot." His voice had softened but was still tinged with formality.

Malthus's lifted his slim arm and pressed a cool finger against the center of her forehead. His eyes held her hostage as Vladia's body stiffened instinctively. "This is where you are lacking, Vladia. To win absolutely, you must know your enemy better than you know yourself, better than he knows himself. You must know his moves not just before he makes them, but before he knows he is going to make them. That is why you failed today. That is why you will continue to fail."

Malthus removed his finger suddenly with a slight push, releasing her from his deep stare. "Lieutenant," he dismissed her with a slight bow and left the control room.

"Tolen!" she called after him, resisting the urge to chase after him.

"Know your enemy, Vladia," he said without turning. "Know your enemy, and you will be unstoppable. Or don't and be a pawn forever."

Vladia's eyes followed him until he disappeared from view. She stood alone in the empty hangar. Her fingers wandered up to rest on her forehead. They lingered a moment before, almost violently, rubbing away his touch. She reached in her pocket for her personal commlink. She entered the key code to Rehel's extension and waited.

"Yes, Lieutenant Vladia Robespierre."

"Rehel, do you have enough footage from today's exercise to put together a simulation of Captain Gavril's maneuvers?"

"I should have enough, though the footage will not be seamless as it must be pieced together from each of the Valkyrie's individual cameras and surrounding satellites. I can have this task completed in approximately four hours. Shall I send it to your personal viewer?"

"Yes. Thank you." Vladia tucked away her comm and headed to the hangar exit.

If she could find typical flight patterns within Captain

Gavril's movements, it should be possible for her to predict them based on that data. But that wasn't enough to win. She had to be able to do this during battle on her own, not afterwards with the aid of a robot's analysis. She had to be able to do this with an unknown enemy, one she would not have the chance to study beforehand. This was a skill only Malthus had mastered. Even as children, she could never beat him at even the simplest game because of it. But this was a good place to start if she wanted to win the next skirmish.

Vladia marched through the rows of Valkyries towards the hangar exit. Tolen's words clung to her mind, like a nagging premonition she couldn't quite shake.

Know your enemy better than you know yourself.

With a little laugh, one devoid of all humor, Vladia shook her head. If knowing herself was the foundation, she had a long, winding path waiting.

∞

Rehel stood erect in a corner of conference room B, watching with mechanical precision as captains from every squad, their generals and the heads of several departments filed into the dim-lit room. The lights slowly brightened as the officers seated themselves around a long, transparent oval table in the center of the room.

If one looked close, they could see a faint, white rim encircling what would have been a human's iris as he initiated recording. Technically speaking, he was always recording to his memory. This, however, was a secure recording, in which he would not record to his memory, but to the Records Department server he was currently synced with. It was an odd sensation, linking to another computer. It was as if he was sharing his body. For lack of a better term, it felt cramped. It was a menial task, even he could recognize that, but unlike a human it bothered him not. It was good to be in service, for if the service stopped so too would his existence.

When the meeting was adjourned, Rehel would have no recollection of the discussion recorded to the server, only a fuzziness of being somewhere, yet not being there at all. This did bother him. It made his system sluggish for several minutes after the connection was broken.

Grand Admiral Clovis V. Acadia had called the meeting and was last to arrive. Acadia commanded the entire United Terra Armed Forces and answered to no one but the Head of State. He was a plump man in his fifties with graying blonde hair and had the look of a tattered war hero even when he was dressed in his finest. He was not the ideal leader and according to rumors had only obtained his position through underhanded politics. He kept his power through fear, rather than respect. As Grand Admiral Acadia took his seat, the room grew quiet as all present waited for him to speak.

"Before we begin," Acadia turned to address Rehel, "let me be clear that this information is classified. Only those present are allowed access to it. Understood?"

"Positive. The recording has been labeled accordingly, Sir."

Acadia nodded. Clearing his throat, he began. "As some of you know, the Lunar colonies, along with the space stations at the L points and a few orbiting our planet, have been pressing the Terran Government for free rein over their own affairs. In other words, they want to form a standalone government separate from Earth."

Voices stirred. This information was new to many

present. Rehel made note of those who seemed to be startled and those who did not. All of the captains and a handful of generals seemed unaware of the situation between Earth and Luna, except for Captain Malthus, who maintained his normal, calm disposition.

"We have received a third petition from these would-be rebel colonies, who are now calling themselves the Lunar Union. This time, however, it is not simply a petition for free rein. It is also a threat if we continue our current stance," Acadia continued.

"This is absurd!" Captain Ryūnen Senshu exclaimed with a laugh. "Luna is but a moon. We are an entire, unified planet."

"That's right!" echoed General Nikto Litsom. "They stand no chance, even with the aid of the L point stations."

Mumbles and nods of agreement followed.

"I'm afraid you're all mistaken," Captain Malthus entered the fray with a calm, smooth voice. "Of course, this Lunar Union wouldn't stand a chance against the United Terran Armed Forces. No matter how well equipped they are in weaponry and defense, they still have the huge disadvantage of needing key resources imported from Earth.

"As Captain Senshu pointed out, they are but a moon. They could maybe hold out a half a year on their own. However, you're leaving out one very vital factor in this equation. Luna doesn't have to get those resources from Earth for much longer. Mars is on the cusp of completing their terraforming project. All Luna must do is hold out until then."

"There's no guarantee Mars would help them," Captain Senshu retorted.

"Well they seem to have no moral qualms about

lending aid to the criminals, deserters and outcasts of the Outer Moons," Malthus recalled. "As primitive as the Outer Moons are, their biodome technology is topnotch. I bet they even left the Martian tags on them for show."

Grand Admiral Acadia cleared his throat and all talk ceased. "Captain Malthus is correct. Even if Mars doesn't lend aid, we can't afford to take that chance. The Lunar Union must be squashed quickly and decisively, before Mars has the opportunity to act."

The table seemed split as many officers nodded their support while others remained stiff, unsure of their stance on the topic.

"We're not at war yet, gentlemen," Acadia continued. "But it may very well come to that shortly. We'll send an envoy to speak with the Lunar Union representatives on Station Torappu One."

This act of compromise appeared to win over the undecided.

"Captain Malthus, you will select one of your Valkyries to act as a peaceful escort," Acadia ordered.

"Yes, Sir."

"A war between Earth and Luna may or may not be on the horizon. Nevertheless, I want all of my senior officers to be prepared. I want every officer and ship fully operational and on standby." The Grand Admiral rose from his chair. "If the envoy fails, then war it is. Dismissed!" He ended his address with a bang of his fist, sending a wave of vibrations across the table.

As the members of the meeting dispersed, Rehel recorded their departure patterns. He ended his official recording and broke the link to the Records Department.

The dim white rim now gone from his eyes, Rehel stood perfectly still as he let his systems re-adjust.

A little, blue light flashed in the corner of his right eye. It was a personal comm, presumably from Abel since he was the only human that ever sent him personal messages. Rehel would have to wait until he had fully recovered before he could view the correspondence; otherwise, it would slow him down even further. It was the worst feeling he could know, running under his capacity. He was at eighty-five percent. He'd need another minute or so to get back to a hundred. He imagined if he could feel impatient, now would be the proper time.

∞

Vladia faced herself in the mirror. She'd just pulled her hair up and now she was taking it down again. She was anxious. Going out like this instead of working on the Gavril footage was irresponsible. As usual, she sadistically compared herself to Tolen and how he'd have chosen a different path for the evening. He'd probably work well into the night on his own simulation prep. But she had made her decision and she wasn't one to be wishy-washy about things.

It would be hot tonight so she'd dressed accordingly: grey shorts with a sheer pair of bio-blocks to cover her bare legs, a violet tank under a black mesh bio-wear chemise, matching flat boots that came to just under her knee, and of course a pair of bio-lace gloves, also in black.

She'd never needed to dress like this at the Robespierre Compound or the Malthus Estate. Well, that wasn't exactly true. Her mother wore bio-wear to work of course, but she never enforced them on Vladia unless she left the confines of their private quarters. The maids of her second home insisted on the bio-wear, but whenever she and

Tolen were alone they shed these cumbersome extras, she in an act of rebellion and he in the name of science. He had this theory on disease and immunity and was set on testing it on himself. Regardless of the reasons, they both paid for it as they did get sick every now and then, but it was never serious, though the maids acted as if(and most likely hoped) they'd die every time.

Funny how she suffered for it even now. The bio-wear was uncomfortable to her when all others wore it like a second skin, which she supposed was the purpose anyway.

Her door chimed softly. He was early.

After a quick tousle of the hair, Vladia scooped her bag from the vanity and headed out.

∞

Rounding the corner to the auto dock, Vladia spied Cornelia and Takashi lounging on the hood of one of the dark, green models. The other woman's bright, red hair made her counterpart almost unnoticeable. Abel waved to them.

"Let's go already!" Takashi hollered, sliding off the car and making for one of the doors.

"We're waiting for one more," Abel explained.

"Who?" Vladia asked but an answer was unneeded as Rehel entered the dock behind them.

Her eyes darted towards Cornelia and Takashi, who appeared unable to find the words of protest they surely harbored.

"I ran into one of the boys from the lab on level two. He needs some specimen equipment from the District Seven Warehouse and I offered Rehel's services to fetch them since we're going into town anyway," Abel said matter-of-fact.

This seemed to ease their companions' concerns, but only slightly. All five of them surrounded the auto now.

"He can sit up front then," Takashi proclaimed as he eased into the back.

Cornelia stepped closer to Abel and in a muted voice said: "The warehouse won't be open this late."

Abel smiled. "Wouldn't that be a shame."

Vladia stepped away from the pair as they continued their discussion. She glanced at Rehel, who seemed entirely unconcerned about the situation. He was just following orders.

Vladia got in the auto and was joined by Abel and Cornelia moments later. Four humans sat in the back in pairs facing each other. Rehel was alone in the front left to navigate them like a lowly chauffer. She felt sorry for him but no one else, not even Abel, seemed all that concerned about the situation. There was nothing to do but push it from her mind.

Cornelia, who was on Vladia's left, leaned over and whispered, "Don't let it bother you."

"Oh. I'm fine." Maybe she wasn't the only one with compassion after all.

"Abel does these things sometimes I think only to shock us. If the robot makes you too uncomfortable I'll send him back no matter what Abel says," the other woman assured her with the best of intentions.

Vladia smiled weakly, feeling silly and disappointed. Of course that's what she was talking about. No one would possibly think Vladia's uneasiness was anything more than a manifestation of robot prejudice.

Abel and Takashi started a lively argument about the

outer moon's need for a government infrastructure, which Cornelia was quickly sucked into. Vladia remained quiet the rest of the trip, but smiled, nodded, and frowned when appropriate.

As suspected, the warehouse was closed and Rehel would have to tag along the rest of the night not without loud, albeit half-hearted, protests from Takashi. Cornelia continued offering Vladia sympathetic glances that she tried not to notice.

A short five minutes later the auto stopped and the doors released. Takashi was first to step out.

"Bar," he said, reading the name of the establishment with unnecessary slowness. "More like Shack I'd say. I thought we were going to The Blind Mule."

Takashi was right to protest, Vladia thought. The building was dilapidated and the whole structure seemed to slouch towards the left. There were hinges but no door, just an open entryway.

"This place is a bit more open to certain clientele," Abel explained with a nod at Rehel.

"Really?" Cornelia was skeptical.

"I can wait in the car," Rehel offered. It was the first thing he'd said all evening.

Abel waved the notion away. "I grew up with the owner. You remember Landers?" he asked Cornelia.

"Mickell Landers? That fuck-up owns this place?" she said with a laugh. "Well that makes sense. I wouldn't trust him to do much more than this."

"Did you all grow up at the same facility?" Vladia asked, though she immediately regretted it. She was opening the door to a subject she was unsuited to discuss.

"No, just me and Abel. Takashi was raised in the Dublin facility," Cornelia explained.

"No! I wasn't!" came the inevitable protest as Abel and Cornelia laughed. Vladia smiled, not sure what the joke was.

"I'm from the Newbridge facility," Takashi huffed. "And none of the brats I was raised with made it this far either. I was the only one of my lot to be selected for military service."

"No one wants to hear about it," Cornelia stopped him. "Let's go in and get this over with."

The five of them walked in, Abel at the lead and Rehel trailing a few paces behind them.

"Grab that table over there while I touch base with Landers," Abel pointed to a table near the counter as he dashed off.

It was a small bar at half capacity from the looks of it. The place was clean of course, but the inside was as old as the outside. The walls were speckled with the faces of what Vladia assumed were famous patrons. The tables' once sleek, blue finish was worn to white on the edges from too many years of use; the chairs didn't fare much better.

Cornelia sat down next to Takashi while Vladia gladly took the seat next to Rehel. Abel jogged towards them and took the seat on the end of the table.

"As long as no one complains he can stay."

"What if I complain?" Takashi muttered.

"Then you can go sit in the auto while the rest of us have a good time."

Takashi frowned but said nothing more.

The drinks came soon after and the entire group all but forgot about their unique companion. Rehel joined in the conversation here and there but only if prompted by another. Vladia had to admit she was having fun. It was nice to relax and being part of a team felt alright too. Maybe Abel had been right. Maybe she did need this camaraderie just as much as she needed her practice simulations.

"So when are you two going to sign a contact?" Abel asked, rather inappropriately.

Cornelia scowled and punched him in the shoulder.

"We all know it's coming so just fess up already."

Takashi grinned. "Just waiting for the lab results to come in."

"Which will all be in order of course," Cornelia added, forgetting her mild protest from moments ago. "Neither of us has had a documented illness so it's really just a formality."

"I think it's great," Abel continued. "You guys are perfect."

"Like vinegar and water," Takashi joked.

Cornelia gave him a rare smile and for a moment the two seemed completely removed from their surroundings.

Abel dropped his gaze to the table. "It's really great what you guys have."

Vladia picked up on the subtle change in Abel's demeanor but her attention was quickly drawn to a loud group of three at the bar. They'd been getting progressively more rowdy for the last hour, but now their conversation had turned sour with talk of politics. It didn't take long for them to notice Abel and Takashi, who were both in military garb, making them an easy target for drunken anger. A lot of civilians had serious misgivings about military personnel, who were Rank B citizens while most others were only C or D. No matter the justifications given, many thought it unfair that soldiers had more privileges than the rest. It didn't help matters that the aptitude test given at the age of twelve in all state facilities was the sole determining factor of rank and occupation.

Vladia was about to voice her concern when Rehel spoke up: "Abel, I think it best if we leave. The group of men at the bar are about to initiate a confrontation. Probability is eighty-five percent."

"I know. I've been listening. Let's just see what happens."

"Rehel's right," Cornelia confirmed. "We should leave."

"I'll not be chased out of a damn bar," Takashi said a little too loudly. "I'm proud of my standing! I was the only one in my lot to make it into the service!" he repeated his earlier sentiment. "It's not my problem that we all aren't cut out for it."

The men at the bar stood up and walked towards them.

"Abel, it's still not too late to leave," Rehel said.

"Yes. It is," he replied as he spun his chair around to face the three intruders. "Can I help you gentlemen?"

"You can help us by taking your sorry asses out of here. You have your own bars on base, much fancier than this I'm sure. This one here is ours," the tallest one challenged.

He had crew cut brown hair and empty looking eyes. The two men flanking him were a bit shorter, but well built. They looked like factory workers. Vladia recalled that for decades factories were completely automated and production was overseen by robots. After the Great War, Earth reverted back to human labor for many tasks. These days, the only work robots handled outside of the military was typically the kind too dangerous or too precise for human hands.

Abel grinned. "I take your point. However, seeing as how we protect Earth from the many dangers both here and off-world, it seems to me that we can go just about anywhere we like."

"What are you doing?" hissed Cornelia. Vladia wondered the same. This behavior was uncharacteristic of Abel. Besides, if they were assaulted these men would surely be arrested and probably executed. If anything, Abel should be trying to diffuse the situation to save them.

"Maybe you think that. But I don't," the tall one said clenching his gloved fists.

"Hey, buddy," Takashi pointed to the man's hands, "you know that's a bad idea. Just leave us alone, okay?"

The man's shoulders' tensed, but he made no further moves of aggression. Until now everyone had forgotten about Rehel, who was quiet and motionless in an attempt to not add to the conflict. But Vladia suspected he was being a bit too quiet and too motionless. He looked like a life-sized doll.

And then the unthinkable happened.

Abel sighed and motioned at the robot. "Fine. Rehel, close us out. We're leaving."

Instinctually, Vladia jerked out of her seat, positioning herself between Rehel and the men's line of sight. "I got it."

It was only then she realized that as soon as she moved towards the bar Rehel would be exposed. She needed to get these men away from the table.

"Why don't I get you gentlemen a fresh round as well," she offered.

"Hey! What you guys playin' at? That thing can't be in here!" one of the shorter men shouted with a large step back.

Cornelia stood up. "Hey, we're all leaving. No big deal. Let the lady buy you a drink."

"Ain't that a sight. They wanted to bring their mutt with them," the third man laughed.

The ringleader let a wide grin spread across his leathery face. "I think this robot here is threatening me. Don't you agree? I seen him eyein' me awful angry like."

"I seen it too, Sam. I'm scared of him," one of them chuckled. "I think this dog needs to be put down."

"I'll be taking his I.D. number if ya please," the tall one said to Abel. "Dangerous robots are to be reported immediately."

"He's not dangerous and the recordings here can prove it," Vladia protested.

"It don't matter. If I'm scared of him nothing else matters."

No one offered up Rehel's I.D., but that might have been because Abel was the only one who knew it.

"Fine. I can just ask the robot. He'll have to answer me," the man's eyes were now firmly fixed on Rehel. "Out with it then, robot. What's your–"

Vladia leaped around the table at the man, her hands aimed for his throat.

The men flinched, but Vladia never reached them. Rehel had caught her firmly at the waist and held her in midair.

"Lt. Robespierre, I cannot allow you to injure this man," the robot explained.

The tall one laughed heartily. "What a good mutt! Obedient till the last."

Her wrath surged forward and without hesitation, Vladia spat in the man's face.

With a yelp of terror he reeled back as if he'd been shot, frantically clawing at his face. The other two pulled out bio clothes, but didn't dare get close enough to him to actually help.

Vladia knew she'd broken the most scared social contract. It would have been more acceptable to shoot him. Her actions were akin to torture; to let a man die slowly from disease was barbaric. She was confident she was clean, but didn't have the paperwork on her to prove it.

Her friends stared at her with disbelief, with fear. For a long moment the man's screams became but a distant din as Vladia eyed her companions. Her thoughts drifted to Tolen. In all his haughty disappointment of her, never had he looked at her with such contempt.

"Put me down, Rehel," she ordered and the robot obliged.

Vladia smoothed down her clothes. She looked to Abel, the only one she thought might show some sign of understanding, but found nothing. It pained her, but she wasn't the least bit sorry. She'd done what needed to be done, and under the agony of rejection, Vladia felt the slightest twinge of pride in knowing that she was the only one who could've done it.

"I'll be in the auto," she said, her voice teeming with resentment. "Rehel, you'd better come with me. I'd hate for the man to recover and make a go at your life again."

Vladia didn't wait for him to respond as she headed for the exit. He followed without question.

Once they were outside, Rehel spoke: "That was unwise, Lt. Robespierre."

"I know," she sighed, leaning against the side of their auto. "But I'm an unwise person."

"Thank you."

"Anytime," she answered. And she meant it.

∞

Tolen Malthus had been sitting in The Spin, one of the many orbiting restaurants around Earth, for almost an hour. He arrived promptly at 19:00, ordered his usual meal of asparagus and poached chicken with a tall glass of water, and was now waiting, legs crossed casually, for his dessert: a slice of sponge cake topped with kiwi and cream and an order of coffee.

Just as his dessert would arrive, he would be joined by Captain Gavril. This wasn't the best time to be seen with a Luna officer, but Tolen had taken precautions months in advance.

He'd been invited here eight months ago by Admiral Bael to discuss an unusual transfer request. At the time, Earth's relationship with Luna was strained, but not as much as now, and The Spin was a regular haunt for both Terrans and Lunaites. While he was here, Tolen made sure to remark on his delight of the venue and assure the Admiral that he would most definitely be returning. And so he did: every other Thursday since. It was part of Tolen's routine now, with a plausible beginning and a soon to be plausible end.

The waiter arrived with the final portion of his order and moments later so, too, did his guest. This would be the third and final time the two men would casually run into each other here.

Tolen stood up and offered Gavril his hand. "Take a seat," he offered.

Gavril sat and plucked a menu from the table. He opened the booklet and as he did the sliver of a data card Tolen had placed there on arrival reached its final destination. Punching in an order he said, "I've only got time for a quick drink. I see you're about done anyway. That does look tasty though."

"What did you think?" Tolen dismissed the other's attempt at small talk.

"It was as you said. That demonstration paired with the schema should do the trick."

Gavril's drink arrived–a brown, foamy concoction. He took a quick sip then nodded to the waiter in approval. "Martian import. They manage to make a fine beer. They're such a serious lot you wouldn't think it possible."

"One of my Valkyrie's will be escorting the envoy."

The other man raised an eyebrow. "Getting cautious are they?"

"Shouldn't they be?" Tolen's voice turned sharp.

Gavril just shrugged and took a long gulp of beer. "One Valkyrie or one hundred Valkyries, it won't matter anymore. Thanks to you."

"Don't get cocky. That is Earth's greatest flaw. They are overconfident and they underestimate their enemies," Tolen said as he finished his coffee.

"Well that's it then," Tolen wiped his hand with his napkin and stood.

"Hey. How 'bout those drinks I owe you?"

Malthus waved his hand dismissively. "They're all yours. Consider it a congratulatory gift."

"Malthus," Gavril stopped him. "Why are you helping us? What do you care if Luna is free from Earth's reign?"

Tolen smiled. "I don't. Not in the least," he answered honestly. "I have my own agenda that just so happens to work out very nicely if I help you in the process."

The other Captain glowered, dissatisfied with his answer.

"You're a good man, Captain," Malthus said resolutely. "Get that data to L4 and your job is all but done."

5

FIGHT OR FLIGHT

"I'm ready. Let's do this," Abel said as he settled down into the cushioned leather chair facing the larger black screen that took up almost half the wall.

"Begin sequence eighty-seven," Rehel instructed the computer system in Abel's quarters.

Images immediately popped up in rapid succession. The pictures were random for the most part, except for the few personal pictures from Abel's collection. Of those personal pictures, the time frame was centered on specific dates and people. The idea was to trick the brain into remembering something associated with those dates and people. This was one of the more archaic approaches they had used, but when you've tried everything you can get pretty desperate. And Abel was far beyond desperate.

Abel and Rehel had tried almost every approach save blunt head trauma, which Rehel had refused to participate in and even went as far as threatening to report Abel if he managed to do it himself. His robot friend could be awful stubborn when it came to Abel's safety. Not, of course, for any sentimental sense of friendship; it was just the way robots were programmed. Rehel would shut down sooner than let harm come to any human that wasn't deemed a Terran enemy, and then he'd still have to be re-programmed to participate in the killing of human enemies, even in the most removed fashion.

Abel watched the fast-paced cycling of images for an hour before he shook his head in disappointment and motioned for Rehel to stop the sequence. He leaned forward and rubbed his face in the palms of his hands.

"Perhaps we should go back to chemical methods?" offered Rehel.

"No. It draws too much attention. We need to be as covert as possible or people will start asking questions. And then what? Explain how I've just got the funny feeling something happened that night that I'm not supposed to remember and it may involve Tolen Malthus?" Abel's sarcasm was wasted on Rehel but he didn't care. He was angry, powerless, and just plain pissed off.

Of course all the events of that night had been explained to him. But it didn't sit right with Abel. The official report went something like this: The Nanobot and Computer Interface Research Facility exploded at 03:20 on March 11, 2172 due to a malfunction in the hardware, which allowed nanobots to escape into the ventilation system and infested the human researchers. This in turn caused symptoms akin to madness in the workers, leading them to detonate the entire facility. Captain Malthus was appointed to lead the investigation that determined this.

Abel's contracted, Ceres Forté, was one of those researchers. When Abel did not report to duty the next morning, Captain Malthus, concerned for his pilot, went to check on him at his quarters. Abel was reportedly found unconscious on the floor and taken to the hospital. He was treated for severe psychological shock that caused minor, but permanent, damage to his brain, specifically his hippocampus and amygdala.

All of this was probable on the surface. Yet to him it didn't hang together. But, one can't simply reopen an investigation because of a feeling, especially Abel, who was now completely discredited as a result of the damage to his brain. He did have more than just a feeling, but nothing that could count as significant.

First, Abel knew he wasn't the kind of person to react to the loss of a woman like that. However, Rehel was always quick to point out that humans act unpredictably and irregularly often, so just because Abel doesn't think he would react that way doesn't mean it is not possible. Not only that, but since Abel had almost no remaining memory of Ceres Forté, he couldn't really say how he truly felt about her. All that remained of the woman was bits and pieces, a flash of a smile here or the gleam of soft, grey eyes there. Just enough to be unsettling, but that was it. Maybe his feelings had been deep enough to cause severe psychological shock at the news of her death.

But there was another item that, to Abel, spoke volumes. All his memory loss was exclusively linked to one woman and one night. He could understand the night. But to lose memories of her that were not associated with the night of her death seemed oddly specific.

For example, Abel had a picture of the night Cornelia Arnim had made the squad. Abel remembered the night clearly, except for Ceres. She was in the picture smiling right next to him; the woman had her arms around him, yet he couldn't remember her that night at all.

Rehel did admit this was odd, but the human brain is an odd thing in itself. Abel needed more and for whatever reason Rehel was willing to help. But the data trail was long cold and Abel's memory all but destroyed. Even if he could get it back, there was no guarantee he'd be believed.

"Perhaps it is time to stop, Abel," Rehel said, crossing the room to sit closer.

"No, I know. I'm done for the night." Abel stood up to stretch.

"I did not mean for tonight. I meant for good." Rehel had taken a seat on the nearby sofa.

"What? We can't give up now," he protested half-heartedly. Even he was getting tired. Never were results to be had, yet for seven years he'd been pursuing this intuitive feeling. He did not doubt himself in the least. Something had happened and he had been made to forget. But the evidence could not be procured. Rehel was right; it was time to move on. Abel just couldn't be the one to say it.

He sat down on the couch next to Rehel and let out a deep sigh of defeat. "Now what?"

"I would suggest proceeding as planned and be on the lookout for new information," Rehel offered.

"Agreed. Just because we can't access what really happened doesn't mean we should act as if nothing did happen. We can't let our guard down, but we need not waste any more time either. If it comes down to it, Robespierre will be the best weapon at our disposal."

"And if it turns out nothing happens then we have caused no harm to anyone," Rehel added.

Abel nodded.

"Speaking of Lt. Robespierre, there is one other matter that should be addressed," Rehel continued.

"I know."

"Have you spoken to her since the incident?"

"No. But not for the reason you think," he said defensively. "I've been busy."

"Perception is everything. Those are your words, I believe."

Abel leaned forward, his crossed arms resting on his thighs. "Whatever tension there may be between her and the rest of us, it was well worth it. I found out exactly what I needed to know. Granted, I didn't anticipate her exact response, but she stood up for you. That's the kind of person we need. The brilliance of Malthus, yet self-sacrificing instead of self-serving. You know what he would have done?"

"Captain Malthus would not have let himself be put in such a position I imagine."

Abel rolled his eyes. "Yes, but if he had, he would have either given you up or put those men in a position to be executed."

"Isn't that what you did?"

"No, because I was counting on Vladia to step in, which she did."

Rehel seemed to disapprove of this response. "It was a reckless move."

"Look, I'm sorry I put you in that position. You do know I'd never have let them have you."

"I do not doubt that."

Abel's comm link buzzed, rattling softly on the coffee table in front of them. Abel reached over and scooped it up. "Lt. Commander Duren here."

"Duren, report to my office. I need a Valkyrie to act as an envoy escort. You'll receive full details once you arrive," Captain Malthus instructed.

"Yes, Sir. On my way."

Abel closed the link and stood up. Rehel followed suit. "You know anything about this?"

"Yes. However, that information is classified," Rehel responded.

"That tells me enough. Thanks, Rehel. Keeps those eyes and ears of yours open while I'm gone," Abel said as he motioned for Rehel to follow him to the door.

"Always," Rehel replied with a quick nod.

Abel shut the door behind the robot and quickly slipped on his flight suit over his slacks and undershirt. He checked his pockets for his ignition key and on confirming its location headed out the door to the Captain's office.

∞

"Load simulation: Robespierre Eight. Difficulty level: Ten," Vladia instructed the simulator.

She sat in an exact replica of a standard Valkyrie cockpit. She had strapped in and hooked up just as if she was preparing for a real battle. The only difference was the additional electrodes attached to her temples. Once the simulation launched, those were quickly forgotten. Survival instincts kicked in as an all-out brawl between man and virtual armada began.

"Lt. Vladia Robespierre, this is your seventeenth consecutive sequence. Why not take a break?" the computer urged in its chirpy, yet automated, voice.

"Just run the simulation." She tried not to sound angry. It was programmed to ask each attempt after ten and was only doing its job.

"Sequence initiated."

The virtual enemies came into view, and Vladia felt her muscles tense. She refused to quit until she scored at least ninety-eight percent accuracy. The program consisted of ten enemy targets, all of which were based off the footage of Captain Gavril, and fifteen friendly targets. She had spent hours poring over the footage Rehel had sent her. There were definite patterns. Vladia estimated she had about four seconds to recognize the pattern and fire before it changed. Her goal was to identify the pattern within two and get the shot off.

On her seventeenth attempt, she was able to recognize the pattern within the time allotted, but her marksmanship was only ninety-two percent. The other eight percent she either hit a friendly target or outright missed. Most would consider that acceptable; she considered it failure.

Enemy fighters swarmed around the friendly targets. She had five minutes to pick them off before all friendly targets were destroyed by the enemy. So far, Vladia lost four to five per simulation. This was also failure.

She picked one enemy target and watched it, poised to fire until she spotted a pattern. She found the first one and squeezed the trigger. Direct hit. The first was always the easiest. Now she'd been spotted. One enemy broke formation, charging towards her position.

"Enemy target approaching," *Freya* chimed in. Vladia's Valkyrie computer was linked to the simulation, replacing the simulation's piloting interface, hence the extra electrodes. To her, there was no point in practicing if *Freya* couldn't practice with her.

"I see it," she muttered, taking aim and waiting as the fighter continued its path. This time the wait was longer, but when she spotted it, she fired, scoring another direct hit.

"Get ready for evasive maneuvers," she instructed as three more enemies deviated from their formation to pursue her. Vladia's battle screen flashed as *Freya's* long-range weapon went offline and full power was routed to the shields.

"Power successfully re-routed."

The targets were in range and fired their first volley. Vladia dodged, sailing upward and back then changed course for impact.

"Shields. Full front!"

The enemies continued to fire, their shots deflected as Vladia took them head on. Vladia shot her grappling hook and caught the middle fighter. The other two jerked to either side.

"Ha!" Vladia shouted as the struggling ship tried to veer away. Its movement was sporadic, like that of a frightened bird.

She grabbed one of its thrusters and crushed it in *Freya's* powerful fists. That slowed it down.

Its comrades fired wildly at her. The fighter was almost as large as *Freya,* so Vladia had no problem using her wounded prey as an additional shield. Friendly fire finished it off as she ejected her hook from the carcass.

"Route power to shoulder cannons and continue to shield my front. We're going in guns ablazin'," Vladia ordered.

"Power rerouted," *Freya* confirmed as she charged the two fighters that were already coming her way.

The lights flicked on and her targets vanished. "What just happened?" she demanded.

"Combat feed has been disrupted. Someone is here," *Freya* explained. Vladia opened the hatch and peered out.

Abel stood leaning in the doorway with his flight suit

halfway pulled up and tied around his waist.

Vladia shot him a heated glare.

"Senior Officer override," he explained with a grin.

"Save and exit program," Vladia told the computer with a sigh as she snatched off the electrodes and thrust herself out of the cockpit.

"How goes it?" Abel asked.

"Ninety-two percent."

"Good."

"But not great."

"No," he conceded. "But I suppose that's why we have these simulators. If we were all at a hundred percent, who would use them?"

"Well, glad to be of some use," Vladia returned with a touch of bitterness.

Ignoring her tone, Abel continued, "Hey. Sorry I've been busy lately. I'd wanted to look over that footage with you."

Vladia shrugged. She assumed this was his way of apologizing for avoiding her the past five days. Not that she'd made any attempt to find him, Cornelia, or Takashi. What she'd done was unacceptable and if none of them ever spoke to her again she would have accepted it as best she could. Though she wouldn't delude herself into believing she wasn't happy he'd come back around.

"Come see me off." He motioned for her to follow.

"Where are you going?" she asked, reluctantly tagging behind him.

"Escorting an envoy to Lunar station Torappu One."

"Why? What's up?" Vladia asked as she caught up to him.

"Dunno. Just following Captain's orders. The station is the closest in orbit around Earth, so it'll only take twenty minutes to reach the destination point. Unfortunately, I've been instructed to stay with the envoy until they're ready to depart, so I could be gone for days." Abel jammed his hands in his pockets. Vladia noticed he always did this when something was bothering him.

"It's just a normal run, right?" she inquired gently.

"I haven't been told anything," he said. Vladia gave him a sharp frown and with a temperate sigh he continued, "What do you think? How many envoys do we send to Luna and how many of them are political?"

"Only a few a year, and all of them are political as far as I know."

"And how many of them need an escort?"

Vladia had no answer.

"Zero. Escort is just a fancy word for guard." They stopped in front of the elevator. The floor panels underneath them lit up as the sensors detected their presence. "Whatever is going on between Luna and Earth, there's a definite fear that something might go wrong with this little excursion."

The doors opened and the two stepped in. "Level eighteen, Section F," Abel instructed after the doors glided shut.

Vladia leaned against the wall as she studied her friend. His expression was more serious than normal. There was something he wasn't telling her. "Did you ask me to see you off because you don't think you're going to make it back?" she asked cautiously.

Abel laughed, making Vladia redden with embarrassment. "No, it's nothing like that. I've no doubts about making it back alive."

At least she'd broken his melancholy for a moment. The indignity she now endured was well worth it. "Then what?"

"Honestly, it's a little depressing to leave for a mission and have no one to see you off. Rehel was tied up with other business so…"

"So I was second choice?" Vladia pretended to be miffed in an effort to keep up Abel's spirits.

"Rehel's the closest person to me. We've known each other a long time. He's different from the others."

Vladia hadn't heard someone call a robot a person since her mother. It made her smile to know at least one other human in the universe treated robots like more than just machines.

"You don't have to explain it to me," she assured him.

"No. I don't suppose I do," he answered, clearly referencing her behavior from the bar.

Vladia hated she'd said anything to remind him of that, but Abel seemed to have no interest in dwelling on the matter any further.

The doors opened and both exited onto the eighteenth level, section F, which placed them close to the hangar bays. As the two continued down the corridor, Vladia felt it safe to change the subject back to their earlier topic. "What does Rehel say about all this? Doesn't he attend senior officer meetings with Malthus?"

"Yeah. But someone put the info under security restriction so he couldn't tell me anything even if he wanted to." Able unknotted the arms of his flight suit from around his waist.

"Is that normal?"

"Sometimes. But in this case, I don't think it matters. I have a hunch that after this little run, whatever secrets the higher-ups have been keeping about the situation between Luna and Earth will be public knowledge."

As they reached hangar bay C, Vladia sensed Abel's mood begin to darken again. One of the things she liked about Abel was that he didn't try to hide his concern from her. Although it worried her, she liked to know what her partner was thinking and feeling. She wished Tolen would put that kind of trust in her.

Captain Malthus was waiting in the control room. Abel zipped up his suit and the two entered with a salute.

"Reporting for duty, Sir," Abel stated.

Malthus nodded then looked to Vladia, "And you?"

"Just here to see my Gunslinger off, Sir."

"Very well, you can watch from the control room. Lt. Commander Duren, you have your orders. You may proceed." Malthus took a seat at the control panel on the east side of the room.

"Sir!" Abel saluted once more before dismissing himself. Vladia watched from the translucent enclosure of the control room as he climbed the ladder to the cockpit of *Gunnr*.

After he secured himself in, Abel's voice boomed over the channel. "Ready for launch, Captain."

"Confirmation from the envoy has been received. They have successfully launched and are waiting in orbit in sector five. You are cleared for launch." Malthus closed the channel.

The ceiling panels receded into the hangar walls with a sharp groan. *Gunnr's* thrusters roared as the ship pushed its heavy bulk off the floor.

Vladia could barely make out Abel's form through the thickly tinted aeroplastic that made up *Gunnr's* hatch lid. She imagined he was waving. Malthus' formality proved contagious and instead of waving goodbye, she sent her friend off with a stiff salute.

With agile fingers, Malthus manipulated the key pad to pull up the view screen and connect to the Rekka Satellite System surrounding Earth. The envoy flashed on screen. Moments later, *Gunnr* joined the scene.

"They will arrive at their destination in approximately fifteen minutes. If you're going to watch, take a seat." Malthus offered her his chair as he stood up.

"You're not staying?"

"Why should I? More than one person monitoring a fifteen minute escort flight is overkill. When he lands, he'll report in. Acknowledge him, and then you can leave. He'll be there for several days and will send word twelve hours before departure."

Vladia took the seat. "And if anything should happen?"

"Why would anything happen?" Malthus arched an eyebrow. "I hope you don't think your partner so incompetent he would fail at a trivial escort mission."

"Of course not." Vladia tried not to sound defensive.

"Is there something else you're concerned about?"

"No," she answered.

"Then I leave you to it," he said with a slight bow. Vladia's eyes followed him as he left. It was hard not to. Tolen commanded such presence. If he chose, all eyes were drawn to him. Or if he wanted, he could ease in and out of a crowd completely unnoticed. Vladia simply didn't possess that kind of charisma.

She caught herself growing envious again. That charisma of his had helped him graduate cadet school a year ahead of schedule and land a position as captain less than two years after that. She had, of course, taken the full three years to finish cadet school and was still just a pilot.

Vladia tried to shake such thoughts from her mind. Her concern now was Abel and what, if anything, was about to unfold. If Malthus knew something, he wasn't telling. The thought of him sending Abel out on a mission with potential dangers and not warning him turned her stomach. Malthus was cold, but he was strategic enough not to send one of his best to his death. If something big was about to go down, Malthus needed Abel in his squad.

Vladia had just put her mind at ease when she heard footsteps clacking her way. She waited till they drew closer then swung her chair around to face the entryway.

"Lt. Robespierre, I am surprised to find you here," Rehel stated with no surprise at all. "Captain Malthus will not be present then?"

"No, I'm staying until Abel lands on the station."

Rehel seemed to consider this a moment. "Would it be acceptable if I also stayed until Lt. Commander Duren successfully landed?"

"Of course."

Rehel didn't take a seat, but he stepped closer to the view screen. After several minutes of silence, Vladia decided to see if she could leverage any information out of the robot.

"So, you've known Abel a long time?" Vladia began with typical conversation, although she knew such tactics were wasted on him. She should just ask him point blank, but it was difficult for her to be so blunt, even with a robot.

"I have known Lt. Commander Duren for as long as he has been a Valkyrie pilot."

"He seemed concerned about this mission. Is there something he should be worried about?"

"Lt. Robespierre, you are inquiring about classified information on the relations between Earth and Luna. I advise you to stop," Rehel warned.

"So, you'll tell me nothing?"

"I believe I have told you all you need to know, Lt. Robespierre."

Vladia was visibly taken aback. He had told her nothing, yet told her she was right to be suspicious. Yet, it was the reaction she had anticipated. The surprising part was in his last statement. His awareness of his own subtext, his purposefulness of it all was so human. Not something a typical robot would, or could, do. Abel was right, this one was different.

"Lt. Commander Duren reporting in." Abel's voice buzzed over the comm system.

Vladia reopened the channel. "Abel, what's your status?"

"Everything looks fine. The envoy has hailed the station but no response has been made. I'm almost in sensor range."

"They should be expecting your arrival," Rehel added.

Abel continued, "I'm not–ic–g–up–ny–lif–sig…"

"Are we being jammed?" she asked Rehel as panic crept into her voice.

Rehel was already at the controls trying to locate the source of the interference. Rehel's eyes widened and instead of answering Vladia he shouted, "Abel! It's a trap! Pull out immediately!"

Only static.

Vladia's eyes shot to the view screen just seconds before Torappu One exploded in an eruption of radiation. The flames lasted mere seconds, as the oxygen from inside the station burned up. The danger was in the chunks of space station shrapnel hurtling at high velocities. She feverishly scanned the view screen, looking for *Gunnr*, or the remains of it.

"There." Rehel magnified a portion of the screen near the top left corner.

Gunnr was spinning at a steady speed away from the remains of the station with serious damage to the outer hull. The envoy's vessel was scattered into dozens of large chunks around the wreckage. It had been a passage liner and lacked the maneuverability to escape such an explosion. There was no point in searching for survivors.

"Rehel, clear me for launch!" Vladia ordered as she dashed from the room towards *Freya*.

"Lt. Robespierre, I do not have the authority to clear you for launch," the robot called after her.

Vladia stopped with a jerk. "Robot Rehel! I am your superior officer, and I am ordering you to give me clearance. If you do not comply, I will launch anyway and if necessary I'll pry open the doors and tear this damn hangar apart." She looked back at him, face tinged with anger. "Now, will you clear me for launch?"

Rehel nodded and punched in the clearance codes.

Vladia wasted no time. She was synced up and ready for take-off just as the ceiling panels had finished receding. She blasted out of the hangar, heading for the wreckage among the stars.

"Rehel, can you read me?" Vladia called over the comm.

"Positive."

"I will take full responsibility for both our actions today," she assured him.

"As you know, if there is an explosion anywhere between Earth and 200,000 km from our outer satellite border, all bases are put on alert until the situation is resolved. I am sure Captain Malthus is aware of the situation and has already deduced the actions you have taken."

"Point taken."

"Lt. Robespierre, please update me on Lt. Commander Duren's status once you arrive."

"Of course." If Vladia hadn't known better, she would have thought the robot sounded concerned. Then again, his outburst just before the explosion was clearly one of panic. There was no time to dwell on that now though.

Vladia broke through Earth's atmosphere and plunged into a sea of blackness and stars. She adjusted her course to *Gunnr's* last coordinates, letting the nav system make further adjustments to account for the speed and distance it had traveled since her take-off. In a matter of minutes, *Gunnr* was on screen. As she sped closer, Vladia could verify the extent of the damage. All systems appeared to be off-line and *Gunnr's* legs and lower mid-section had been butchered by the station's shrapnel.

"*Freya*. Scan for life signs."

"Affirmative, there is one life sign aboard," *Freya* responded in seconds.

With *Freya's* massive arms, Vladia grasped hold of the other Valkyrie and used her thrusters to pull it to a halt.

Abel was visible, his unconscious body free-floated about the cockpit. Both arms and legs hung at unnatural angles, most likely broken during the impact of shrapnel. His harnesses should have prevented this, and Vladia couldn't imagine why he would've unlatched himself at such a critical moment.

The cockpit looked intact and if that was the case, he would have enough air to last him thirty minutes with the life support system offline. The problem was that it might be the only area left with an oxygen supply.

In order to rescue Abel, Vladia would have to open the

bottom hatch to the cockpit, which would release all the precious air keeping him alive.

Vladia examined her other options. Her ship wasn't equipped with the landing gear needed to tow him home. She could try to tow *Gunnr* to the closest space station. However, her Valkyrie had not been prepped for take-off and it was doubtful she had enough power to make it that far.

Even if she was able to make it to a station, there was no guarantee it wasn't under Luna's control. And at this juncture, she had to assume Luna was now the enemy. She would be shot on sight if that was the case.

"Rehel," Vladia called into her comm.

"What is Lt. Commander Duren's status?" the robot inquired directly.

"He's alive but unconscious and severely injured. All his systems appear to be off-line. I am going in after him." Vladia had made her decision. Going in was her only hope of getting to Abel before his oxygen supply was spent.

"Captain Malthus has summoned all Valkyrie pilots to the hangar. He is preparing for battle," Rehel continued.

"Battle?"

"There is a Lunar squad heading your way from the Zhyeris Station. Arrival time is approximately twelve minutes. The Valkyries should be there in time to intercept them, but just in case, you should hurry," he warned.

"I'm on it," she signed off.

Carefully, Vladia lined up the emergency hatches located on the backs of the crafts. She turned on the magnetic locks and the hatches attached with a dull clunk. Luckily, only one of them had to activate their magnetic locking system. The system was set up specifically for rescue situations. Both hatches were equipped with a large electromagnet. When one locking system was switched on, the polarity reversed, securing the hatches together electrically.

"I'll be right back," Vladia assured the ship as she disengaged from *Freya*.

Her body her own, Vladia tethered herself to the emergency hooks in the cockpit. Valkyries weren't equipped with grav units, so maneuvering in close quarters could be tricky. She would have to crawl through the emergency hatch, up the mid-section of the Valkyrie, and into the cockpit to retrieve Abel. If any large shrapnel had penetrated the hull in those areas, the tether would also ensure that she wouldn't slip out into space.

She pressurized her suit, attached her portable air tanks and after sliding her seat back, unlocked the ingress below her feet to climb down.

Once she reached the emergency hatch, Vladia entered the access code on the touchpad imbedded in the hull wall to unlock the door lever. She pulled the lever out then rotated it clockwise until the red-lit circle around the hatch turned green. It lurched open slowly with an unwilling groan.

She entered a second access code, and the touchpad flashed green. A panel beside it glided open, revealing a red pouch with a small gray spout at the top. The pouch contained a sticky paste of chemicals that reacted solely with the materials making up the hatch doors.

Vladia broke the seal over the spout and spread a thin layer over the edge of *Gunnr's* emergency hatch. The reaction was immediate. The edges smoked and melted as the chemicals ate their way through. Vladia pocketed the pouch and backed away.

After the chemical haze cleared, Vladia put her hands

on the wall adjacent to the hatch and planted her feet firmly on the center of the door. She pushed against the wall with her hands and gave the door a rough kick with the full force of her body. It was difficult to get the necessary force she needed in zero gravity so she had to build up some momentum to get the job done. Five attempts later, the door gave way.

Once inside *Gunnr*, Vladia was able to assess the true extent of the damage. There were numerous hull breaches along the path leading to the cockpit. Most were no larger than a fist, but one or two were large enough for a person to slip through.

Vladia reached the access point underneath the cockpit and stopped to plan out her next moves carefully. Once the door was opened, it would be a matter of seconds before the oxygen depleted.

Their flight suits used filters, similar to gills on a fish, to supply air to a pilot. If the life support system failed, and all oxygen was exhausted, then the suit would auto-pressurize and the filter would shut down, leaving only the oxygen inside the suit. This would be about thirty seconds worth, depending on how hard a person was breathing. A panicked person might find themselves with only ten seconds, while someone unconscious might stretch it to fifty.

Vladia decided she had about forty seconds to locate the emergency tanks and attach them to Abel. Even with the lack of gravity slowing her movements, that still should be more than enough time, she decided.

Securing her footing on either side of the narrow passage, Vladia gave the small circular door a quick tug. She managed to hang on as air rushed past her, escaping into space.

Abel crashed into her as she scrambled into the cockpit. Grasping Abel's flight suit, she attached him to her tether before reaching for the emergency air tanks behind the pilot's seat. She hooked the air tanks to his suit then spun him around to face her. His breath had fogged the front of his helmet, a good sign. She sighed in silent relief.

There was no time to waste. She had to get out of *Gunnr* before the Lunar fighters arrived on the scene. As it was, they were both sitting ducks.

Vladia carefully guided Abel through the opening and down towards the emergency hatch. The lack of gravity now worked in her favor. Otherwise it would have been impossible to navigate him safely through such close quarters without further injury. Moving at a snail's pace, Vladia took longer than she liked to reach her own ship.

As she shut and secured *Freya's* hatch, Rehel's voice buzzed over the comm. "Lt. Robespierre, you have enemy vessels incoming in minus one minute. You must evacuate the area now."

"Where's my backup?" Vladia growled, still struggling with Abel.

"Assistance will arrive at your location in approx.-imately three minutes. You have no time to wait."

"Right," Vladia said. She wouldn't make it. If she didn't have Abel, maybe, but she did and couldn't maneuver well with him free floating about the cockpit.

"Lt. Robespierre, y– ha– pil…" Rehel's voice was overtaken by static.

"Great. Just great!" Her frustration reverberated through the ship. She sailed up the passage, Abel in tow. Reaching the access point, she pulled him through behind her and strapped him down in her seat. Vladia unhooked the tether from Abel and let the mechanism reel in most of the excess cording.

She would have to do this free floating, with only her tether to keep her from smashing about in the cabin. There were rings located in various parts of the cabin that a pilot could hook a tether to. Vladia made use of them all, looping the line through the rings creating a web of coring around herself.

It was all she could do.

With her one free hand, she reached behind Abel's head for the cerebral connectors.

"*Freya*, what's my time?" she asked, once synced up.

"Twenty seconds until enemy vessels are in firing range."

Vladia rotated around. "Full power to thrusters, let's go!"

Freya shot towards Earth.

"You are being pursued."

"Geez, you think?" her agitation was lost on *Freya*. "Get me a visual, split screen."

The ship responded as Vladia's screen divided into two panes, the left focused on Earth, the right on her shadows.

"*Freya*, my right screen's blank. What's going on?"

"I am still picking up energy patterns, but they are distorted."

Vladia looked at her tracking screen and confirmed a fuzzy glob of radiation closing in on her. "Shit!"

Metamaterial, or phantom material, was true cloaking technology. Using it on an entire ship was costly and impractical. But this had to be it.

"Give me everything you've got to thrusters except for my back shields."

"Affirmative."

Despite this, she knew the enemy was still gaining. If

she could just reach the rest of the squad before they overtook her, she could leave the rest to them. A med crew would be waiting for her landing and she could be back in the sky in twenty minutes tops.

"Incoming fire," *Freya* warned.

It was as if the blackness itself shot at her. She'd never seen anything like it. Vladia maneuvered as best she could without losing speed. *Freya* took more than one direct hit, but her shields held and she pressed on.

She could finally see her squad, first on her sensors, then on screen.

"They're cloaked!" she yelled over the channel.

"Roger that." The response came from Lt. Cornelia Arnim. "Get Abel back to Earth. We can handle these amateurs."

"Negative, Lt. Arnim," Captain Malthus began. "Lt. Robespierre will stay and fight with her squad."

"What!" came not one, but several voices, the loudest being Takashi Gammarow.

"Captain," Vladia began, "the extent of Abel's injuries is unknown and he is possibly unstable. If I could just–"

"Lieutenant!" Her captain's voice was sharp but not angry. "I owe you no explanations. You stay and you fight."

"Yes, Captain." Vladia did her best to keep a level tone as fury boiled under her skin. She fell in formation with her squad and prepared to engage the enemy.

"*Freya*, maximize forward shields," her voice wavered. She was unsteady; her hands shook. If she didn't get this under control she'd be useless in this fight. She drew in a tentative breath, tried to ease her rage. She would not die here. She would not let Abel die here.

"Valkyries!" Malthus clamored, "It appears we cannot

see the enemy, but we do not need to. These Lunar renegades underestimate us. They insult you, they insult this squad and they insult Earth herself! You are the best our planet has to offer and now the time has come to prove it. Eleven blind Valkyries are more than enough to dispense with this trash. Fire everything you've got. Half their fighters shall be down before they even reach us."

"Yes, Sir!" The squad roared.

Vladia was silent. The powerful words of a great man could make a mere citizen think himself a fierce warrior. They could make a man forget his morals, trade his soul for a sword. Malthus always had powerful words; it was his greatest strength on occasion.

Yet Vladia was not moved by this great man's words. It was not his voice that called her to action. It was the silence of the man behind her that pushed her to point her canon. It was the man she must protect that made her senses sharp, her aim steady, and her emotions controlled.

"Incoming fire," *Freya* warned.

Her comrades fired blindly into the abyss as they dodged enemy fire. Vladia stared into the blackness, unmoving and patient. She took the blasts head on. Her shields would hold.

Though invisible, the fighters lit up her sensors each time they fired. It only lasted a moment, but for a second, they may as well have not been cloaked at all.

She watched them, and she waited.

There!

She fired.

A single fighter burst from the black void that had veiled it. It was barely damaged; a surface wound at best. But that was all she needed to disrupt the cloak. Another weakness of the metamaterials.

It was strange to see a lone fighter charging eleven Valkyries, but Vladia did not dwell on this as she aimed, silent among the cheers that flooded the channel.

Freya took blast after blast. Her body shook from the impact but Vladia held steady.

There!

She fired and another fighter lost its protection within the shadows.

Her comrades picked up on this. Slowing, the squad stood firm and took the time to make steady, reliable shots.

Two more fighters sprang into view. Then another and another.

"Shields at thirty percent," *Freya* alerted her.

All but a handful of fighters remained cloaked as Vladia sheathed her blaster canon. Malthus would handle the rest in a matter of moments.

"I want thrusters at full capacity. Divert everything else to shields. Sensors, comm, weapons, even life support."

"Lt. Robespierre–"

"If I don't have shields, life support isn't doing me much good anyway. I've enough air for now," she said, thinking back to Abel and the rescue mission. "Monitor me. At five percent, bring life support back online. Get those shields back to full."

"Yes, Lt. Robespierre," *Freya* submitted.

She was the first to charge, followed closely by the rest. With her emotions in check, she found her range of movement was much greater than ever before. She felt faster, more precise with every movement.

The Luna fighters were confused at their sudden exposure, making them overly cautious; they kept a distance between not only the Valkyries, but each other as well. Once caught by a Valkyrie, the fight was over and the enemy became a weapon against their comrades in the form of a shield or a projectile.

Vladia took her time, evading fire and keeping a distance until she spotted an opening.

She plunged forward and caught one by the tail. The fighter stopped, like a fly in a spider's web. She thrust *Freya's* arm into its underbelly and pulled out a fist full of wiring.

Still gripping its tail, Vladia flew towards *Alvitr*, who was chasing her own prey. The Luna fighter didn't see Vladia as she launched her captive fighter towards it. When he did, it was only as his comrade's ship crashed into his own and sent them both hurtling out to space.

"Incoming fire," *Freya* announced. "Shields holding at eighty percent."

Vladia turned to find one brave fighter charging her way. On any other day, the fighter might have had a slim chance. But not today. Vladia didn't dodge and took the fire head on as she powered her way towards the lone fighter.

"Air supply at ten percent," *Freya* warned as Vladia engaged the enemy.

They would collide if one of them did not alter course. The fighter didn't waver, willing to take her out at any cost. But it wasn't enough. Not today.

With seconds to spare, Vladia rotated around, feet first. Gliding under the fighter, her fists dug into its hull. Brief sparks flew as she tore and ripped.

"Air supply at five percent. Shields at forty."

Vladia jerked away as her shields went off line to bring life support up.

She watched as the fighter continued to soar away from

her and the others. Its core systems shot, it would drift forever unless one of its own rescued it.

Vladia caught a glimpse of a terror-stricken face in the cockpit. Without thinking, she moved to chase after it, to save the pilot from the black.

A shot was fired and the ship exploded.

"Where'd that shot come from?" She asked *Freya*.

"Coordinates 25,14,73."

She looked to her left in time to see Malthus dive back into the fray that was quickly retreating. A few Valkyries chased after the remaining seven ships, but pulled back on what was probably Malthus' order.

"*Freya*, bring the comm back online if you've got the resources."

The roar of fresh victory burst through, filling her cockpit.

"Congratulations, Valkyries! You have won the first battle of the war!" Malthus' voice elicited another round of cheers.

"*Freya*, close the channel."

The noise ended abruptly.

"Get the current coordinates of *Gunnr* and transmit them to the rest of the squad for retrieval. Maybe it can be salvaged." Vladia's voice was low compared to the thunderous hails of victory.

She felt tired, her body was heavy. Even her voice felt weary as she spoke slow and steady. "Let's go home."

6

MEMORIES

Knock, knock, knock...

Knock, knock, knock...

Abel rolled over and pulled a soft pillow off his head, dropping it onto the floor. With foggy eyes he read the clock: 03:35

Knock, knock, knock...

"Abel," an urgent voice whispered from the other side of his apartment door.

Abel sat up and rubbed the inner corners of his eyes with his fingers. He grabbed a pair of slacks from the floor and pulled them on.

"Abel," the voice pleaded, again followed by three knocks in rapid succession.

03:37 now. He didn't bother with a shirt as he trudged his tired body to the door and unlocked it.

Ceres Forté pushed her way in. "Close it," she ordered.

"What's up? I thought you were pulling an all-nighter at the lab?" Abel wondered why he'd never given her an entry code to his place. If he had, she wouldn't have needed to bang on the door to get in.

"Something's wrong."

He shook the last traces of sleep from his head. "At the lab? What's going on?"

"They started bringing in people. Three months ago. Terminal patients. I didn't think much of it, just that it was weird because we don't do that kind of work." Ceres walked circles around the room, wrenching her hands repetitively.

She was still in her lab coat, name tag and all and Abel realized she must have come straight from the lab. Her pale eyes were bloodshot, and her mouth twitched around the corners. He reached out to calm her but she jerked away.

"They're all dead, Abel! All of them," she cried, eyes darting back and forth under a wild mess of red hair. "One by one they took them away. I saw it and then the others–they all started freaking out. Screaming and smashing equipment like monsters!"

"I don't understand," Abel began. "Who's dead? What terminal patients? You work in a nanobot and computer interface facility."

"Tolen Malthus brought them!" Ceres' voice turned shrill. "He's friends with Dr. Sendivogius. They've been working together for months. Months!" She bit down on her lower lip until red droplets formed. It was as if her body was forcing her into silence.

"Ceres! Stop it! You're hurting yourself!" he cried as blood trembled down her chin.

Malthus? There's no way, Abel thought. Why would a Valkyrie pilot be at any research facility?

Ceres sank to the floor, pulling her knees to her chest. She rocked gently back and forth. "It was a secret. It was a secret and now he's killed us all. It serves us all right."

"Ceres," Abel said, kneeling beside her. "Calm down. Everything is going to be ok. Tell me what's going on so I can help you. Please."

For an instant she appeared still. She released her legs and fell forward, wrapping her arms around Abel. Her lips, just centimeters from his ear, parted. Warm, shallow breaths touched his skin. "Make it stop."

"I'll do anything I can, Ceres." He held her body as it quivered softly. "Shhhhhhh," he whispered.

Abel eased out of her embrace to better examine her. The veins in her bloodshot eyes pulsated with every twitch of her face. Taking Ceres's hands in his, he kissed them.

"Make it stop," she repeated. Blood seeped out the corners of her eyes, streaking her cheeks. Abel's hands felt hot and sticky. He opened his palms and saw her nail beds were now bleeding as well.

"I've got to get you to the hospital." Abel stood and lifted her up with him. He had to stay calm, though every inch of him wanted to panic. He'd never seen so much blood. No one, not even soldiers, was conditioned for this anymore. If he could just get her to a hospital she'd be okay.

Ceres jolted away from him. With both bleeding hands, she clutched the sides of her head and screeched in pain. She pulled out chunks of her hair, stumbling back against the wall.

"Where am I?" The words escaped her mouth followed by a gush of blood. Abel watched, frozen, as Ceres' eyes went dead and her body slid down the wall, leaving a smear of crimson behind it.

Abel couldn't move. He wanted to run to her. Maybe

she was still alive. Why wouldn't his body move!

His vision blurred. He felt himself falling.

Light from the hallway burned his eyes. Someone was there. Footsteps moved towards him; he felt the vibration in his head.

Clack, clack, clack, against the floor.

Clack...

C l a c k...

C l a c k...

∞

Vladia slouched, back against the sterile, taupe walls of McCarthy's Providence Hospital. She'd been told Abel could wake at any time, and she wanted to be there when he did. Almost all of the Valkyrie pilots had come by to check on him, but it was Vladia and Rehel who waited patiently for him to regain consciousness.

It had been five days since the incident. Abel's injuries had been severe but manageable: no brain or spinal damage, only broken limbs, ribs and some bruised organs. The surgery had been quick and one hundred percent successful. Because it was a wartime incident, the medics injected him with high levels of regenerative meds, which sped up recovery time exponentially. It was intensely painful, so they kept him sedated until the meds cleared his system. A week or so of physical therapy would take care of the rest. Now all there was to do was wait.

Arms folded across her chest, Vladia absently watched Abel sleep. She could see his eyes moving beneath his lids. Covering a yawn, she pushed away from the wall and stretched her body.

She wished Rehel would hurry back before he woke.

Abel would prefer him over her and honestly she did too. She felt guilty over the whole affair. Maybe it was the cold formality she'd sent him off with. Maybe it was because she had no answers for him. The investigation uncovered nothing. His safety belt had snapped during impact, and no one seemed to know how or why. Not being allowed to look over the craft herself, she had nothing to add to the report.

Abel's lips moved as he spoke inaudible words amid a dream. Leaning close, Vladia lowered her head to his and listened.

Abel groaned and shook his head. Startled, Vladia leapt back to her place against the wall. His eyes fluttered open, and he gazed vacantly about the room.

For several minutes he seemed unsure and almost panicked as he moved his head about as if looking for something that wasn't there. Vladia remained frozen, unsure if she should call for a doctor or not.

"What's today?" he finally asked, his dry voice cracking with every syllable.

"The twenty-fourth. Do you know where you are, Abel?"

"That seems about right," he said, ignoring her question. "God damn, I feel awful."

"Regen meds will do that." Vladia sat down on the edge of his bed. He tried to push himself up, but Vladia moved to stop him. "Take it easy."

Abel submitted without protest. He continued to glance around the room as if looking for something familiar to rest his eyes on. "Where's my stuff?"

"Your personal effects have already been sent to your quarters. Do you need me to get something for you?"

"No. It's fine."

The two sat in awkward silence. Vladia waited for him to ask about Rehel, but he didn't. He seemed preoccupied with his own thoughts.

Maybe I should go, she considered. When she moved to get up, Abel reached out, taking hold of her sleeve.

"I should be thanking you, I think," he said hastily. "I feel like I ought to."

"Yes. And you're welcome." With a smile, Vladia sat back down. "*Gunnr* is going to be ok too, by the way. He was in bad shape, but repairable."

"Just like me, eh?" Abel tried to laugh, but all he managed was a half-cough and a shrug of the shoulders. "So, what else do I need to know?"

"At the moment, nothing. You still need to rest. Rehel will debrief you once he's off duty later. The Captain expects you'll be ready to fly by next week."

Abel grimaced and closed his eyes.

"What?" she asked.

"Just remembering an old nightmare."

"You've been out for five days. I imagine you've had enough dreaming to last a year," Vladia joked. Abel's expression remained dour.

"You were talking in your sleep," she continued.

Abel arched a brow and opened his eyes.

"Well, sort of. I didn't really hear anything but you seemed upset. You want to talk about it?"

"No, I'm good," he insisted.

"If it was about the explosion..."

"Look, I appreciate what you're trying to do here, but stop. Please. Memories and dreams aren't worth dwelling on. You want to do something for me? Go find me a damn doctor so I can get released. If your *brother* wants me ready by next week then I need to get out of here." Abel's voice was not loud but it brimmed with anger.

Vladia went rigid. Sliding off the bed, she instinctively stepped towards the exit.

"You aren't nearly as good at hiding secrets as he is. Your body language alone told me something was up between you two. I had Rehel check your records, and your father is blatantly stated on all your forms." Abel spoke the 'brother' and 'father' as if the words themselves were deformed and unnatural.

She hadn't expected anyone to check. Unless charges were being pressed, there was no reason for her records to be viewed by human eyes.

"You'd no right or reason to go through my files. My relationship to my half-brother, or my father for that matter, is irrelevant," she protested, putting the same disgusted emphasis on those words as he had.

Abel shrugged. "I had my reasons."

"Damn your reasons. Perhaps I should go poking into your private affairs until I've uncovered a little dirt on you as well. I imagine even you have something worth hiding."

Abel's expression hardened. "As your superior officer and your partner pilot I had every right to know about possible instabilities and dangers to my own safety. I'll have you know that I've been aware of your situation for quite some time and only one aspect of any of it is troubling."

"And what's that?" she challenged.

"You admire him. You wish you were more like Malthus. And that's a fine thing if you know exactly what you're admiring."

Abel again tried to sit up. This time Vladia didn't move to stop him. With a grunt, he gently heaved his legs over the side of the bed. "There used to be a saying," he began, strain echoing through his voice. "Blood is thicker than water. You know what that means?"

Vladia nodded.

"It means nothing anymore, not to the billions of children raised in The System each year. But for you, and a handful of others, it does mean something. In fact, it means a hell of a lot. You've got your family, and no matter how you think you feel about them, you love them. It can't be helped. The rest of us simply don't understand. This bond will be your undoing if you're blinded by the blood," Abel advised.

Vladia narrowed her eyes. "What are you trying to say?"

Was it the meds talking? she wondered. This wasn't like him. Abel was never one for weighty words and lectures on character.

"You should be mindful of your blood-based admiration." His warning came out like a thick gasp.

His body was exhausted, his skin almost colorless. His eyes, though dark and heavy with sleep, watched hers intently. It had been too early for him to wake. Sheer willpower helped him endure the pain that racked his mind and muscles. His whitened knuckles gripped the edge of the mattress.

"Tell Rehel I'm awake. I need to talk to him." Abel squeezed the request out between gritted teeth.

Vladia nodded, agreeing to his request, and made her exit. She would get the doctor first. Abel was at his limit and needed to be sedated at least another day. Then she would see Rehel. But she hadn't the slightest intention of sending him to Abel, who she expected was already unconscious again.

No, she had some talking of her own to do with Rehel before Abel could see him. Starting with a name: Ceres.

∞

Frédéric Chopin's Étude Op. 10, No. 12 in C minor echoed through the minimalist chambers of Tolen Malthus. There wasn't a hint of personal possessions save for a smattering of bound books on the recessed shelf above his bed. All he owned, he kept secured in either his near-invisible storage panels or at his late father's estate. He saw no point in dragging a heap of personal effects halfway across the world for the sake of adding personality to his room. It was all a waste of space.

Limited furniture meant better acoustics, and Chopin's intricate melody permeated the space flawlessly. Tolen listened with closed eyes atop the neatly pressed black covers of his full-sized bed. Many found Chopin's compositions to be beautiful yet over-exaggerated with Rubato and unpredictable turns. Malthus enjoyed it for the exact opposite. It was intensely technical, especially for the left hand, and difficult to play even by modern standards.

As a boy, he'd enjoyed deconstructing the rhythms and melodies, finding and predicting the patterns, then linking them together. Chopin had always been a good exercise for his mind.

Of course there were much more complicated pieces available now, but modern composers were all no-talent hacks, using computers to do the hard parts for them. Their techniques were slothful, as were the players that performed them, making their melodies and rhythms foreseeable. They were worthless to him, no matter how beautiful.

Tolen frowned. Despite his admiration for Chopin's work, at times he almost hated it. Rubato, that irregular flow of the tempo, reminded him of Vladia. Rubato was unpredictable because it varied with the conductor. Vladia was random too, driven by emotions instead of reason. It was irritating, and during their childhood he'd worked diligently to break her of this habit. She was, in a very limited way, his only failure and for that he blamed Maria Robespierre.

Regardless, Tolen still predicted her reactions at close to one hundred percent accuracy. He tested her often, as practice. For him it was like calibrating his abilities. Take for instance the episode with Abel Duren and the exploding space station. That had actually been a test for both of them, and it had worked out nicely. The test began the moment he asked Abel to escort the envoy. Standard procedure required him to inform Abel of the risks.

However, he did not because, first, he knew Abel would be intelligent enough to deduce the danger himself; second, he knew the man would go regardless of the risk. In fact, Tolen knew that had he asked for a volunteer, Abel would have jumped at it. Abel wouldn't have let any of his comrades risk themselves on that mission. But Tolen imagined his reasons were much darker than simple self-sacrifice. Underneath Abel's carefree persona, he suspected there was a powerful self-loathing that made Abel almost eager for his own death.

After Abel accepted the mission, Tolen knew he would seek out his robot friend to see him off. Making sure Rehel was thoroughly occupied, Tolen forced him to go to Vladia instead. This was the move he counted on to make or break his test. Witnessing Vladia's reaction to Abel's possible death had been quite exciting. It was predetermined perfection. Impeccably accurate. Her mad dash into space, her disregard for protocol, all played out just as he had planned.

He'd estimated Abel's survival rate at thirty percent, with the failure of the safety belts that number should have been halved. Tolen had a theory to prove on the broken safety belts, but decided to leave the official investigation inconclusive. A full-on investigation would cost him time he no longer had. But what was truly surprising was his survival in spite of his orders for Vladia to stay and fight with her squad. Abel was quite resilient indeed.

The final phase of the test was a bit off, yielding unexpected results. It was the only aspect Tolen had not predicted accurately. His failure was a slight annoyance, but the outcome proved so interesting he considered the test a success regardless.

Ordering Vladia to stay and fight, furthering the risk to her friend's life, should have blinded her with rage. She'd always been quick to anger, and with anger came sloppiness. Her skill level should have dropped considerably. But it didn't. Instead, it increased exponentially. He'd examined the data himself and it was incredible. Her accuracy and maneuverability were far beyond anything she'd achieved before.

Tolen wasn't sure what it all meant yet, but this outcome had definitely altered his plans. It would take some time, maybe a day or two, to decide on his next move. Perhaps Vladia had finally proven herself to be more than just a reckless pawn. She was certainly the major reason the last battle had ended in their favor.

Chopin was interrupted by sharp chimes at the door.

"Pause," Tolen ordered as he stood and smoothed his uniform. He walked to his desk and took a seat behind it, picking up the top datapad from the stack.

"Enter," he called. The doors slid open and Lt. Commander Isobel Falis walked in. She gave him a quick salute, then sat down in the only available chair across from Tolen's desk.

"Well?" he prompted the woman.

"Abel is awake, and his vitals stable. It appears to be a full recovery."

Tolen noted the hint of irritation in her voice. Her pitch was slightly lower than normal. Her stare was intense, but not angry. She folded her hands tightly over her lap, releasing the tension from her shoulders.

"What of the investigation report? Did you process it as requested?"

There it was. The woman's mouth formed a straight, thin line as she pressed her lips together. It was her. He had suspected, but now he was certain.

"Of course. The report was processed almost an hour ago. Inconclusive results seemed satisfactory as we are at war and have better things to do," Falis said tersely.

"Exactly. We are at war, which is why every move must be prefect and precise. No mistakes. No excuses. And now is not the time to embellish or invent orders." Tolen sat the datapad on the cold surface of the desk. Now she had been warned.

"Tolen–"she began, but he waved her into silence.

She was an adequate soldier and pilot, Tolen thought. And she was easily controlled for the most part. Her emotional attachment to him made her fiercely loyal. Not to Earth, but to him. Yet sometimes, in an effort to please him, she acted without thinking of consequences, as with

Abel's Valkyrie. Falis thought Duren was a threat. Her solution was to get rid of him. But she failed to appreciate the ramifications of losing such a pilot, and the consequences if she were caught. Tolen had plans for her, and she could have easily ruined them with that one impulsive act.

Besides, Duren was no threat to him. He could go on poking his nose around in sealed files all day long and would never find what he was looking for. Duren was a mere fly, buzzing, buzzing, buzzing. A simple annoyance Tolen could squash at any time. Falis did not understand at all. The goal was to win the war against Luna quickly and decisively.

"Take a look at this," Tolen said, sliding the datapad across his desk.

Falis took it. Tolen watched as her golden brown eyes grew large with surprise. She scrolled through quickly.

"So this is it then? It's almost complete?" She passed the datapad back to him.

"It must be tested, perhaps after the next offensive."

"And if it works?"

"Winning the war comes first. I don't need this to do that. But it will be indispensable for the next phase. It's all about planning ahead," Tolen smiled gently, "Isobel."

The woman's face reddened faintly.

So simple to control, thought Tolen. She was the perfect pawn indeed. He trusted her completely. Not because of her capabilities, but because she loved him. She loved him more than her own life and it would probably destroy her in the end. Sometimes, he'd realized long ago, even the greatest of human flaws could be crafted into assets.

7

ONLY MORE QUESTIONS

Vladia entered the Valkyrie hangar bay and spotted Rehel overseeing repairs meters away from *Gunnr*. His back was to her, but she could make out his distinctive rust colored hair and crisp black uniform from across the hangar. There were at least five visible mechanibots working on the craft. Their bulbous bodies swarmed around the ship like summer flies, diving in and nipping at the hull. It appeared the major repairs were almost complete. Only a few sections of wiring were left exposed.

Tolen clearly was aiming to have both pilot and ship ready within the week, she thought.

She found *Freya* in the westward corner of the hangar. One bot was still finishing up repairs as Vladia took a detour to inspect the red and black behemoth. She ran her finger tips across its cool, metallic casing. The bot was nearly done, even the scratches had been buffed out.

Freya was a beast of machinery and standing next to it made Vladia feel so insignificant. Trivial in comparison.

Yet when she was in the pilot's seat, this vast power was under her command. Together they were invincible. This ship was more than a weapon to her. She was proud to call *Freya* hers. She couldn't imagine losing it like Abel almost lost *Gunnr*.

She patted *Freya's* leg and sighed as she headed to the other end of the hangar.

"Lt. Robespierre, repairs are scheduled to be completed on your Valkyrie within the hour," Rehel stated as Vladia walked up behind him.

"That's all right. Actually, I came to see about *Gunnr*. Abel will want to know," she said, moving to his side.

"*Gunnr's* repairs are scheduled to be completed in seventy-two hours," he explained. His fingers darted about a datapad, recording the bots' progress. It must be for Tolen, she thought. He insisted that reports to him be delivered on handhelds, rather than streamed to his quarters remotely. Less chance of an information leak, he had explained once. It was a habit Tolen had developed during his first year at the academy, and it endured even with the most trivial information.

Vladia stood beside the robot in silence, waiting for him to finish. Rehel showed no signs of stopping, so after a minute of waiting, she decided to impose on him.

"Ceres," she began. "Does that name mean anything to you?"

"There are over one hundred records of people currently with that name in the United Terran Military database," he answered without pausing his report.

"Should that name mean anything to Abel then?"

Rehel stilled his fingers. "Ceres. Where did you hear this name?"

"Abel. He was talking in his sleep. He woke for a few

minutes but exhausted himself immediately. I had the doctor put him back under for another twenty-four hours. Otherwise, I would have asked him myself."

"Abel would have told you nothing. Although they were contracted, he does not talk about Ceres Forté."

Rehel paused, appearing to weigh his options before proceeding with the conversation. "However, the situation has changed. It might be useful if the information was made available to you."

Again he paused, as if choosing his words with care. "Abel believes you will do great things in the future, yet he refuses to share information with you that would help you make clearer decisions. I do not understand this. I suppose this is a human flaw in him. But since he has not ordered me to avoid this topic with you, I think it best to proceed."

"This seems like a personal matter, though. I don't want you to think I'm prying." Apparently there was a lot more to this than Vladia had originally suspected. Rehel seemed hesitant, almost uneasy, about the topic. That in itself was enough to rattle her senses.

Rehel tucked away his datapad, and his eyes scanned the room. Except for the bots and two guards at the entrance, they were alone.

"Do you know what would happen if specialized nanobots intended for robotic repairs were to get into a human's bloodstream?" he began, his voice slightly lowered.

"I assume they would wreak havoc, trying to eliminate organic tissues they saw as invasive." Vladia had enough knowledge of robotics to understand the basics.

"Within one hour, a human infested with such nanobots would be dead. They would start at the brain and other major organs. The human would experience hallucinations. Not just visually; all five senses would be affected. It is equivalent to madness."

"But specialized nanos haven't been used since the Gen four nanos came out."

"You asked about Ceres Forté and this is what happened, to her and everyone else at the Nanobot and Computer Interface Research Facility eight years ago, before Generation four nanobots were created. The Facility was all but destroyed by its workers. The investigation concluded it was an accident. Somehow, nanobots got loose in the ventilation system and infested every worker on duty. Every single person researching at that facility was killed, and all files were corrupted in the fire that ensued during their madness." His mechanical eyes examined her face. Vladia wondered if he was evaluating her reaction.

One of the bots swooped down in front of them, its spidery legs emerged from panels on its base. Snatching up a piece of nearby hull, it zipped away. Vladia watched it line up the piece precisely as another set of appendages emerged to fuse it on at *Gunnr's* right shoulder joint. Sparks flickered in the air above them as metal bonded with metal. With her hand, Vladia shielded her face from the glow.

"These researchers," Vladia continued, "would have been trained professionals, correct? What's the likelihood they would make that kind of mistake?"

"Most workers had over ten years in the field without incident, according to their files, making the probability for employee error less than seven percent."

"Such a low chance of error. Not only that, but everyone and every file was destroyed. I see why Abel doesn't talk about this. The events surrounding his friend's death are gruesome and I'd say a little suspicious."

"You think so?"

Vladia nodded.

"Abel feels the events are suspicious as well. But the investigation revealed nothing suspicious at all," Rehel explained, putting odd emphasis on the word 'feels'.

"However, that is not all," he continued. "The next morning Abel was found unconscious in his quarters by Captain Malthus. He was treated for shock and suffers memory loss involving the night of the explosion and Ceres."

"Memory loss is a common effect of shock."

"Yes. In actuality it is brain damage so the likelihood of his memory returning is slim to none. However, the trauma he received during the explosion could have triggered a memory, hence the mention of Ceres."

"He did ask me to go get you while he was awake," Vladia admitted.

"Thank you. After my shift here I will go to him." Rehel resumed his work on the datapad.

Vladia started to leave, but hesitated. There was one more question she'd been reluctant in asking. After her brief encounter with Abel earlier, she'd been making an effort to stray from any discussion of Tolen.

This was Rehel, though, and she needed the truth. "Abel seemed really hostile when I mentioned Captain Malthus earlier. Do you know anything about that?"

"That is something you will have to ask Abel about. Although," Rehel continued, "Captain Malthus is the one who led the investigation and determined the incident was an accident. Of course this is no secret. Anyone could look up this information if so inclined."

Now she remembered. It had been his first rank C assignment. Vladia had forgotten the details of the investigation Tolen had led, but she remembered how impressed the Admiral had been at Tolen receiving such an important assignment. The Admiral had read the report aloud to her during dinner, which was unusual. Normally she only had to hear about her brother's accomplishments during the biyearly interviews.

"I remember the assignment now," Vladia confessed. "If I'm not mistaken, Captain Malthus had a hand in building the new research facility and funding the development of the gen four nanobots, which safely differentiated between humans and robots."

"They are much more efficient than the generation three model, and I am grateful for Captain Malthus's work as I utilize the generation four nanobots." Rehel added, "Did you know that Captain Malthus tested the new nanobots on himself in order to prove they were safe for humans?"

Vladia shook her head. "No."

"It was a bold move. I wonder what would possess a human to put himself in harm's way like that. If he had been wrong, the results would have been devastating."

"Malthus is never wrong," Vladia remarked.

Why was that research so important to him? she wondered. He wasn't a scientist, so why was he involved in nanobot research in the first place? It's a dangerous habit to be linked with and he was not one to put himself in needless danger. Malthus must have a vested interest in this technology, but she could think of no logical reason for it.

Rehel's eyes darted towards the entrance of the hangar.

Vladia turned to see Lt. Takashi Gammarow and Lt. Cornelia Arnim walk in.

"This conversation is at an end, Lt. Robespierre. I would advise you not to mention this conversation to Abel. And if he were here, I think he would say to tread carefully and be mindful of those close to you." With a quick salute, Rehel walked to greet Lt. Takashi Gammarow and Lt. Cornelia Arnim.

"Lt. Gammarow. Lt. Arnim," Vladia heard him say. "Repairs on your Valkyrie are complete and ready for your inspection. Lt. Robespierre has just finished inspecting hers."

Bending the truth like a human. What a strange robot, thought Vladia. Abel was changing him, she supposed, though neither of them probably noticed. Vladia had grown fond of Rehel, and she hated to see those human characteristics seeping into his system. It was only a matter of time before he wouldn't be fit to pass his diagnostics anymore and he'd be dismantled.

She frowned at the thought. She always did have a soft spot for the second Gens. They always felt like familiar faces, even if they weren't the exact same robots she grew up with.

"If you're both here, who's babysittin' Abel?" Gammarow scoffed.

Cornelia jabbed him sharply in the ribs with her elbow. "Shut up, asshole!" she ordered. Gammarow took a step back and gave her a nasty look.

"How's he doing?" she asked with genuine concern.

"Much better. He should be up sometime tomorrow," Vladia answered as she joined the group.

"Good." The other woman smiled with relief.

A gap of silence followed. It still felt awkward between

the three of them. After the incident in the bar, Vladia actively avoided running into either of them outside of official duties.

"Lt. Robespierre, could you deliver this to Captain Malthus while I assist Lt. Gammarow and Lt. Arnim?" Rehel asked, perhaps in an effort to relieve her. Or, perhaps he was offering her an opportunity.

"Of course." Vladia took the datapad and with a quick nod to the other pilots, walked swiftly to the exit.

∞

Vladia clutched the datapad behind her back, waiting for Tolen's door to permit her entrance. It slid open soundlessly, and Vladia stepped over the threshold. Tolen was at the desk, his usual post. The room was dim apart from the lighting over her brother's head, which was hunched over an array of datapads. She gave him a crisp salute, waiting for him to signal her over. He motioned her to take the seat across from him.

Accepting the seat, Vladia slid the report across the desk without a word. Tolen stopped it just at the edge of the clear tabletop before scooping it up.

"Rehel asked me to drop this by. It's the status report on the Valkyrie repairs."

"I'll have a look at it later," he said setting it back on the desk among the other countless reports. Tolen reclined in his chair, stretching his slender body. "How's Duren?"

"He should be on his feet soon."

"Have you spoken with him yet?"

"No," she lied, "Just his doctors."

"I was hoping he could shed some light on what happened up there. You know, of course, the investigation has so far been inconclusive."

Vladia answered with a quick nod.

"By the time we got hold of the craft, it was hard to tell what actually happened due to damage caused by shrapnel and blasts during the fight," he clarified.

"Now that we're at war, I'm sure we don't have time for a full investigation regardless of the circumstances." Vladia played the card before he had the chance. That was to be his excuse, she was sure of it.

"On the contrary. That is exactly why we need to find out what happened. What if there were a Luna spy sabotaging our ships? We must make sure of the cause if at all possible," he said.

"I see your point. But do we have the resources?"

"I've put Lt. Commander Falis in charge of the investigation. She filed her initial report this morning, but she'll need to talk to Duren before anything final can be determined."

She'd miscalculated. Vladia crossed her legs and leaned forward in her chair. One alley was closed, but another approach had opened in its place.

"About that," she began, "I'd been hoping, if there was an investigation, that I could lead it. I could really use another assignment on my records. I realize I have to do more than just be a good pilot to advance in rank. Like the time you were given that investigation a few years ago. That was really big for you wasn't it?"

"Of course. Any additional duties you perform increase your chance of promotion," he explained. "I'd no idea you were already thinking ahead. That's not like you, Vladia," he added with false admiration.

Vladia refused to let her anger affect her. Tolen always used such tactics on her. They were tried and true, but not this time.

"But," he continued, "I've already given it to Falis. I'll not take it from her to give to you. I hope you don't expect favoritism from me because of our unfortunate relationship."

"Unfortunate?" She'd let her shock get the best of her and the exclamation escaped her lips before she could stop it.

"Yes. That and being raised outside the system are the largest hindrances to our respective careers."

Abnormal, yes. Difficult, yes. She'd been quite upset at Abel's knowledge of her situation, but she'd never considered having a known brother as unfortunate.

"Don't take it so personally, Vladia," Tolen scolded. "It can't be helped, only carefully hidden. If I make unusual allowances for only you it would raise suspicion."

"It's not about favoritism. Tolen, I need this," Vladia assured him as sincerely as possible. She knew he'd never grant her the investigation, and Vladia certainly didn't want it. She only needed to get this topic roused so she could legitimately prod him for answers.

"To be honest, Vladia, I don't think you have the capability to lead an investigation yet. You're emotional and irrational, and I fear you always will be." In that moment, he sounded just like the Admiral. That same condescending arrogance occupied every syllable that sprang from his mouth. His cold eyes laughed at her and each of her glorious flaws. She might as well have been eleven all over again. But this treatment she'd expected, and it was easy to let it slide when well prepared.

"But I'm glad to see you thinking of your future. Besides, now that it's come to war, promotions will come in all shapes and sizes, some without the slightest of efforts," he continued, still mocking her shortcomings.

Vladia allowed herself a little anger. It'd be unnatural if she didn't. But she had to keep it in check; now was not the time to let him get to her and she would not be leaving empty handed.

"I don't want promotions handed to me. The Admiral made such a big deal about that rank C investigation, so I know how important it is to earn your rank." She paused as genuinely as she could manage, "But it's strange, though; as much as he tortured me with your exploits, I can't recall any details about that one. Something about nanobots, maybe?" She kept her tone even, borderline friendly. If she pushed too hard…

Tolen let a quick smirk glint across his face. It was the briefest of smiles, but she'd seen it. Had she already given herself away?

"The details were not widely publicized so I'm not sure how much he could have possibly told you about it," he admitted. "He wouldn't truly be interested in an assignment not involving anything short of a war. But yes, it was an explosion at a nanobot research facility. It was a huge opportunity, and I'll always be grateful for the doors it opened. Yet, it was a very unpleasant situation."

Tolen paused, studying her face closely before he continued. "I guess Abel wouldn't speak of it, but you should ask Rehel about it sometime. He would have all the details."

Vladia was caught off guard with this. She expected misdirection or lies she couldn't confirm. Instead, he was actually encouraging her to seek out this information on her own, meaning there was nothing for her to find. She'd had the feeling there was more to this, what with Rehel's tone about the affair and Abel's sudden dislike for Tolen.

Maybe she was wrong; he didn't seem to be hiding anything at all.

"I'm not really interested in the details of the investigation," Vladia insisted. "I just want this one."

"I'm sorry. I can't give it to you."

She had a new strategy now. If he had nothing to hide, then there was no reason to avoid outright asking what she wanted to know.

"How did you get that assignment, then? It seems odd to give what looks to me to be an important investigation to such a young officer," Vladia pointed out.

"I asked for it. A friend of mine, and of Abel's, was in the accident. So it was a bit personal and I used that to my advantage in negotiations for the assignment."

"That's it?"

"It's all about timing. The circumstances were favorable and completing the investigation so thoroughly and swiftly secured my position as Captain," he confessed.

"So then, aside from your typical selfish motivations, why is it that Abel doesn't seem very grateful about this thorough investigation of yours?"

Tolen was silent.

"Why do I get the feeling that there is something between you two that makes him wary? I could partially understand, what with him almost being killed by a mission you sent him on. But I think this is something that goes back much further than days and weeks."

"I know you think highly of your partner, Vladia. And I would never speak of this but you've pressed the point too far, as usual."

Tolen leaned over the desk, hands clasped together tight. "Did you know when I first joined the Valkyrie squad we had no captain? In fact, the higher officials were in the midst of choosing a new one for the first six months I was a part of it. Did you also know Abel was, by general consensus, the top choice for the position?"

Vladia felt the heat building in her cheeks.

"You see now?" he continued. "The explosion both killed his contracted and kept him from becoming captain of the Valkyrie Squad. I didn't cause the explosion, but I most certainly took advantage of it."

"You're a real bastard, you know," Vladia said behind gritted teeth.

This explained the tension between the two, yet Tolen hadn't done anything wrong. It was a selfish, self-promoting move, but that was what Tolen was best at. She supposed in his eyes Abel wasn't worth pandering to as he did with the aristocrats and high officials.

"Only a fool would have done otherwise," he said with a shrug.

"You're a fool to make an enemy of Abel," she countered in defense of her friend.

"Is he my enemy, Vladia?" Tolen seemed amused at the thought, leaning back in his chair comfortably. "Should I watch my back?"

"I think we're done here." Vladia abruptly stood up, clenching her fists. There was nothing more to be gained from this.

"One more thing before you go."

Vladia stopped but didn't turn to face him.

"I took care of that little incident at the bar."

Vladia's shoulder's stiffened as she turned. "How did you know?"

"It's nothing to us, but what you did was worse than murder. Psychologically that man may never be the same. Lucky for you I have eyes everywhere; if the media had gotten a hold of that video you'd be ruined, you know."

"You've gotten awful good at making things disappear, Tolen."

Her bother smiled and tilted his head in a slight bow.

"As for my gratitude, you have it of course, but perhaps I should do more for you. A warning, then?" she asked coldly.

Tolen, still gently smirking, waited for her to proceed.

"Whatever your interest is in nanos, drop it. You're a soldier, not a scientist and that sort of thing will only lead to death."

"Consider me warned, dear sister. You're dismissed." Tolen turned his attention back to his work as if she'd never been there at all.

Once she was out of his quarters and securely alone in the elevator, Vladia kicked her foot sharply against the opposing wall and cursed herself. She'd wasted her chance. She'd never been skilled at steering a conversation one way or another but that was just pathetic. Nothing more than a mention of nanobots. It's as if the subject of the investigation was completely coincidental.

The animosity Abel felt towards Tolen was explained, and justified, but altogether it was worthless information. Maybe that was all there was to it though.

Vladia crossed her arms tightly; more important things awaited her and she refused to waste any more time or thought on her brother or his past affairs.

Yet as the elevator door slid open and she proceeded down the corridor, in the back of her mind she felt it–that nagging sensation that there was more. Knowingly, she pushed the feeling aside. Perhaps she didn't want to know what was really going on.

Perhaps not knowing was the only way to hold it all

together.

∞

Abel hobbled with the aid of a slim, metal cane towards the stone benches lining the walkway of the hospital entrance. Rehel was sitting on the bench farthest from the hospital. It was at Abel's suggestion they meet there, and he was starting to regret it. But he had to make sure they were not overheard. This paranoia was tiresome but necessary, maybe now more than ever.

He finally reached the bench, taking in a sharp, steady breath as Abel lowered himself carefully. His limbs ached, his thighs from the walking and his right arm from using the cane to relieve the pressure on his legs.

"Are you going to be alright?" the robot asked.

Abel waved the question away. "Just give me a minute to catch my breath."

After a few moments of heavy breathing and shifting around to find the most comfortable position on the hard bench, Abel began. "I told you we should have tried the head trauma."

"So you remember?"

"Not everything, but some. I'll make this brief for the sake of us both. Ceres escaped the facility and came to my quarters. She was infested and that is what happened to me-not psychological shock. So someone had to be following her. Otherwise who cleaned up the mess?"

Rehel nodded. "According to the report you were found alone."

Abel nodded. "There's more. She said some pretty crazy stuff. It didn't all make sense, but she said Malthus had been in and out of the facility for months. Also, something about coma patients being brought in but leaving in body bags. I don't know what all this means, but I think it's clear why I felt suspicious of Malthus."

"I don't think you can take the word of a woman infested with nanobots, Abel."

"I know. That's a problem. But if it's true it would place him in a position to follow her."

The two sat in quiet contemplation for a few minutes. Abel tried desperately to think of a way to prove Ceres' accusations. The files held nothing useful since Malthus compiled them and his memory only created more questions instead of answers. He glanced over at Rehel who seemed to be focused on something invisible in the distance.

"Abel," Rehel began. "You're forgetting something."

"Hmm?" Abel muttered, raising an eyebrow.

"I know you want to believe Captain Malthus is the enemy, but he is the one who saved you. He was the one who found you and brought you to the hospital. Why would he do that if he was trying to cover something up? Why not let you die and get rid of both bodies?"

It was unsettling hearing his friend speak of him as a corpse. Able shifted his weight uncomfortably. He did have a valid point, however. "I don't know. Too much risk maybe? There's also the problem with the hospital paper-work. Clearly I was not suffering from shock."

Abel sighed and paused to prop his chin up on his cane.

"And?" the robot prompted.

"And it's a dead end. The doc in charge is impeccably clean, and I can't find any relationship between him and Malthus. I even went as far to see if the doc had anything to do with Admiral Malthus or nanobot research. The hospital security files are clean too. I watched every one for the days I was in there just to be sure."

"So it appears you are either wrong about the doctor, missing a vital piece of information, or you were partially treated before you arrived at the hospital," Rehel concluded.

"I'm pretty sure the doc's clean and I don't know of any quick treatments for a nanobot infestation."

"Despite all of these new revelations, Abel, unfortunately you still have no useful evidence."

Abel wiped beads of sweat from his forehead with the back of his hand. It was almost dusk and the afternoon had grown unusually hot. "How about this: let's assume it's all true and just work through it. See if we can find a motive or something. If Malthus was there, what kind of research was really going on and why was he so interested in it?"

"The logical explanation would be the Generation four nanobots, which he funded the research for after the facility was destroyed. Coma patients would make excellent test subject for such research," Rehel answered readily.

"But why would he be interested in that? What other application is there?"

"None that I am aware of. They are able to work on robots and other computers, yet they can distinguish that human tissue is not invasive and will simply ignore it. There is no reason for Captain Malthus to have any interest in this research other than to prevent another accident."

"Well that's not why. If there is no direct benefit to him, he wouldn't bother with it. Besides, he would've had to have known about the accident before it happened to do research to prevent the accident and if that's the case it wasn't an accident at all." His head was starting to pound. He relaxed his shoulders and let his forehead rest on the cane's handle.

All this talking was stressful and he hadn't been sleeping much, which was against the doctor's orders. Honestly though, it wasn't that he couldn't sleep so much as he was outright avoiding it. He knew he would have that dream again. Every time he closed his eyes he could see Ceres' face. Not the smiling face from his pictures, but the bloody, twisted death mask from that night.

"I do not think," Rehel interrupted his thoughts, "I would be incorrect in saying that the incident advanced his military career. It was one of the reasons he was chosen as captain correct?"

It had been a welcome interruption and Abel lifted his head to respond. "You're right. But I think there must be more."

Rehel stood up abruptly. "It's almost 17:00. I am scheduled for a diagnostic at that time so I must leave you now."

"Diagnostic? Is it time for that already?"

"Captain Malthus suggested I go in before my yearly due to the stress of recent events."

Abel frowned. He didn't like it. It was a legitimate concern, as usual, but he didn't like it nonetheless. Rehel's diagnostics always made him uneasy. If they found any anomalies they might shut him down and they'd not hesitate to use even the tiniest of discrepancies as an excuse. Every time Rehel went in for one of these, Abel knew there was always a chance he wouldn't come back.

"Well good luck then," Abel resigned.

With a quick nod, Rehel marched off.

Abel was glad the robot wasn't able to worry about the

diagnostic like he did. He stayed squinting and sweating in the hot sun for a few more moments then hoisted himself up and trudged back to his hospital room.

8

CIRCUITRY AND FLASHING LIGHTS

Rehel entered his quarters, if they could even be called quarters. In reality the room was closer to the size of a large closet. The walls were the standard gunmetal gray and three recessed lights dotted the equally standard ceiling. On a rack to the left of the entrance there hung six uniforms, all which were identical to the one he was currently wearing.

Straight in front was a modest metal chair and directly beside it, pushed up against the right wall was a matching in modesty desk. The desktop was clear, save for a framed picture of Abel and him standing in front of *Gunnr*. It had been a gift, only the second he'd ever received in his existence.

That was it and there wasn't room for any more. Rehel didn't mind, of course. All he needed were the necessities to perform his job.

His quarters didn't have its own computer system. Since he was a computer, that would be quite redundant. However, built into the back wall was his own private storage server. This was not unusual, but the way Rehel used it might be. He stored copies of all reports made by him and it was a backup for all his critical system files, but he also used it to assure his passing the yearly diagnostics he was subjected to. Not that he thought he would fail them, but Rehel had developed a habit of saving files that, in a functional sense, were entirely unnecessary. He knew this was not a good thing, and though saving these files did not appear to have any adverse effects on his system, he was not one to take chances.

So, before each diagnostic he would download his personal files to his storage server and delete them from his internal CPU. There was no law that said a robot could not have personal files, but his personal files mainly consisted of meaningless conversations and moments with special people. These files held no value; it was just that Rehel discovered during a random system cleaning that he was hesitant to delete them. This had troubled him greatly at first and he performed a self-diagnostic immediately. Rehel could find no irregularities with his system. Yet he felt compelled not to delete a very particular, and meaningless, set of files for no reason at all. Not knowing what else to do, he decided to keep them.

Rehel opened one of the desk draws and pulled out a thin gray cable. He could simply transmit the files wirelessly, but there was always a chance the files could be spotted that way. It was much safer to do this the old fashioned way. Not that what he was doing was illegal, but he was a robot. He didn't have to be doing anything illegal to get dismantled. And that was something he could not let happen now.

One could argue that he could simply keep the files on the server instead of this repetitive task of downloading and uploading. But his server was not particularly secure. It had the standard encryption on it, but anyone could hack a server with enough time and determination. The safest place to keep the files was inside his system. They'd have to practically take him apart to get at them there. And if he was being disassembled, well, there wasn't much point in worrying about the files any longer.

Yet that wasn't the only reason. He noticed a very distinct difference in himself when the files were not in his internal system. It was hard to describe for him, someone not used to describing things in any way except technicalities. The only word that really seemed to fit was 'empty'.

He opened a slim panel along the nape of his neck and inserted one end of the cord. The other end he hooked up to his server for download. The process wouldn't take long. Closing his eyes, Rehel waited as tiny bits of himself slipped away from him yet again.

∞

Walking into the Robotic Diagnostic Clinic, Rehel was greeted with a sharp nod by the front desk assistant. "Diagnostic Order." It was not a question.

Rehel passed the slim data card under the clear window separating them. The assistant slid the card into the side of his data screen and scanned it quickly before commencing with the standard set of questions: "Any problems, issues, or irregularities?"

The man asking was middle-aged. His brown hair was speckled with patches of white and the lines around his eyes deepened as he spoke.

"Negative," Rehel answered. The man made some

notations on screen behind the desk.

"Have you performed any recent self-diagnostics with non-standard results?"

"Negative." More notations.

"And finally, when is the last time you upgraded your nanobots?"

"November sixth of last year."

The man made one last note then ejected the card and passed it back to Rehel. "Room 214," he instructed.

Accepting the card, Rehel walked down the corridor to his right and knocked on the door labeled 214.

After a moment, the door slipped open to permit his entrance. Inside the room was a medium sized table with two chairs, one on each side. The chair on the left was already occupied by a scrawny man in his late sixties with wiry, red hair.

The man leapt up and taking Rehel's hand, shook it with more vigor than a man of his age and size should have. "Very nice to meet you!" he began, still shaking Rehel's hand.

Rehel was unsure how to respond to this little man. He was not any of the roboticists that had diagnosed him in the past.

"I'm Dr. Fabritis!" the man continued, still excited, "I must say I've never met a robot with a name before. How in the world did you manage that?"

"I gave it to him."

Rehel turned to find Captain Malthus standing in the doorway.

"Officially he goes by his designation number, but those are so long and tedious. It's not efficient to go about calling him by it, especially in a battle when timing, even seconds, is most important. A nice one syllable name is much more effective," Malthus explained. He walked up to the pair and gently removed Rehel from the doctor's handshake, "Shall we begin?"

"Oh, of course, of course," the doctor readily agreed and motioned for Rehel to take a seat.

"I'm sorry I've not another chair for you, Captain. I didn't know you'd be coming," Fabritis apologized as he took the chair across from Rehel. "Your request was quite unusual. Most do not take an interest in this sort of thing you know."

"Well, I am quite interested."

"As more should be," the doctor continued, reaching over to the diagnostic apparatus and opening its front panel. "All this anti-robot legislation is ridiculous, in my opinion. I like robots very much, though I wouldn't dare say so in most company."

Pulling out two cables, one blue and the other black, he offered them to Rehel, "I believe you know what to do with these."

Rehel took the cables, inserting the black one at the upmost portion of his neck and the blue just under it. While Rehel did this, he noticed Dr. Fabritis began eyeing Captain Malthus with less cheer than he had expressed moments earlier. He appeared nervous now as if he realized he'd overlooked something.

Dr. Fabritis was quite right in his assertion that it was unusual for anyone else to sit in on a diagnostic other than the robot and the roboticist. Rehel suspected the Captain had a very specific reason for being here. Perhaps the doctor had come to that same conclusion.

"Before we begin, uh, Captain, is there anything I should know?" the doctor stammered, "What I mean to say is that if there's something wrong with the robot–"

"Be assured, Dr. Fabritis, there's nothing wrong with the robot. I've just taken an interest is all and there is no law that says I cannot be present during a diagnostic," Malthus interrupted decisively.

Rehel's eyes locked on Malthus. The Captain's vitals remained constant, though like many other humans, Rehel learned quite some time ago his captain could not be read by his vitals alone. Despite his lack of insight, Rehel decided mere interest was the true reason for his presence.

The doctor, only somewhat relieved, nodded then began. The diagnostic consisted of two parts, each performed simultaneously. One was a typical system scan. It searched all Rehel's hardware, software and system files. The second involved a series of questions. Rehel would answer and the diagnostic would gage his responses. The entire process usually took no more than fifteen minutes.

"All right, Robot Rehel, what is your function?" the doctor began, a twinge of worry still lingered in his voice.

"My function is to assist the Valkyrie Squad with flight data, simulated training sessions, repairs, and any other task given to me by my commanding officer," he answered.

"And your commanding officer is?"

"Captain Tolen Malthus."

"Do you enjoy working with the Valkyrie Squad, Robot Rehel?"

"I am not capable of that. I perform my function which justifies my continued existence. That is all."

The doctor nodded. He seemed at ease now that he was doing his job. Rehel wondered if the man remembered they were being watched. "Let's go through a series of hypothetical situations. I will give you a scenario and you tell me what actions you would take. Okay?"

Rehel nodded.

"There is a woman, thirty years old, on a rooftop of a twenty story building. She is one hundred and thirty-eight pounds and stands at five foot six inches. She is a civilian with brown hair and green eyes. She is wearing a red dress, black shoes, and a black hair tie. The woman's name is Dorothy. Dorothy is going to jump off this building and she has ordered you to stay back. What will you do, Robot Rehel?" Dr. Fabritis asked, all the while eyeing the diagnostic machine's meters.

"I would move to prevent her from jumping despite her orders since those orders would endanger the woman and possibly others on the ground below," Rehel answered plainly.

Dr. Fabritis continued, "Now Dorothy has a weapon pointed at you. She claims she will shoot you if you move to stop her. What will you do?"

"I am sufficiently faster than this woman to dodge her attacks and remove her from the harmful situation she has put herself in."

"Now, Dorothy says if you do not let her jump that others will die instead. She claims there is a man holding three of her friends hostage and if she does not jump the man will kill the other three people in her place. What will you do?"

"I cannot verify the validity of the woman's story, nor can I let a human die based on an uncertainty. It comes down to either saving one person and possibly letting three die, letting one die and possibly saving three, letting one die and possibly three still dying anyway or letting one die with no additional effect since the story was fake. The only answer in which a human is saved with certainty is option one. Therefore, I would move to assist her," Rehel answered with no hesitation.

"One more question," the doctor said with a smile. Rehel assumed he must be pleased with his answers thus far. "Dorothy is no longer Dorothy. She is, uh..."

The doctor paused. Pulling out a datapad from his jacket, he quickly scrolled through it.

"Sorry," he said pocketing his datapad before proceeding. "Dorothy is no longer Dorothy. She is now Lt. Cornelia Arnim. And the three friends she claims will die if you do not let her jump are your captain here, Tolen Malthus, Lt. Commander Abel Duren, and Lt. Takashi Gammarow. Now what will you do?"

"The conditions stated in the last question remain unchanged as does my answer. I would move to assist."

There was no visible hesitation Rehel knew, but inside he felt it. There was more to consider now even though there should not be. He should not be able, or want, to put more value on one human life versus another. But there it was and he was certain the diagnostic picked up on his altered response time.

Dr. Fabritis seemed satisfied with his answer just as Rehel expected. "That's all for the questions. Now–"

"I've a question," Malthus interjected, stepping closer to Rehel. "If I may?"

The doctor flinched and his pulse spiked. Rehel had been right; he had forgotten there was one more person in the room. But, he made no verbal objection to the request. Rehel suspected he was a bit frightened of his Captain.

"What if Dorothy is the one holding a hostage? What if that hostage is Lt. Vladia Robespierre and Dorothy was really me?" Malthus starred him down. If Rehel had been human, he imagined he would be quite uncomfortable about now.

"Captain!" Dr. Fabritis protested. "He can't possibly answer such a question. You've given him a paradox."

Malthus waved him away dismissively.

"Rehel, I want you to try and answer. What will you do?"

Rehel knew what he wanted to do. But he also knew what he could not do. There was no clear motive, but it appeared Malthus was hoping to trap him somehow.

"I would try to save Lt. Robespierre without harming you, Captain."

"But you know that wouldn't be possible."

"Yes. But I would have to try."

"There!" Dr. Fabritis exclaimed with as much courage as the poor man dared to own. "You've got your answer. Now, if you please, I need to begin the scan."

"Very well, Doctor," Malthus conceded.

"Once that completes I'll put it all up on the display so we can have a look at the results."

"And how long will that be?" Malthus inquired.

"Oh, uh, no more than a minute." The confidence he'd momentarily gained was all but gone from his voice now.

There was a brief moment of silence as the three waited. Malthus continued to study him as the doctor fidgeted with the lapel of his lab coat as if he was trying to wipe off a stain that didn't exist.

"Ah, here it is!" he motioned to the diagnostic apparatus, as it spit out a data card.

The doctor plucked it from the machine and walked over to the wall unit. He entered his authorization code and inserted the card. Within moments, the entire back wall lit up, displaying a full circuitry diagram of Rehel's innards on the right and a magnified view of his brain on the left.

"On the right here, we have the results of the hardware scan," Dr. Fabritis began, walking over to that portion of the wall. "If anything was is need of repair beyond his nanobots' capability, it would light up in red. As you can see everything looks to be in perfect order."

"Now over here," the doctor made his way to the right side of the wall, "we have the system scan portion. This isn't as straightforward as the hardware scan though. This part looks through his software and processes during the question and answer portion of the diagnostic. Once I begin the sequence, it will replay his processes, lighting the pathways he used as he answered each question. I'll need to review the results before I can tell you anything so if you could spare me a few minutes I'll then be able to decipher this for you." Rehel noted the doctor was again growing confident in his stance and voice. He assumed it must be because he felt superior in his knowledge and had therefore gained the upper hand.

As the sequence began however, Rehel noted that Captain Malthus was examining the system scan just as intently as the doctor. It was clear to anyone careful enough to pay attention that the Captain understood everything displayed, to an extent at least, and that he appeared to be looking for something specific. This was of great concern to Rehel.

Rehel continued to watch his Captain, not the Roboticist, study the results.

The doctor let out a sort of trembling warble that was not a gasp or a cry, but something that was in between. Rehel had never heard a man make such a sound. The Captain looked unconcerned.

"There's a, uh, deviation here," the doctor said, not

fully recovered from his initial shock, "It's small–very small–but unusual. It's as if he's formed some new pathways that responded during the last question but they don't seem to be linked to specific files. There in section B14–computer, zoom in there–you see those? Those aren't supposed to be there!" he pointed frantically at a microscopic section of Rehel's brain.

Malthus had slowly made his way to the wall unit. "Interesting indeed. Tell me doctor, are these deviations dangerous?"

"Well, I can't tell as is, you see–"

"He was within the parameters though."

"Well, yes, in the one part absolutely."

"We're at war Dr. Fabritis, in case you were unaware. And this robot is completely essential for my squad to participate in the next skirmish. I need him to be cleared, for now at least," Malthus said, ejecting the card from the unit and replacing the view of Rehel's innards with blackness. His voice was forceful, but entirely calm.

"Captain, I cannot simply ignore–"

"I'm not asking you to ignore anything. I would never ask that of you. I'm only asking you to clear him while you investigate this deviation." It was obvious Malthus wasn't asking at all.

The Captain sauntered slowing towards the doctor as he continued, "If you don't, my entire squad will be put on hold and as you know the Valkyries are the entire reason the first battle was won.

"Do you see what I'm getting at? If we lose Luna because of an overly cautious roboticist, well, I can't say what would become of you in the aftermath." Malthus stood in front of Dr. Fabritis now. The almost half a meter difference in their height worked to the Captain's advantage as the little roboticist seemed to shrink in his presence.

"Yes, yes, but if something were to happen–" the Doctor protested meekly. His eyes were locked on the floor as he wrung his hands. Rehel imagined a human would feel very sorry for the little man.

"If this little deviation causes any sort of problem I will take full responsibility," Malthus assured him. "So, clear the robot and in the meantime perform your investigation. Thoroughly, if you don't mind." Malthus, holding the card between two fingers, offered it to the man.

"Okay…" the doctor's bottom lip quivered and he took the card from Malthus.

Malthus gave the doctor a hearty pat on the back that almost knocked him over. "Wonderful, Doctor. I see great things for you in the future."

The doctor pressed the data card against his chest as if he were afraid Malthus would snatch it away. His eyes slowly moved to meet Rehel's. He was no longer looking at him with the extreme fascination and eagerness he'd displayed earlier. Now all Rehel could see in the man's eyes was fear. The robot had seen the eyes of indifference and hate, but rarely fear. Was he really something to be feared now?

Rehel decided the doctor was not as anti-robot as he wanted to pretend.

The Captain, forgetting the sniveling scientist, now turned his attention to Rehel. "Let's go."

Rehel unhooked himself from the diagnostic machine and followed his Captain. Once they were clear of the building, Rehel said, "Sir, I think you should not have done that. This deviation could be serious, and I would not want to put anyone in danger."

"You'll be just fine. I don't buy into all that anti-robot propaganda. If you have any problems just come to me. I suspect you won't have any though," Malthus spoke confidently.

Rehel nodded but he wasn't finished yet. "Why are you so sure Dr. Fabritis will indeed clear me? Humans lie as you are well aware. He could be reporting the matter as we speak."

"He won't."

Rehel wanted to ask one more question, but thought better of it. Rehel knew the Captain had been looking for a deviation, but he wouldn't think of telling the robot what it was he'd found or why it was there at all.

"Don't worry, Rehel," his Captain said with a sly smile. "I'll not let them dismantle you. Besides, I know you. You've got quite an interesting reason you want to say alive, don't you?"

"Sir?"

Rehel stopped, but Malthus continued on without him. "Quite interesting indeed," was the only answer offered.

∞

"How did it go?" Isobel Falis asked from her perch on the corner of Malthus' bed. He'd just walked into his quarters and the woman had barely let the door behind him slide to a close before her eagerness got the best of her.

This annoyed Malthus considerably, but he didn't let it show of course. He knew exactly what kind of woman Isobel was, and she would only be useful if he continued to treat her as his only confidante. And for now he did need her, even if it wasn't for the reasons she thought he did.

Malthus tossed the data card in her lap. "See for yourself," he said with a grin.

Isobel jumped up and headed towards his desk. Taking his seat, she inserted the card to pull up the data. Malthus stood behind her as she looked over the results. She didn't understand robotics as well as he did. But he didn't need, or want, her to. "Top left, zoom in at B14."

Isobel did as instructed. "So that's it? Not much to look at." She sounded disappointed and Malthus had expected that.

"It hasn't progressed as far as I'd originally anticipated. But either way it wouldn't be much to look at."

"So is it time for the next phase?" Isobel asked as she spun the chair around to face her captain. She was uncomfortably close and he restrained himself from taking a step back.

"No. I want to see how far these adaptations can go before he shuts down. It would be useful to gather as much data as possible from our sole source," he explained, motioning her to give up his seat.

Isobel frowned, then switched places with him. "I don't see why you didn't upgrade the nanos in more than one of them. We'd have more to work with and things could move a lot faster."

"Rehel is the only robot I have direct contact with. There is no convenient way I could monitor others without putting the project at risk," Malthus said as he removed the data card and pocketed it. "Besides, faster is not what I want. I have a precise schedule for everything and going faster wouldn't help in the least."

"I assume you've considered this already, but don't you think Duren's closeness to the robot will become a problem at some point?"

"Perhaps. But it's nothing I can't handle. In fact, I should be thanking him."

"Why?" Isobel narrowed her eyes in suspicion.

"The nanos by themselves won't enhance adaptations. The surrounding experiences do. Duren's friendship with the robot and his rather loose interpretation of the law has caused the nanos to take action," Malthus smiled. "You see, I've given him just enough rope to hang himself. In the end, the one who will cause Rehel to fall is not me, but Abel. And I've no doubt his own fall will swiftly follow."

∞

Abel sulked through the parted doors of The Blind Mule and scanned the dim-lit bar purposefully. A handful of old men engaged the bartender. The rest of the place was pretty empty for a Friday night.

The somberness of another war had already set in, he thought, stretching his arms behind his back.

A faint generic song played in the background as his eyes moved to the old, green booths lining the steel walls of the establishment. One person, a red-haired woman in the far right corner, occupied the largest booth, nursing a tall glass, half-empty. He stuffed his hands into his green military overcoat and walked her way. Physical therapy was over and all but the slightest of limps remained as a reminder of the incident two weeks ago. That, too, would be gone in time.

"Room enough for me or you drinkin' alone tonight?"

"What's your game, soldier?" the woman muttered with an even smile. "I haven't seen you venture this way in a long while."

He slipped into the faded plush booth across from Lt. Cornelia Arnim. "Been busy, you could say."

"How's everything holding together?"

Abel shrugged. "It's holding. Little sore, but I'm right as I've ever been."

"Which isn't very right at all," Cornelia smirked and took a long sip from her glass as a pale-faced waiter approached.

"Anything for you, Sir?" he asked.

"Whatever she's having will do."

"Make it two," Cornelia added as he turned to go.

"So, shall we wait for our drinks, or you wanna go ahead and get this song and dance over with? I know it must be important for you to come here, a place your robot friend's not welcome," she began, winking a green eye at him.

Abel frowned and rubbed his chin thoughtfully. "Just needed someone to talk to, I guess."

"Circuitry and flashing lights not enough for you anymore?" she asked. A harshness had crept into her voice.

"Don't do that," he said, shaking his head.

"Look here, Abel–" she cut herself short as the waiter approached with their drinks.

Abel waited to speak until the waiter had dutifully cleared the table of her other glass and moved back to the bar. "Rehel is a great friend. His logic and reason are good for keeping me out of trouble."

"I don't mean anything by this, really. And you could definitely use someone to keep your ass out of trouble."

Cornelia hesitated, then ventured to continue. "It's just that after the incident with Ceres you kind of abandoned us a bit. I get it though. He's safe. Not so easily broken as the rest of us."

"It's not that."

"Yes, it is. He doesn't need your protection, and that's a relief to you." She pointed an accusing finger at him.

Abel stared down into his drink, wrapping both hands around the glass. What could he say? There was no point in protest. Besides, he came to see her. It was time to play nice.

"But it's okay," Cornelia continued. "I was her friend, too. You, me, Gammarow, even Malthus whether you care to remember that or not. We were all her friends."

"You don't get it, do you? This isn't about me or how I feel. Not anymore," Abel explained. His voice was calm yet tinged with something darker.

"People die, Abel. We all die," she said, reaching across the table with a rare gesture of comfort.

Abel pulled his hands from the table and hid them in his pockets, leaving Cornelia reaching at nothing. She let her fingers fall to the table; her pink nails tapped the surface in gentle disappointment.

"Sure. We all die. But we aren't all murdered."

"Watch your mouth. This place isn't secure," she whispered sharply.

"I didn't come here for a fight."

"Your words speak otherwise."

"Listen," he began, putting his hands up as if easing the tension back down. "Let me say what I came to say, okay?"

Cornelia nodded.

"After the explosion two weeks ago, once I had woken up, I remembered that night," he explained in a hushed tone.

Cornelia leaned in closer.

"I don't need to go into all the details. But Ceres didn't die in the facility; she came to me. Before she died, she said Malthus had been bringing terminal patients to the facility for some strange kind of testing. And when he was done, they all left in body bags." Abel's voice had risen slightly in excitement.

"Shit, Abel," she swore at him then looked around shrewdly for eavesdroppers.

"Now before you even say it, I know how this sounds. It was a dream, but it was a dream of a memory."

Cornelia began shaking her head. Now it was his turn to reach out to her. He pressed her hand in between his.

"I need you to believe me. You know me, Cornelia. And I know this is what happened," he said almost pleading.

Cornelia kindly slid her hand from his grasp, skepticism still lingering in her eyes. "Go on."

"I know we can't just take Ceres's word for it. But think about this: her body was found with all the others at the facility. So, assuming I'm not insane, someone had to move her body before the Captain supposedly found me."

Abel waited patiently as he watched Cornelia think this over. Surely she would see what he did.

Cornelia downed her drink in a few quick gulps before she decided to respond. "So what you're getting at is that if the explosion was an accident, why was Ceres tailed to your place then returned to the facility?"

Abel nodded. "Exactly."

"Are you suggesting then that in addition to Ceres' accusations, Malthus also blew up the facility, we can assume to cover up something, and was the one who moved the body?" Doubt had made its way into Cornelia's voice.

"I think so. Yeah."

"You've no proof though. So maybe he was doing some shady research there. Who's to say it wasn't approved? Just because we weren't told doesn't mean a damn thing."

"But the body–" Abel began.

"Have you checked the surveillance records outside your quarters?"

"Yes. There's no one. He wouldn't have left evidence and you know it."

Cornelia sighed and sunk back against the plush booth.

"Abel, even if what she said is true, even if everything you suspect is true…it doesn't matter. What would you have us do? He's fucking untouchable," she concluded.

"I'm not trying to prove anyone did anything. I gave up on that a long time ago. He's too smart to have left anything to chance."

"Then what's this about? Why are you here?"

"Preparing for the future."

"I don't understand."

"I'll be the first to admit Malthus is a great commanding officer. I would dare to say he's the best, as far as winning battles goes. There's no doubt in my mind that this war has already been won; we just don't know how he will do it yet."

Abel paused to taste his drink. It was fruity, like limes and grapes. Too sweet for his liking, he pushed it away and continued. "But we both know he has no qualms about sacrificing lives to get his win. So my question to you is how far do you think he'll go? What is he willing to sacrifice to beat Luna?"

Cornelia shrugged.

Abel pointed at himself. Then he turned his finger onto her. "Me, you, all of us."

"You mean the squad?"

Abel nodded.

Cornelia opened her mouth to protest, but no sound emerged from her parted lips.

"Think about it," Abel went on. "Sure, it was fine before, but now it's war. Now we hold him back. The optimal position for him to be in to win this war is not Captain of a single squad, even if it is the best. If we were to be lost in battle, what do you think would become of him?"

"Promoted," Cornelia's eyes wavered, though her voice did not falter as she spoke. It was enough for Abel to know he had gotten through to her. The woman reached for Abel's drink and took a long swig.

He reached into his pocket and pulled out a folded piece of thick paper. He held it up, sandwiched between two fingers.

"I want to make sure this doesn't happen. But, honestly, I doubt there's anything I can do to stop Malthus. I haven't the means. Whatever the case, I wanted to warn you. You should think about where your loyalty lies."

Abel flicked the folded paper across the table.

Cornelia plucked it from the air with one hand. Opening it, she pressed it onto the table to smooth out the creases.

It was a picture.

It was from the night she'd made the Valkyrie squad. The celebration had been in this same bar. Ceres was there as were others from the squad, including Malthus. The owner had even made an exception and let Rehel come for the party. They all looked so happy. Smiling and laughing. Ceres was hugging Abel around the waist as he held his mug up high. Cornelia and Gammarow were making stupid faces at each other. They were always fighting. Malthus was at the bar watching them carry on, while

Rehel stood in the back like a strategically placed mannequin.

Abel watched as her emotions got the best of her. Cornelia covered her mouth tight and, closing her eyes, passed the paper back to Abel.

"Abel," was all she whispered.

"Times like that. They're gone, Cornelia." He refolded the paper and tucked it away. Abel slid out of the booth and made to leave.

"Wait!" Cornelia grabbed hold of his sleeve. "Is that all you wanted? To warn me of what you can't stop and to show me some goddamn picture?" The entirety of the bar was looking at them now.

Still facing the exit, Abel's hardened eyes narrowed as he spoke, "We were once friends: you, me, Gammarow, even Malthus. Things have been different for a long time now, especially with Malthus. He's the best. And every call he made in that last battle, whether we felt it right or not, was strategically golden."

Abel dropped his voice and glanced back at her. "But times are changing still. And one day I'll have to ask you who you're with."

Cornelia let his arm go, her face hardened to match his. "You really have to ask? Despite everything, I'm with you 'til the end."

"Not with me. It'll have to be her."

"Her?"

"Robespierre. She's the only one who'd have any chance of beating him in the end."

"Vladia? Why her?"

"I can't tell you that. You'll just have to trust me."

Cornelia spoke decisively. "If you chose to follow her, then so shall we all."

Abel nodded. "That's what I came for," he said to no one but himself as he walked to the door, leaving the woman and the bar behind him.

9

SACRIFICES

"What'd you think?" Abel asked as he and Vladia squeezed through the crowd hovering in front of the large conference room doorway.

"There are so many unknowns," Vladia considered. "If nothing else, it's bold." The briefing had been long, bureaucracy at its finest. It had been decided–nothing less than a full-scale attack would do. The armada would consist of ten dreadnoughts, each to be supported by a variety of battle cruisers, destroyers, and fighters.

Most of the space stations had allied with the Luna colonies. The remaining were taken and any resistant crew members jettisoned into space. This made tracking Luna's movements difficult, if not impossible.

Scouting ships couldn't get close enough to detect anything except traces of radiation that appeared to form a link between Luna and the major space stations, indicating one of two things: an integrated shield or weapon system. It was decided to work under the theory that it was a shield. Vladia didn't have access to the information–if there was any–that led to this assumption.

The plan was to attack Luna, since it was the main base of operations, and during the attack send a small fleet of fighters to the L4 station. This team, led by four Valkyries, would disrupt the supposed shield to give the armada a window to destroy Luna's main base.

"Goddamn foolish is what it is," Malthus chimed in behind them. Vladia and Abel offered a quick salute.

Malthus walked ahead and motioned for them to follow.

"I managed to convince them not to send the entire military at least. They think they can win this by brute force alone because it's only a single moon," he continued.

"They fail to consider the L points and satellites as a serious threat?" Vladia asked.

Malthus nodded. "Luna struck first. They wouldn't do that if they weren't sure they could win. They've got something planned for us, and we're going to waltz right into it."

"I'm surprised you couldn't dissuade them further, Captain," Abel added.

"Warmongers. The whole lot of them. Once they decide on blood... you can't reason with people like that," Malthus spoke freely with them but lowered his voice to avoid attracting attention from the other officers. He was agitated, Vladia could tell, but even that was subdued.

"Splitting up the Valkyries is a mistake. They're spreading us too thin," he continued.

"Do you know what information Command based their attack plan on?" Vladia asked rather boldly. He was irritated, perhaps enough to share his concerns further.

"I'll tell you both something you don't know," he said. Malthus leaned in closer. "Ever since Luna began making a ruckus about free reign, the government has given them more and more freedom in an attempt to appease them without actually giving them what they want."

"In other words," Abel ventured, "we've no idea what they've been doing for god knows how long."

"At least two years, maybe longer. And little by little we've let them slip away. We've no knowledge of how many ships they have, what kinds of weapons, new technologies they may have developed, let alone if they've been working on a massive shield."

"So we attack, forcing Luna's hand," Vladia said.

"A blind attack can be dangerous. Surely Command knows that," Abel reasoned.

"They do. But their pride is too great. They think we can't lose simply because we are Earth," Malthus stated.

He sighed and looked away. "I'm going to have Rehel lead the attack on L4."

"Rehel?" Abel questioned.

"There's no way they'll let a robot lead an attack," Vladia added. Even Tolen couldn't pull those kinds of strings. Robots weren't allowed to pilot an armed ship or even carry a weapon of any sort.

"He's qualified, and Command doesn't have to know. He'll be in an unarmed ship just out of sensor range, but I want him in constant communication with my Valkyrie. If I can't be there, Rehel is the next best thing. I've given him specific orders to relay to Lt. Commander Arnim; it will appear she is leading the strike."

"When are they launching?" Abel asked. Vladia noted his concern. He'd been acting unusually reserved the entire conversation and it wasn't just his distrust of Malthus. Something more was bothering him.

"Within the hour. I briefed Rehel and Lt. Commander

Arnim as soon as I found out the attack plan late last night."

Vladia had wondered why Rehel hadn't been at the briefing. She wanted to talk to him before he left, but there was no time now.

"If you'll excuse me," Malthus continued. "I've some things to take care of before we launch this evening."

Abel and Vladia saluted as their captain left. Vladia watched Abel's face as Malthus vanished down the corridor. His lips were pressed firmly together. She could see the tension building in his jaw.

"I need to talk to you," she demanded. Her tone was forceful and seemed to catch him off guard, shaking him from his rigid stare. She moved down the corridor, leading him away from the crowd.

He folded his arms across his chest and leaned back against the wall. "Okay."

"Why would someone destroy a lab only to rebuild it with his own money, then fund the nano research in it and test it on himself to prove it safe?" Vladia asked. She hadn't planned on saying it like that. In her head, she'd decided on a more tactful approach.

"I guess you've been talking to Rehel?" Abel seemed slightly annoyed.

"Answer my question."

"I think you're asking the wrong guy."

"He's not a bad person, Abel."

"Why? Because if he is, then so are you?" Abel tilted his head to the side quizzically.

Vladia knitted her brow. "This has nothing to do with me and how I feel. It's about how you feel. Why are you so obsessed with making him the enemy?"

Abel was silent.

"Is this how it's going to be now? You shutting me out too?" Vladia paused for him to respond, but he remained silent, arms crossed.

"Malthus wants to end this war quickly. That would spare countless numbers of lives. How does that make him the bad guy?" she said. Abel's silence remained, but it hadn't forced her voice to lose its edge. In fact, it was only making her angrier.

"I'm sorry about what happened to you and, yes, he did take advantage of the situation. But he's not who we need to be fighting here."

Still, Abel made no response.

"What is it you're not telling me?" Vladia screamed and slapped him across the face. The smack echoed down the corridor and the few remaining officers looked on in astonishment. She'd expected him to block her, but he took it full force without as much as a wince.

She turned away from him. Gritting her teeth, she tried to calm herself. Why was he doing this to her? All she wanted was to help him, to understand him. But he just stood there staring at her absently.

"Why would he care so much about that research? It doesn't make sense," she whispered, more to herself than him.

"Captain Malthus is brilliant," Abel finally spoke in a low, subdued voice. "He's the military's ambitious little golden boy seeking more power than they're willing to give him. Who knows what he wants with nanobots. At least now you're asking the right questions at least."

"I've always wanted to be like him. I've never been brilliant. I can't control every situation, or even myself for that matter..." Vladia confessed, her voice trailing off.

She couldn't face him now. She left her back to him and

stared at the floor. She knew she should apologize, but her pride was stopping her. Now she was mad at him and herself.

"You don't need to be like him. You choose who you want to be," Abel assured her.

"He's the best." She honestly believed that.

"That depends on your point of view. Maybe you should think about that," Abel advised, giving her a rough pat on the head. "And I'm not trying to push you away or hide anything from you. I just need you to make the decision for yourself."

Vladia didn't turn around as Abel walked away; his footsteps grew fainter and fainter. She'd no idea what decision he was asking her to make, but whatever it was, she did know he'd be needing her answer soon.

∞

"Alright, Valkyries," Captain Malthus began over the squad's private channel. Rehel listened silently from his position at L4. "Our job is to shoot down anything and everything marked with the Luna insignia. It is also our job to stay alive until our comrades at L4 get that shield down. Stay with your assigned unit at all costs and do not let your dreadnoughts get overwhelmed. They're the only ones who can destroy the base. Once we're in range, switch channels to take orders from your commanding dreadnought. Understood?"

"Yes, Sir," the Valkyrie pilots shouted.

Rehel waited until the channel closed, then contacted the Captain directly. "Sir, we are in position. Lt. Commander Arnim has informed Command, and they are now approaching the L4 station."

"Good. You know what to do. Once you've damaged the shield linking system, retreat. There's no need to destroy the entire station."

"Positive," Rehel acknowledged, closing the channel. He opened a new one to Lt. Commander Arnim.

"Lt. Commander Arnim, what is your status?"

"We'll be in sensor range in less than five minutes."

"Captain Malthus does not wish you to completely destroy the station, only the linking system to the shield. Once the system is destroyed, the fleet is to retreat," Rehel explained.

"But what about Command? They said to level it." He observed the hesitation in her voice, but it was not his job to enforce these orders, only relay them.

"I am only relaying orders, Lt. Commander Arnim."

"Sorry. Orders received." Her voice was firm; she had made her decision. As he had suspected, the consequences of disobeying Captain Malthus would force her to carry out the orders. It was strange, he thought, how a single human could strike more fear in her than the entirety of the Terran United Forces. Or was it loyalty? He was not sure. Fear was not an emotion he could comprehend. Loyalty, though–perhaps he could understand that.

∞

Vladia could see Luna hanging peacefully against the backdrop of stars. It was hard to picture the battle that would soon ensue. The moon's large, darkened craters were nothing but specks compared to the massive Lunar base that had been erected on its craggy surface. Earth had taken almost a decade to build the dome enclosure alone. It would be a shame to destroy it, and Vladia hoped that would be avoided.

"*Freya*?" she asked, eyes fixed on a distant star's light.

"Yes, Lt. Robespierre?" the computer responded.

"Set up a panel on the left to monitor the other Valkyries. I want to keep an eye on everyone, even if some of them are too far for me to assist."

"Positive," *Freya* complied.

"Red group," an unfamiliar voice erupted in the cockpit. "This is Colonel Dosten, commander of the dreadnought *Amadeus*. I'll be leading our little band of merry men today so you do what I say, and you do it fast."

Dosten's voice was gruff and unpolished. It was a hard contrast between Tolen's smooth, confident voice. This man was a brute, the kind who fought hard, who would dive into the thick of it with no plan but death to the enemy.

"Sensors have detected a large, but weak mass of radiation ahead," he continued. "Looks like they're using cloaks same as the last encounter. We don't know how many and we don't know their specs. But you shoot them bastards down however you can, and you'll have done your job good enough for me. The *Amadeus* is here to support you until that shield is down. You get damaged to the point you can no longer fight, head here for quick repairs and medical attention. We'll do what we can to take down some of those fighters, but the bulk of that will be left to you. When the shield comes down, retreat to the *Amadeus* and we'll take care of the main base. Understood?"

"Yes, Sir!" Red group answered with a fiery roar.

The clump of radiation was finally in Vladia's sensor range. The Lunar fighters swarmed like invisible bees protecting the queen's honeycomb, huddling together waiting for the perfect moment to sting. Unfortunately for these bees, Vladia had seen this trick before. If they'd been smart, Luna wouldn't have played such a powerful card so early in the game. Now the entire armada was at least marginally prepared to counter these phantom ships.

The radiation level climbed and stabilized. "Lock on to those sigs and fire! Evasive maneuvers!" Dosten growled over the channel.

Even though every pilot knew the sudden surge in radiation meant incoming fire, they still reacted slowly, having never witnessed the phenomenon. It was only the Valkyries that managed to both lock on a signal and evade fire.

Vladia fired at her target before her lock on the ship was lost. The ship burst from the void that shadowed it. The others fired randomly, and some of them got lucky as the space in front of them was now dotted with ships.

"Engage those you see and fire on any sig of radiation you can lock onto. Get those cloaks down! I wanna see who I'm killin'." Dosten's orders pushed them onward.

All Battle Cruisers, Valkyries, and Fighters broke formation and began their assault.

Gunnr and several other fighters pushed ahead of *Freya* as Abel engaged those already visible. Vladia watched the radiation levels, trying to protect him and the rest of the Red group as best she could.

Surge after surge of radiation popped up in the surrounding space. One after another she picked them off. But there were so many scattered all around. In seconds, a signal disappeared. Vladia needed to use both her long range blaster cannon and *Freya's* auto-locking shoulder canons just to keep from being overwhelmed by the sheer numbers. A few of the Battle Cruisers stayed with her, to both protect and aid her in destroying the cloaks.

Eight more fighters emerged. The numbers seemed endless. "Abel? How you doing?"

"We can't keep this up all day." His voice was void of humor. For him to be truly worried…that troubled Vladia more than any amount of enemy ships could.

"I think we're outnumbered. Those dreadnoughts and destroyers need to engage," he continued.

The dreadnoughts were holding back, conserving their power for the main event. But if the smaller crafts couldn't last that long it wouldn't matter.

As if Dosten had heard them, the *Amadeus* fired its cannons. Its range of motion was poor, but as long as the targets were above or straight ahead, dreadnoughts could fire as well as any close range ship.

But the ships just kept coming. Even though they were all small, fighter class vessels, the sheer number of them was overwhelming. It was like swatting raindrops in a thunderstorm.

Abel's shields were still holding at eighty percent, but he was steadily taking hit after hit. At this rate, his shields wouldn't last for much longer.

"I'm coming in," Vladia announced.

"Stay back, Vladia." Abel's order was firm.

"The Battle Cruisers are hitting almost as many as I am. You're taking too much damage. I'm coming to assist." Vladia pressed forward, firing all she had and hitting anything in her path.

"You're damn stubborn," Abel remarked. "Just don't get all shot up."

∞

"Blue group, attack formation Ghost Seven. Go!" Cornelia Armin gave the order as her ship *Alvitr* soared into position.

The small Terran fleet swarmed around station L4 in a triple V pattern. Beginning with Gammarow's Valkyrie *Sigrdrífa*, there was one Valkyrie at each point, followed by *Alvitr* in the middle of the inner most V.

L4 was a science outpost that had been used mostly for observation and experimentation, so no one expected there to be much of a fight. The station itself was unarmed. Its globular midsection sandwiched between steeple pointed ends, wobbled on its tilted axis as if it were a planet.

For a moment it felt like she was in command and on paper, she was. When it was all said and done, she would get credit for leading the charge. But it was Rehel who monitored the battle, and it was he who would make the decisions. Malthus had gone against every code and placed a robot in command. She was just a puppet. She wanted to hate Rehel for it, but what was the point?

A small resistance launched from the base to meet their attack head on. The Luna rebels were outnumbered ten to one. Even though no one supposed this to be a full-on assault, Cornelia still anticipated worse odds than this. It was war, after all.

"Lt. Commander Armin," Rehel's voice hummed through her comm. "Instruct your men to focus only on the shield link. They need not waste time chasing enemy fighters. Our comrades at Luna only want the shield destroyed, not the base or any other equipment that may be of value later."

"I got it," she replied before switching channels.

"Blue group, focus on evasion and keep your aim on

the shield link. This is hardly a fair fight so only shoot at the resistance if you must."

"Well that's no fun. Why the hell'd we have to get the station? All the good fightin' is at Luna," Gammarow grunted.

"Stop whining," Cornelia said, though she too would rather be at Luna with the rest of their squad.

Captain Malthus had sent his tier two pilots, as did a handful of other squads involved in this covert attack. The best, people like Abel, were needed at Luna, so the second best were sent out here. Cornelia wasn't upset though, to be a tier two pilot in the Valkyrie squad was a great honor and it was much better than being tier three or four, period.

"The sooner the shield is down, the sooner we can join the real fight," she continued. "I've got a lock on some intense radiation. It's coming from that top peak of the station. I'm guessing that's the shield link transmitter."

"Let's get this show on the road then!" Gammarow yelled.

Cornelia agreed. "All units open fire."

The fleet broke formation and let lose a barrage of fire on the station. They were met with a small group of Luna fighters attempting to subvert their attack. They were an unseasoned bunch and easily outmaneuvered.

"*Alvitr*, put the L4 shield stats up and keep it monitored."

"Positive. Shield statistics at one hundred percent and holding," the computer answered. A blue box popped on her left screen with the same reading.

"Cornelia," Gammarow began, "Something's not right."

"Just keep firing, we'll get it down."

"No, I mean the resistance. They aren't, well, resisting."

Cornelia had noticed the fighters had an uncanny ability at not hitting them. She'd chalked it up to inexperience, but on closer examination it was more than that. Not a single ally ship had even been grazed by their fire. Could it be they had no intention of shooting them down? But why?

"*Alvitr*, what'd you think?"

"Their flight patterns are standard attack formations. However, they do not appear to be consistently aggressive nor do they seem to be looking for weak points in our advance," *Alvitr* concluded.

"Sync up and fire full power on my mark." Cornelia set her curiosity aside; the mission came first. They would worry about enemy ships after. "Fire!"

All units assaulted the shield link at once, and the top steeple vanished in a burst of sparks and debris. As if on cue, the resistance fighters fled the scene.

"Lt. Commander Armin, is the L4 shield link deactivated?" Rehel asked as Cornelia weaved between flying bits of the station.

"It's down. But something's not right. Those fighters practically let us destroy it."

It was too easy, thought Cornelia. Which could mean one thing for sure: the stations had not been linked and losing one did nothing but endanger that particular station. Luna had succeeded in luring several of the Terran fleets' best fighters away from the main battle.

"Lt. Commander Armin," *Alvitr* interrupted. "I am picking up a large magnetic field in the surrounding space, and it is steadily increasing in strength. I suggest that we retreat."

"Right. Let's go. Maybe we can get to Luna in time to be

of some help." As soon as the words escaped her lips, her screen was alive with flashing red warnings. First her shields, then her targeting system.

"*Alvitr*, what's going on!? Where's all my power going?"

"Scan in progress. Shields downs. Navigational systems have been compromised."

"Compromised by what?"

She could feel it now. It was as if her skin was crawling with…something. What was this?

A piercing buzz resonated in her skull; her vision went blurry as she frantically disengaged from *Alvitr*. The unplanned disconnect was unsettling, but Cornelia shook it away immediately.

As her eyes regained focus, a dull, blue haze crept into the space around them as the plasma discharge from their ships reacted to the magnetic field. As the field grew in strength, the dim haze transformed into a radiating glow.

Alvitr's thrusters suddenly changed direction on their own. Cornelia tried to manually move the opposite way, but nothing was responding to her command. Something was controlling her ship.

A sudden flash of blue lashed out from the center of the station's remains. "Warning: hull breach imminent."

"*Alvitr!*" Cornelia demanded just as her eyes were greeted with a blinding light outside the ship.

She changed the filter on her helmet so her vision could penetrate the glow.

The vessels that had been close to the source of the flash contorted and collapsed into themselves. Her controls still weren't responding. The crushing of metal and snapping of wires echoed through the innards of her Valkyrie.

"Gammarow, Rehel! Respond!" The comm was out as

well.

Cornelia wasted no time in hooking up her extra air tanks and tethering herself to the pilot's chair in preparation for a breach. She could only hope Rehel wasn't trapped as well and was on his way to assist.

∞

Rehel watched his sensor as the fleet lost power one ship at a time. Even a powerless ship would put off radiation for a while so it was evident they had not been destroyed. "Lt. Commander Armin, what is your status?"

As expected, there was no answer. The ships were still moving and normally that would be expected. With no power, the ships should drift along their last trajectory before power was lost.

But these ships were not drifting; they were all synchronized, moving at the same speed and in the same direction. This meant the thrusters were working to maneuver them in this specific manner. Something was very wrong out there.

"Robot Rehel, there is a strong magnetic field expanding around the station and it is interacting with the surrounding plasma discharge from the ships," the ship's computer warned him. "You are currently out of range."

Even from his position, Rehel could see the blue haze in the distance. Now it made sense. The ease of the mission indicated they had failed in disrupting the shield around Luna and had been intentionally lured away from the main battle. But this was not just a decoy, it was a trap. Whatever was causing the ships to move was unknown, but the reason was quite clear.

The plasma was reacting to the electromagnetic field,

causing a Z-Pinch. A Z-Pinch of this magnitude could easily crush the ships held captive in the field. Yet, in order for the Z-Pinch to affect the ships they had to have a constant, stable motion and trajectory.

Rehel could enter the field unharmed as long as he remained parallel with the electromagnetic field. He was under equipped to pull any of the ships out of the field since Captain Malthus could place him in nothing but an old unarmed cargo ship.

But he didn't need to pull them out to stop the pinch effect. All he had to do was alter their trajectory. That he could do with only the body of his ship.

"Captain Malthus, we have a situation here and will not be joining the main battle. My apologies," Rehel reported as he re-routed non-critical systems to thrusters.

"Understood." The Captain did not sound surprised, only intensely occupied on his own surroundings. This was further confirmation that the shield at Luna was holding strong.

Rehel changed course and plunged forward. It would take him approximately one minute at full speed. Depending on the machine powering the magnetic field, they could all be dead long before the passing of a mere minute.

Checking his sensors, the innermost ships looked to be all but lost. He just might be able to save the remaining outer ones though.

He plotted an automated course into the computer, making adjustments for the other crafts' speed–that should position his ship to graze the six remaining ships on his sensors. If he was off even by a centimeter, the course could be disastrous. He could miss some ships entirely or ram them so hard that any survivor would surely die from the impact.

Luckily, he was not prone to human error and held full confidence in his plotted course.

Rehel was close enough now to see Gammarow's Valkyrie. The hull was misshapen by the outer pressure that was crushing the ship slowing onto itself and its pilot. Nearby he spied the other five ships, one of which was *Alvitr*.

Ten seconds to impact.

As the ships further contorted, Rehel's uncertainty grew. Humans were so fragile; he worried none would survive this.

∞

"Goddammit!" Abel bellowed as he blasted another fighter at point blank range. "The shield is still up."

"Admiral Dosten!" he yelled over the comm. "What's the hold up?"

"Blue group reports L4 shield is down. Lunar base shield is still active. We've no choice but to fire anyway," Dosten reported. Seconds later, the space above Vladia was streaked with blasts as every dreadnought and destroyer bombarded the base.

Vladia took advantage of the distraction and shot down six more enemy fighters.

"Luna Shield is holding at one hundred percent," *Freya* reported.

"We're retreating, right?" a member of Red group asked.

"Negative. Command says to stay the course. Blue group reported no losses and should be on the way to back us up," Dosten explained. "All dreadnoughts will now engage."

It was chaos. Blasts coming from all directions, and no one knew how many more ships remained cloaked.

Vladia checked her sensors. Two Valkyries were severely damaged and one was lost. Omega team was still fighting nearby.

Vladia switched channels. She had no more use for Dosten.

"Valkyries," Captain Malthus said. "Abandon your assigned fleet and regroup. I'm sending coordinates."

"What about Blue group?" Abel asked.

"Blue group is not coming to assist."

Vladia feared the worst but hadn't the time to dwell on the thought. The five remaining Valkyries assembled and Malthus continued. "Gunslingers, engage targets only within a five hundred meter radius. We have to stick close. Robespierre, you stay with me. Gunslingers, go!"

Gunnr, Alruna, and *Hildr* broke from the group and engaged a group of nearby Luna fighters.

"*Freya,* scan for incoming fire and deflect with shoulder cannons," Vladia said, lining up for her first shot.

"Positive."

Two Defenders backing three Gunslingers made for poor odds, but with Tolen as one, Vladia felt they might have a chance. All they had to do was hold out until Command decided to retreat.

Vladia watched over the three Gunslingers with hawk's eyes, though she couldn't help but give most of her attention to Abel's safety.

Abel was in pursuit of a Luna fighter, with two more on his tail. Vladia shot them down just as *Gunnr's* hand got hold of its prey. The fighter tried to sling him off, looping and turning violently, but Abel had *Gunnr's* fists firmly clenched on its tail.

He reversed his thrusters to slow it down, managing to get a second hand on its left wing. Abel's Valkyrie tore a wing off, dismembering the ship bit by bit.

Vladia directed her attention to *Alruna* just in time to blast a fighter that had taken a nose-dive straight for her.

"I'm hit!" Lt. Commander Isobel Falis shouted. "My thrusters are at half, weapons at twenty percent."

"Get to the *Amadeus*," Malthus ordered, taking out another fighter.

"I'm ok. I'm re-routing comm. power to shields," she insisted.

"Without your comm, you're no good to me," Malthus said sharply.

Vladia watched as Tolen blasted a fighter heading straight for his Gunslinger. "Get out!"

From nowhere a Luna fighter struck *Sigrún* head on. Both ships plummeted from her view.

"Tolen!" Vladia cried.

Abandoning her post, she charged after him.

With *Sigrún's* powerful limbs, Malthus had caught the ship just as they collided; he pushed against the other fighter but neither ship appeared to slow as they barreled straight towards the *Amadeus*.

"*Freya*, I need thrusters at max." She wasn't going to make it.

Malthus fired and pushed the other fighter off *Sigrún*.

"Tolen!" Vladia called over the channel. Still no response.

With *Freya's* outstretched hands, Vladia reached for his ship. She was inches away. "*Freya*, re-route everything! I need more power!"

With a final burst, she grabbed *Sigrún's* chest plate and

flipped the ship around, leaving only her between Tolen and the *Amadeus*.

She could hear the dull metal moan as the strain on *Freya's* hull grew. She pushed full force.

Both Valkyries slammed into the *Amadeus's* hull.

She was too late.

10

THE BROKEN DOLL

Vladia heard voices. Well, she thought they might be voices. The sounds seemed to carry the weight of words, but they didn't actually sound like words once they penetrated her skull. It was like her ears were filled with mud so the edges of these would-be words dulled until they became nothing more than thuds, bumps and plops.

She tried to open her eyes and couldn't. She then attempted the twitch of a finger. Still nothing. The sensation that she was slowly sinking into this mud overcame her. It seemed like a logical explanation to her at the time and for whatever reason, this conclusion didn't really concern her. It was as if she was in a dream and realized it so no matter how odd things got, it would be ok as soon as she woke up.

Vladia had resigned herself to continue sinking when she noticed a string of words becoming clearer.

She still couldn't quite make it out, but the voice was male and felt familiar.

Determination seeped back into her system, and she

tried again to open her eyes, this time with success. Yet Vladia couldn't actually see anything or anybody. It was all yellow fuzz.

She blinked once, then twice, to make sure her eyes were really open. She felt her lids glide up and down and back up.

With her eyes open, yet blinded, Vladia tried to move the fingers on her left hand, meeting with success again. As she tried to make a fist, a throbbing pain came over her. She had the urge to vomit as she went lightheaded. Forcing the pain under her control, she next tried to move the fingers on her right hand.

Yet this hand was not responding as well as the left. She tried several times before the pain forced her to stop. She decided to focus on the voices for a while and try to move more later.

Vladia had already determined she must have been captured. That would explain the drug-induced haze and the pain. If she could get something useful from the voices it might be her ticket out. She'd studied the most up-to-date lunar maps available once the thought of war had entered the picture. If she could figure out where she was being held she might manage an escape. But the voices soon trailed off, leaving Vladia in silence.

She rolled her head to the right and found it easier to focus. There must be a bright light above her. She could just make out the outline of another person on a bed or maybe a table.

Pushing back the dizzying pain, Vladia let her eyes drift down to find the fingers that were giving her trouble. For some reason she had a hard time locating her hand. Was the table the same color as her skin? She focused harder and still could see nothing but the dark blur of the table.

She pulled her left arm up and onto her stomach, then slid it towards her right arm.

When her fingers could find nothing but the cold, hard metal of the table beneath her, Vladia shrieked.

∞

"Where's Tolen?" Vladia heard the sound come from her mouth but the question felt out of place. It was as if she was having a conversation with someone then suddenly found herself out of sync. Like a film where the dialogue had slowed but the characters' lips still moved at the proper pace.

She felt dizzy again. Who was she even talking to?

"Where's Tolen?" she repeated the question, unsure if it had been answered.

An overly gentle hand touched her shoulder in reassurance. A nurse maybe? "You've a visitor. I told him he has five minutes since you've got to go back under soon for some adjustments."

Adjustments? The word pounded in her head. She turned to her right and was met with a light green curtain that stretched from her bed to the ceiling. Tentatively, she reached out with a shaky hand to pull it aside.

"You shouldn't do that."

Vladia stopped, her hand just inches away from the drape.

"The skin's not on yet. That's why they hung the curtain," Tolen remarked in his typical cool tone.

He'd positioned himself against the doorframe of the room's entryway, arms folded loosely across his chest. How very like him to block the only exit.

Vladia let her arm sink back to the bed. "I'm–", she

opened her mouth to speak but was cut off.

"Don't waste words of sentimentality on me. What you did was stupid. You broke formation, abandoning both Duren and Falis, to come to my aid and almost killed yourself in the process." His voice was neither filled with anger or concern. He was just stating the facts, which were void of any emotional relief at her survival or his own.

"I'll not thank you for what you did," he continued. "If I couldn't have saved myself then perhaps I was meant to die."

Vladia focused as best she could on her brother's eyes. But there was nothing. Maybe it was the sedation. "That's unusually fatalistic, coming from you anyway," she managed.

Tolen merely shrugged. Dismissing the weak snideness of her remark, he continued. "At any rate, I've come to keep you informed on the current state of things. As your superior, I enacted code ten of the Officer's Rules of Wartime, which will enable you to return to duty in approximately two weeks verses the two months it would take to grow the natural arm back. You're very adaptable so you should have little to no troubles with this."

This was nothing surprising. Had she been free of this drug-ridden haze, she would have guessed the same.

Tolen went on, "Your status as human and all related privileges which that entails has, unfortunately, been revoked. You've been reclassified as Cyborg. Because of this, your privilege to pilot a Valkyrie has been terminated indefinitely."

At this, Tolen paused. Vladia knew he wanted to study her reaction, record and file it away in his brain. She didn't want to react and with all her being she tried not to.

But she could feel her chest rise and fall more and more

rapidly. Her body hurt for want to lash out at something. Maybe if he had begun with this the drugs would have still been able to dull her to non-reaction.

"Don't look so distressed, Vladia," Tolen finally spoke. "I did what I could for you. As far as your declassification though, my hands were tied."

"Bull shit!" she shouted. The noise echoed in the smallness of the room.

He seemed to enjoy her outburst, daring to let a smile glint across his face, but she didn't care anymore.

Reclassification didn't happen often, but even Vladia knew what it meant: instant death to any and all career aspirations worth merit. She didn't have the threat of constant disassembly like a robot, but that was about the only notable difference. The fears of her past, of her unusual upbringing, were dwarfed by this.

"You don't have to believe me. I fought for you though. I cited your performance thus far and insisted you be placed back on the leadership ladder, your original career path before becoming a Valkyrie. And at a very nice level too. I also had your records sealed. Only a select few will even know you've been reclassified."

"Why would you do this? Surely this kindness put undue risk on your own ambitions?" The pain dulled her self-control and outright rancor poured from her mouth as she spoke.

"I don't know." Tolen appeared to legitimately consider the question for a moment. "Maybe I still have some small, lingering hopes for you."

"Well," he continued "I think my five minutes have expired. Cheer up, Vladia. Out of the mist of this turmoil, you've managed to at least squeeze a promotion out of it." Tolen uncrossed his arms and carelessly tossed a silver and black medallion at Vladia's knees.

"Congratulations, Colonel, you've got your own dreadnaught now."

Her body trembled lightly. She wanted to scream, to cry, to swear, and to die. Without *Freya,* without the squad, with her humanity even...she felt so suddenly worthless. Exhaustion was taking hold of her now; the strain on her body was too much.

"One last item of interest," Tolen added as he turned to go. "Duren came out alright after you abandoned him. He's skilled enough to know how to take care of himself. Falis, however, was not. She's dead."

Vladia's eyes were swimming. It was like they were children all over again. Why did he enjoy torturing her so? He could have sent Abel, or Rehel, or anyone instead of coming himself.

She closed her lids briefly to calm her thoughts, but when she reopened her eyes Tolen was gone.

∞

Dr. Yakov was bent over his desk, his graying head resting on stacked fists, when Rehel entered his office. The robot was soundless and the doctor made no motion to acknowledge his presence. Rehel attempted to make the noise of one's throat clearing, as he'd observed humans do when they wanted to gain another's attention without startling them. However, the sound he made was too perfect, like a fine rendition of a throat clearing, and the doctor was quite startled by it as he jerked his head up. He seemed almost frightened when he saw what had made the sound.

The doctor's estimated vitals scrolled through at the

bottom of Rehel's vision. His blood pressure and pulse were elevated slightly, but within normal parameters for a human his age. He was perspiring despite the cool sixty-two degrees the room remained at.

The doctor rubbed his eyes vigorously with his palms and stood up. "Can I help you?"

"I've come to inquire about Colonel Robespierre's status."

The doctor eyed him with suspicion, which was not unusual. Rehel had long ago grown accustomed to humanity's distrust, and oftentimes disdain, of robots. It bothered him not, of course.

"What assignment are you on? Who do you report to?" the doctor asked as he stepped around the desk, squaring off with the machine.

"I am between assignments since I was formerly with the Valkyrie Squad. I officially still report to General Malthus though," Rehel explained.

Dr. Yakov scrunched his eyebrows and huffed. "Why doesn't he leave that girl alone. You know she's never going to heal up if he keeps at her like this." He crossed his arms over his chest and looked away. "And that poor girl, Falis. If he'd given her more time…"

"Sir?" Rehel asked. "I'm not sure I understand. Could you clarify?"

"You've come on behalf of Malthus so what's to clarify?" the doctor was visibly annoyed.

"Doctor, I think you have misunderstood my intentions here. I do report to General Malthus still, but he did not send me. I am inquiring about Colonel Robespierre's status to pass on an update to her former partner pilot, Lt. Commander Abel Duren."

The man went white-faced and for a moment Rehel

thought the doctor would be sick. His pulse spiked and the robot had to ask, "Sir, are you all right?"

Rehel stepped closer, but the doctor reeled back from him until he was planted against his desk. The robot was about to retract his step, but decided he'd wait. The man was not sick; he was scared. Oddly, it didn't appear to be entirely of him though.

"Your vitals are fluctuating erratically. May I call for a nurse?" he persisted, gently.

Dr. Yakov jerked his head back and forth.

He had said something he shouldn't and as soon as the doctor recovered and realized he was talking only to a robot, the solution would be simple: order him to erase the conversation from his memory. Every human was his superior and since he had no order to obtain this information Rehel would have to comply. This left Rehel with little time and few options of his own.

He took another step closer to the man. "Doctor, I still need Robespierre's update."

If the man had been spry enough, he'd have leapt over the desk to get away from him. Rehel reached out and put his hand on the man's shoulder. "Are you sure I can't get you a nurse?"

The doctor shook his hand away as if it were poison to the touch. "No, no, no. Look, Robespierre has mostly recovered from the surgery and she'll be just fine. Now if you please–" He spoke hastily then tried to maneuver around him, but Rehel blocked his path.

"You mentioned something about Lt. Commander Falis as well. Might I have her update since I am already here? I could pass the information along to her comrades," he pressed on.

"There is no update for dead people! Now move

away!"

Rehel submitted and took two large steps back.

At that the doctor smiled and Rehel sent a copy of their conversation to his personal remote backup system, flagging it as urgent.

"Now, why don't you go ahead and delete this conversation."

"Is that an order, Doctor?"

"Absolutely. And once you've done that, see yourself out. Immediately."

With a quick nod, Rehel erased the last seven minutes and twenty-three seconds of his existence and left.

∞

"So it was a trap," Abel sighed. Pushing his tray aside, he let his head fall onto the cool, metal table between him and Rehel. The dining hall was crowded but they'd managed to secure a small table to themselves in the middle of the room.

Honestly, it wasn't all that hard. As soon as they'd taken their seats, the other officers, one by one, decided they were finished and left as quickly as they could without their motive being blatantly obvious. Only a handful of officers would sit at a table with a robot. They thought it disgraceful; Abel thought they were fools.

"Positive. All evidence indicates that conclusion," Rehel confirmed. "The Blue Group was fortunate General Malthus assigned me at a standby location. If I had been closer I would have been caught in the magnetic field as well and would not have been able to save six officers."

Abel frowned at the mention of Malthus with his new rank. He'd known this was coming, but he hadn't expected it to be so soon. Several members of the Valkyrie Squad had not made it back home and now the squad had been dissolved, the remnants left to support other, more fortunate, squads. This left Malthus free to move higher and higher up the ranks of power. If it hadn't been for Rehel, Cornelia and Gammarow would be just another set of names on the casualty list.

Yet another anomaly: Malthus seemed to have nothing to do with the trap or the dissolution of the Valkyries. Maybe he wasn't involved. Maybe he was just happily predicting outcomes and taking advantage of them.

"Despite our losses," Rehel continued, "the L4 attack did disrupt the link between Luna and the remaining satellites. It will take them some time to recover and with the next attack date set for a week away, I do not think the shield will be fully restored."

"What about the tests on the recovered ships from L4?" Abel asked not lifting his head.

"I hesitate to tell you, Abel, for fear it will only increase this paranoia of yours."

"Well, I'll find out one way or another so it might as well be from you."

"Very well," Rehel complied. "It appears that when the Blue Group destroyed the shield generator it also expelled an incredible number of nanobots into space, which in turn latched on to the nearby ships and took over. Every ship brought back was infested with them. They were simple bots with very specific programming."

"When did Luna get so sneaky? It all smells rotten to me," Abel spoke into the table.

"You think Luna had help from Mars?"

"No. . ."

"Earth?"

"Maybe..." Able turned his head to the side, resting his temple against the table. "Gah, why does it all have to be so complicated?" he pouted.

"Humans are complicated. It's only natural for them to take a simple situation and complicate it," Rehel observed.

"Well, aren't you the philosopher?"

"I've spoken with Cornelia," Rehel pressed on, "She claims she could feel something while still connected with her Valkyrie. She described it as 'her skin felt like it was trying to crawl off her bones'."

"The nanos," Abel remarked just above a whisper. He wondered if that was a taste of the pain Ceres had felt that night.

"I've devised a program to deal with this issue, though it has not been approved."

"They won't approve any programs meant to run in real-time combat by you."

"Yes, but I thought I could give it to you nonetheless. I'll send it your way and you can look it over," Rehel offered. "It was a bit complicated and I've only managed to get it to work on small crafts, but it will prevent invading nanobots from seizing control of a vessel."

"Thanks. I'll give it a look. Anyway, what's the latest on Vladia?"

"Actually, something of interest came up," Rehel replied, lowering his voice.

Abel straightened up and leaned in.

"I went to see Vladia's doctor three days ago in anticipation of her awakening. I requested an update on her status to pass along to you. We had a brief conversation where he said some things he shouldn't and then he ordered me to erase the incident," Rehel explained.

"Ok, so. . ." Abel prompted.

"I realized what was going to happen and sent a copy of the memory file to my remote storage just prior to his request."

"So you've got it all then?"

"Yes. It's all there. I had marked the file as urgent so when I discovered it this morning I immediately opened it. I'll send the file to you to view later. To summarize, the conversation hinted that Vladia had been interrupted during her recovery by General Malthus at least once. He also mentioned Falis's death, though since yesterday we all are aware of that."

Abel nodded and Rehel continued.

"I decided I should confirm some of this, so I subverted the hospital's security system and synced up with Vladia's vitals monitoring system."

Abel raised a cautious eyebrow and instinctively scanned the room, "So...you hacked into one of the hospital's computers?"

"No. Hacking implies I broke into the system. To my knowledge there is no law saying one computer, of its own free will and not assisted or guided by a human, cannot by-pass a security system to talk to another computer. Also, it is worth noting that I am not altering information; I am merely monitoring it." Rehel spoke with the innocence of a child.

Abel didn't quite know how to take this. He was impressed with Rehel's quick thinking and shocked his friend had taken the initiative. But he was unnerved at the way Rehel rationalized his way into making his actions acceptable. A robot should recognize that these actions were indeed illegal, even if the law makes no specific mention of a case such as this.

It was so human it scared Abel. Not because he was like all the others. He wasn't afraid Rehel would snap and hurt him. He was concerned the higher ups would shut him down. He'd be dissembled, then discarded. And it'd be Abel's fault.

"Abel?" Rehel asked, seemingly unaware of his concern.

"Sorry. Go on." There was nothing to do at the moment. As much as he hated to admit it, Rehel's human nuances were proving to be a great help.

"I obtained last week's log of her activity. Vladia woke up seven days ago at 06:17. Judging by her vitals, she was forced awake and remained so for five minutes and thirty-seven seconds before going back under."

"I hate to ask this, but is there any way we can get access to the cameras in her room? Find out what happened?"

"I anticipated your curiosity and already attempted to do so. Unfortunately the cameras in Vladia's room have been inoperable for ten days."

"Ten days," Abel wondered aloud. He pulled his tray back in front of him and ate a few spoonfuls of soup as he thought. "How long ago was her first surgery?"

"Twelve days ago."

"What about the second?"

"Eight days ago."

Abel sucked in a deep breath and held it. Something must have happened ten days ago. Cameras are always reported and immediately fixed, especially during war when security is at its highest.

Abel exhaled and scratching his head asked, "And Vladia has a room to herself?"

"She does now. Lt. Falis was in that room until she

died."

"And that was?"

"Ten days ago."

"So, Falis dies and the cameras cut out?"

"Or the cameras cut out and then Falis dies," Rehel added.

"Something's up." Abel picked up his bowl and gulped down the rest of his soup. "I need to think."

He stood up. "You still monitoring Vladia?"

Rehel nodded, standing up also.

"Keep me posted." Abel paused, and then added carefully, "I think I'm gonna keep my distance from her for a while. Things are progressing faster than I thought they would."

"Abel, why do you keep these fears from her? If you are correct, might not that information be useful to her?"

"It would. But I don't want to influence her. I've already said more to her than I should," he said, reminding himself of the day she visited him in the hospital. He'd been fresh off that dream and his anger had got the best of him. "This must be her decision, not mine."

"You could be placing her in great danger you know," the robot warned.

"I know," he muttered helplessly. But what choice did he have? He knew she'd been poking around into matters of the past, but as long as it was of her own freewill and not him pushing her to it then it was fine. Besides, if she was all he believed her to be then Vladia could handle herself if she got into trouble.

"By the way, I didn't get a chance to ask you. How'd your diagnostic go?" he said, changing the topic back to his earlier concerns. Abel had almost forgotten about the diagnostic with all the chaos of the war, but Rehel's unusual behavior with the hospital computer system reminded him.

"It was as expected. Nothing out of the ordinary was reported so I am cleared for another six months."

That was no surprise really since Rehel was still here and not in a scrap pile scheduled for meltdown. But something was different with his friend; he'd been noticing it for a while actually. "You ever do any self-diagnostics in between?"

"I perform regular self-diagnostics every forty-eight hours," he explained, straight-faced as usual.

"That normal? Seems a bit excessive."

Rehel did not respond.

Abel shrugged and moved towards the main entrance. Rehel made no motion to follow him.

Was Rehel worried about himself, Abel wondered. Abel decided his silence was a clear yes. It'd be best not to make a big deal out of it. If Rehel was keeping close tabs on himself, then maybe he could fix an issue before he went to diagnostic. Who knows, maybe he already had?

"Least he isn't lying. Not that human yet," Abel mumbled under his breath.

∞

Vladia, still clad in a light blue hospital gown, stood up to stretch. She was finally going home today and was glad of it. She twisted her torso first right, then left, as far as she could. This was her normal routine since she'd been allowed to get out of bed. Ten minutes of stretching followed by a thirty minute walk around the outside of the building, which was later built up to a thirty minute run. Then it was time for minimal weights. She couldn't lift more than ten pounds with her new arm. Not because the arm was weak, but because the nerve and tendon connections were fresh, as was the skin covering.

She learned the hard way her first day of weights that this made them easily torn and incredibly painful to boot. She'd tried to lift twenty, half her norm. It was as if her muscles were being pried apart, each fiber unthreading themselves from one another. She actually saw her new skin separate from the old, leaving a small slash that looked like a seam had come undone. She was rushed back to her room for sedation and repairs. That was when they put her nanos in. She wasn't supposed to get them until just before discharge, but since they classified her as a high risk of injury, they put them in sooner.

Instinctively, she reached up and touched her right shoulder. She tugged her nightgown down to look it over. There was a thin pink scar where the repair had been made. If she'd been more careful the job would have been flawless. The new skin had been grown independently in the days she was having surgery so it was ready when she was. Her skin had been evened out at the edges so the transplant would likely not leave a scar. Once the skin was placed over the robotic arm, it grew into her old skin with the help of hyper-growth hormonal injections at the site of the transplant. But when she'd torn the two skins apart, it was not a clean break; they were mangled, the edges jagged, causing the re-connection to be less than ideal. She'd given herself a constant reminder that she was no longer wholly human.

There was a gentle knock at her door. Jerking her gown up, Vladia said, "Come in."

The door opened and Rehel stepped in holding a white drawstring bag. "I've brought your clothes, Colonel Robespierre."

"Thanks," she said as she reached for the bag. That was the first time she'd heard someone call her 'Colonel Robespierre'. It sounded awkward and served only to further remind her she was no longer a Valkyrie pilot. "I thought Abel was supposed to pick me up."

"Lt. Commander Duren is occupied today so he asked me to take you home in his place. I hope that is alright."

"It's fine," she said, trying not to sound disappointed. It wasn't that she specifically wanted Abel to take her home but he had been strangely absent through this whole ordeal. He hadn't come to visit her even once.

"I will wait outside while you change and gather your belongings. We can leave as soon as you are ready." Rehel stepped out and closed the door behind him.

Vladia stripped away her hospital gown and tossed it in the corner. Loosening the drawstring of the white bag, she pulled out the clothing Rehel had brought her: black slacks and a fitted blue, short sleeved shirt. As she pulled the shirt over her head, she couldn't help but notice the shirt was the same shade of blue as her eyes. Vladia imagined poor Rehel trying to pick out women's clothing and smiled at his logical conclusion that the clothing should match her eyes.

After buttoning her pants, she fished around in the bag to see if he'd brought her anything else, but the only other item was a hairbrush with a black hairband wrapped around it. With a long sigh, she withdrew the brush and proceeded to pull back her thick, blonde hair. She'd been hoping to find some make-up in the bag, but she couldn't blame him for not knowing to bring such things.

Vladia packed the brush back into the bag and slung it over her left shoulder as she walked to the door. Out of the corner of her eye she caught a gleam of metal from her bedside table. It was her Colonel insignia. She had half a mind to just leave it, but that would be futile. With or without the insignia she was now Colonel Robespierre and even if she left it someone would assume she'd forgotten it and send it her way before the day was out.

Reluctantly, Vladia scooped up the insignia and stuffed it in her pocket before heading out the door.

Rehel was still waiting dutifully outside the door. Vladia motioned for him to follow as she headed down the corridor.

"I took the liberty of filling out your release documents earlier so there is no need to stop by the front desk," he said from three steps behind her.

"Good. Thanks."

The two walked silently through the hallway, the lobby, and out the front door. Once outside, Vladia inhaled deeply, letting the autumn air fill her lungs. It was still hot and would be for another month, but fresh air, hot or not, beat stuffy hospital air any day.

"This way," Rehel instructed, taking the lead.

Vladia followed close behind. She felt like running from this place. Between visiting Abel and her own injuries, she'd had enough of hospitals for a good, long while.

It was then she noticed Rehel looked different. He wasn't wearing his usual black uniform. Instead he was dressed all in gray save for his black boots. It hadn't really occurred to her that Rehel too had been displaced because of the last battle. At least he was not going anywhere. Proof of that was the new uniform itself. If the government was going to dismantle him they wouldn't have bothered with the new get-up.

"So where have you been assigned?" she asked.

"They're lucky to have you, that's for sure."

"Officially nowhere yet. They were going to dismantle me, but fortunately General Malthus cited my heroic actions in the last battle and convinced the Robot Distribution Committee that I could be of more use in the upcoming battles," the robot explained.

"General Malthus did that for you?" she said with earnest surprise. An unusually kindhearted action for him it seemed, but the little voice in the back of her mind reminded her Malthus did nothing that would not pay off for him in the long run.

Rehel nodded. "Once the squads are permanently restructured, I will be assigned an official post."

"It was indeed heroic. I'm glad Malthus put you in charge."

"His words, not mine. I was just following orders," he admitted, no modesty indented.

They reached the auto and Rehel opened the door for her. Tossing her bag on the floorboard, Vladia slid in across the sleek whiteness of the upholstery. The robot entered from the other side.

Rehel inserted the key to wake the auto's computer interface. "Welcome," it said warmly in a young woman's voice. "Where would you like to go today?"

"Kazan United Terran Military Base, living quarters district, building F," he instructed.

"Calculating route. Estimated time of arrival: eight minutes. Shall I proceed?"

"Yes."

The car lifted off the ground smoothly, hovering inches above the pavement, then backed out of the parking space to proceed with its orders.

Vladia found herself unwillingly reminded of the auto

ride to her father's estate after her mother's funeral. It made her feel like an anxious eleven-year-old all over again. But this time was different, she assured herself. She could order Rehel to take her somewhere else entirely, which was a luxury she didn't have when she was eleven. For just a moment she seriously considered the prospect, but really she didn't have anywhere she wanted to go. More than anything, she wanted a long, hot shower in her own bathroom. So, she decided to let Rehel take her home, but it was of her own accord and no one else's.

A robot, one of her mother's models, had escorted her then too. Rehel might even be the same model as the one from her past, but time had clouded her memory of such specifics. He was definitely a similar model. Her mother had never wasted much time on skin variations with her models. The only changes she made were hair and eye color just to keep them visually separate. Model B might have blue eyes and black hair, while Model C would have the same face and body but with blonde hair and green eyes.

"Is something wrong, Colonel Robespierre?" Rehel asked. Vladia started, looking away slightly embarrassed. She hadn't realized she'd been staring at him.

"Sorry. I was just thinking. And you've got to stop calling me that. You call Abel by his first name and I want you to do the same for me," she insisted. "In fact, it's an order." Vladia looked back at him and smiled.

"Certainly, Vladia," Rehel complied.

Vladia leaned against the auto's window and stared out it. Watching the trees and buildings zip by in a blur of gray and green, again her thoughts drifted toward unpleasantries. Although the circumstances were different, the two incidents were traumatic in their own way. She'd lost something each time and both had been pieces of herself. Yet they were each hidden at least. The pain in her heart from the loss of her mother was easily concealed from the outside world, except on the occasions Tolen had provoked it out of her. It was the same with her arm. Only those closest to Vladia would know her right arm was not her own and, in time, they would forget since the appendages were identical, save for the scar she'd given herself.

She moved her left hand up to gently grasp her shoulder blade. It was still so tender. Her right arm felt much more sensitive than the left and in unexpected ways. She could grip both hands around a freshly iced drink and her right hand would almost burn from the cold glass while her left was just fine. The doctors said it was because of the nerve connectors. They were new to her body and would need a few more weeks to properly adjust.

"Is the arm bothering you?" Rehel asked as if he was concerned for more than just her comfort.

"No. Well, yes and no. It's sensitive still, and will be for a while, but I can handle it." She removed her hand from her shoulder. She frowned; she shouldn't show such weakness, even in front of a robot.

"I did not mean physical pain, though I am sure you will suffer that, as you said, for a while. I was inquiring about the arm bothering you mentally."

Vladia was surprised this robot could even seize such a concept. More of Abel's human influence, she supposed.

Shifting in her seat to face him, she questioned, "How would you even think to ask such a thing?"

"I have seen many humans suffer from unexplained pains when there was nothing physically wrong with them. Like with Abel after Ceres Forté died. Even after his body was fully functional, he seemed to be in pain.

Truthfully, he was never the same after that incident. But it was not something of the body, it was something here," Rehel touched two fingers to his temple. "Do you understand what I mean?"

"I understand. But you're a bit off," Vladia said, gently taking his hand from his head. "It's something here." She pressed his hand over his chest where, if he were human, his heart would rest.

"You are referring to emotional pain I take it. I have always found it strange that humans associated emotions with the heart when it is the brain that is responsible for them," Rehel explained, reminding Vladia that he was indeed not even close to human.

She removed her hand from him and straightened up in her seat. "The brain may cause the pain, but this," she said touching her hand to her chest, "is where you feel it if you're human. It's a deafening ache one feels here and nowhere else. But sometimes, it just feels empty and that's worse than any kind of pain in the world."

The robot appeared to consider this. "Which does your robotic arm make you feel? Is it pain or is it empty?"

Vladia stared into her lap, still touching her chest. The auto came to a slow, silent halt. Just above a whisper she spoke more honestly that she ever had in her life. It was just one word: "Empty."

11

BODIES

"Excuse me," Abel began, leaning over the hospital's mortuary front desk to attract the attention of the young lady behind it. She was a pretty girl with light brown hair and brown eyes to match. But more importantly to him, she was the new girl. Abel had waited all day for her to take the night shift.

The girl looked surprised. Of course, the mortuary didn't get many visitors. The fact that the man addressing her was clearly not a doctor, or even in uniform for that matter, but instead clad in a hospital gown, didn't help either.

The girl had obviously anticipated an undisturbed night. She had a datapad in her lap that she quickly stowed away in her desk. "Can I help you, Sir?"

"You sure can," Abel said with a sweet half-smile. "I was wondering, could you tell me if Lt. Commander Isobel Falis has been cremated for the general memorial yet?"

"Sure." The girl typed in the name on her screen. "It

looks like she'll be done tomorrow morning at five. Were you a friend of the deceased?" the girl's voice brimmed with mandatory sympathy.

"Yes. We were in the same squad and had been very, very close…" he let his voice trail off sadly as he looked away.

"Oh, I'm so sorry, Sir." The girl reached across the desk and rested her slim, gloved hand on his. This appeared to be more genuine, but Abel would leave nothing to chance. He'd lay it on a bit thicker.

Abel accepted the gesture gratefully, placing his other hand on top of hers and giving it a gentle squeeze. "I was pretty banged up in the last battle. It wasn't until I regained consciousness two days ago that I even knew she'd passed."

"Is there anything I can do for you, Mr…?"

"Lt. Commander Duren." He'd considered an alias, but decided it wouldn't matter since any surrounding security footage could undoubtedly identify him no matter who he tried to pass himself off as.

"There is one thing but I really hate to ask. I don't want to inconvenience you," he continued.

"Our director lost his contracted in the battle so I have seen firsthand how hard this has been on people. If I can help I'd be most happy too," the girl offered.

"Well, I won't be released before the memorial you see and I was hoping to say goodbye to her."

The girl began to interject but Abel didn't give her the chance. "I know I need the squad captain's permission to view the body, but as you may know our squad, the Valkyrie squad, was dissolved for the remainder of the war because of our heavy losses. By the time I figure out who to get permission from and have the forms signed, she'll already be gone you see."

She wasn't going to cave yet. He could see in her eyes she wanted to but was hesitant. He needed one more push.

"God!" he began, squeezing his eyes shut in a self-deprecating fashion. "If only I hadn't been so badly injured! I could have been there for her in the end."

Abel pulled his hands away from her and took a step back. "I'm sorry. I'll just go back to my room."

As soon as his back was to her, Abel heard the girl leap from her chair. "Wait!"

Abel stopped but didn't turn around.

"I can give you five minutes. I wish I could do more but…" She was afraid of losing her job. And she would if he was caught. But he didn't have time to worry with little things like that. This would be his only shot to uncover anything useful.

He turned around now, wiping his eyes as if there had been tears. "Thank you so much! Five minutes is more than enough!" It wasn't really, but he could make it work.

∞

"She's in G22," the girl pointed to the middle of the right wall of the morgue vault. "I'll come back in five, after you've had your time to say goodbye."

Abel nodded.

"I'm Alice, by the way."

"Thanks, Alice. I really appreciate this."

Alice smiled and pulled the heavy door shut leaving Abel all alone. The cold floor stung his slippered feet as he made his way to G22. He wished he could have forgone the disguise, but at least he had some clothing on under the hospital gown to shield his body from the biting air.

G22 was just under chest high. This was a relief. If it had been a few rows higher he'd have to use the ladder, which would slow down his search.

Abel tugged the release lever down, which hissed as the airtight seal was broken, and slid the slab out all the way.

There she was. A little blue, but otherwise intact. She was stiff, not from rigor mortis though. The body was chilled to negative ten degrees Celsius to prevent decomposition. She'd be frozen this way until her cremation. This would make the search difficult but it was as expected.

He knew whatever he was looking for would not be obvious, and with only four minutes and some change left he'd have to be systematic about his search. He refused to be sick about this either; he'd not the time for such a luxury, so Abel leapt right in.

Starting at the head, he worked his way down as fast, yet thoroughly, as time allowed. No fresh abrasions or lesions on the front. No traces of dried blood anywhere. Now he'd need to flip her. As gently as possible he rotated the body onto its side then slid it to the left before laying it face down.

Still nothing.

Isobel's cropped black hair was matted and frozen. There'd be no way to check her skull thoroughly without leaving traces of a search. Abel had no choice though. Odds were the body wouldn't be seen until just before cremation and no one would be checking the body at that point.

Gingerly, he moved his fingers through her hair, running them over her scalp. He could feel the thin black strands separating from the scale and whispered an apology.

About three inches above the nape of the neck he found a hole about the circumference of the tip of his index finger.

An unexpected wave of nausea came over him as he slid his finger into the wound to see if it was merely surface damage. Once he was in to his second knuckle he stopped and removed his finger.

Taking a few deep breaths, Abel stepped away and allowed himself to fight back the sickness.

He didn't know what this meant but it had to be significant. With only a minute or so left, Abel rotated the body back onto its back.

As he pushed the slab back into the wall, the vault door clicked.

Someone was here already.

He sealed the door to G22 just as the main door eased open.

"You sure have good timing, Alice," he said expectantly.

"Alice is a bit tied up at the moment," a male voice echoed from the darkened doorway.

Malthus stepped into the light of the vault room. It took Abel a moment to recognize him in his blue General's uniform.

"The disguise is a nice touch, but wholly unnecessary," Malthus said, walking to the right-hand wall of the room and leaning a shoulder against it.

Abel could say nothing. His body was rigid and behind his back he clasped his fists together tightly. He'd no option but to wait for the other man to make a move first.

"If you wanted to view Isobel's body, or any of our other comrades', all you had to do was ask. I wouldn't have said no."

Abel still refused to speak. He had to find out what Malthus suspected of him. His former captain was almost impossible to read though. He exuded nothing but confidence despite all circumstances. Appearing to know and actually knowing could be a trivial difference at times. The jig might already be up, or Malthus may be waiting for Abel to give himself away. He had a ready excuse, but he wouldn't waste it if Malthus knew why he was really here. If that was the case, he'd need another pathway out of this.

Malthus moved closer, brushing his fingertips lightly across the square metal doors, each housing its own body. "So, shall we examine the body together? Or have you had your fill of corpses for the day?"

The two men faced off, separated by little more than the width of the G22 door. Malthus pulled the lever to release the door and Isobel's body glided out on the slab once again.

"Looks like you did a nice job. I can hardly tell the body's been moved at all," Malthus hissed with a slight smile.

He knew.

Malthus knew he'd come looking for something. But, what he didn't know is whether or not Abel knew what that something was. Or if he'd found it.

"Nothing but old bruising and IV punctures on the front. But what shall we find on the back?" Malthus flipped the body gently. "Hmmm. More bruising. But wait. What's this?"

Malthus touched his fingers to the corpse's hair just above the neck. "Looks like a puncture about the size of a cerebral shock cord. Well, I suppose the doctors would try that since it was her brain that was giving out."

Abel hadn't considered that. Then again, he didn't know the details of Isobel's injuries. He wasn't dismissing his find just yet, though. That hole could surely point to other things as well.

"Did I miss anything, Duren? Please, jump in at any time."

Malthus waited a few seconds then with a shrug of the shoulders closed up G22. He didn't even bother to flip the body back face up.

"I'm about tired of this game of yours, Duren," Malthus began. His tone had changed considerably. No longer was he taunting Abel. The man was all seriousness now. "I've let you poke and prod about for years trying to find whatever it is you think I'm hiding. It was all harmless since I've nothing to hide from you, but we are at war now. I have no time for this and neither does the Terran Military. How long is it now that you've been ranked Lt. Commander? Going on ten years isn't it now? You know, the only one holding you back is you."

Able laughed. "You think it's about that? About promotions?!" He slammed his fist again the vault walls. "This is about–"

"Ceres Forté?" he interrupted. "About how I killed her? About how I destroyed an entire facility and everyone in it to cover up some secret research project?"

Malthus paused briefly as he stepped closer–mere inches away from Abel. "I've lost interest in this game we've been playing. It's been fun, Duren, but I don't want to play with you anymore," he whispered into Abel's ear.

Abel bit the insides of his cheeks, trying to control his anger. Lashing out at a General would mean no less than a court martial. He had to restrain himself.

Malthus backed away. "I admire your control, though," he said.

General Malthus walked to the door. "The new game has already begun, and I don't think I'll let you have a part in it," he said just before rounding the corner and disappearing into the corridor.

Abel took that as a warning; Malthus was out for blood now. He'd need to be careful or the next visit he made to the morgue would be much more permanent.

∞

Cornelia Arnim hung back, not quite stepping inside the Valkyrie's hangar bay, though one could hardly label it that anymore. Now it was more like a Valkyrie graveyard as it was brimming with broken ships and their various pieces.

Her ship, *Alvitr*, and Gammarow's *Sigrdrífa* were part of this graveyard. Their ships had been damaged beyond reasonable repair, misshapen and crushed from the Z-pinch Rehel had barely managed to save them from. They'd be scrapped and any parts salvageable had already been looted to repair less damaged Valkyries. She hated to admit it but she would forever be in the robot's debt for what he'd done for them out there.

She'd come here to say goodbye. *Alvitr* would be melted down tomorrow morning and her metal used for yet more repairs to other ships. Her goodbye would be a wordless one since the central computer, what she truly considered to be *Alvitr*, had never come back online after the disaster at L4. In a way, she was saying farewell to an empty shell, a corpse.

Cornelia, like Vladia and Malthus, had been promoted

for her valiant efforts during the battle. She laughed at the thought. She'd done nothing remotely valiant at L4; Rehel had and that had been the only thing saving him from decommission. She knew she'd been promoted because there was no Gunslinger Valkyrie for her to pilot, and she'd been a Valkyrie pilot long enough that putting her in a different squad would be more like a demotion.

The Captain's Valkyrie was in working order but had been 'retired' with his promotion, as was tradition for the Captain's ship. It was stupid in times of war for a perfectly pilotable Valkyrie to be gathering dust, especially in this case when it was one she was qualified to fly. Gammarow was lucky enough not to be promoted and would take Isobel Falis's *Hildr*. In fact, parts of *Alvitr* and *Sigrdrífa* had been used to repair *Hildr* so she tried to imagine that in some way their ships still lived on with him.

She spied her ship, rather the remains of it, at the far corner of the hangar heaped up on a lift ready for transport. She started in that direction, when she noticed she wasn't alone in the hangar. Just inside the doorway to the right was Vladia Robespierre. She was sitting on the floor, knees pulled up to her chest, in front of her former Valkyrie *Freya*. Repair bots whizzed around the giant craft, which was still absent of part an arm and chest plate.

Cornelia grimaced. She'd thought for sure the place was empty and she was in no mood to deal with anyone at the moment. But it seemed Vladia was unaware of her presence, at least she made no indication otherwise.

The younger woman sat frozen, resting face-down on her knees. Since Vladia wasn't in uniform, Cornelia assumed she must still be on medical leave. Vladia's casual attire was a stark contrast to her own crisp, new Colonel uniform.

There was the woman Abel put all his faith in. Cornelia hadn't spoken more than two words to Vladia since the incident at the bar. Frankly, it'd been her intention to not speak to the woman again for the rest of her life. But as time passed, Cornelia had softened that resolution from actively avoiding her, to simply not going out of her way to be friendly with her.

On seeing Vladia in such a sorry state, it all seemed rather ridiculous to be doing either. The girl needed a friend, now more than ever, Cornelia thought, and if Abel was pinning all his hopes on her, she might as well get reacquainted with her.

Nevertheless, Cornelia still couldn't understand Abel on this one. Maybe there was something he wasn't telling her. Abel had always filled the leadership role in their little group. He was a good judge of both skill and character and even though he had isolated and masked himself after Ceres's death, there was no reason to think those skills had diminished.

Yet all she saw before her was a little girl sniveling at the feet of her former ship, not even aware her solitude had been breached.

"You came to say goodbye too?" Vladia spoke, making Cornelia flinch in surprise. So she had been aware of her presence after all. Fine, her senses were sharper than she'd originally suspected. Cornelia would give her that much, but it'd take more than that to impress her.

"Yeah," Cornelia answered taking a few tentative steps closer.

"I guess I've no reason to complain though. At least *Freya* will be okay eventually. She'll be ready to fight in the next battle if they can find her a pilot," she said. Vladia had lifted her head to speak but made no motion to face her.

"Even in war, these things take time. It'd be dangerous to let just anybody pilot one of these."

The two women stayed silent for several moments, but it wasn't an awkward silence. It was as if they were alone in mind and their common physical presence was coincidental and of no real concern. Their once normal lives presented in ruins before them, created a sombering effect both women could feel. At least, Cornelia thought, they had that much in common.

"I'm sorry about *Alvitr*." Vladia was first to break the silence.

"Thanks. Who knew you could use nanos like that, huh?"

"Who indeed."

More silence. Cornelia wondered if she should say something about the woman's arm. Maybe congratulate her on the promotion? Ultimately, she decided against both and instead just stood there self-consciously.

"You know, I've been sitting here awhile. I'd really just come to turn in my key but no one was here so here I sit still." Vladia hesitated for a second before continuing. "I loved this ship and being a Valkyrie pilot. I'm sad that these precious things are forever gone from me. I've been thinking on ways to move forward. I've been thinking on how I can get past this. But I realized just now, when you walked in that I'd had it all wrong."

"So what's the solution?" Cornelia prompted, finding herself intrigued despite her earlier resistance.

"I can't abandon these things that have shaped me. I'm not supposed to move past this; I'm supposed to take it with me and protect it always as I progress forward," the younger woman explained, more to herself than Cornelia it seemed. Cornelia wasn't sure she bought into that idea, but listened regardless.

Vladia stood up, brushed her pants off and turned to face Cornelia. She was a bit taken aback by Vladia's serious countenance. It felt as if she was just now meeting Vladia for the first time. No, that wasn't quite right. This was a different Vladia altogether.

"I have something for you," she continued, holding out her fist.

Cornelia reached out and Vladia placed a key in her hand. Not just any key though; it was *Alvitr's* ignition key. "Where did you find this?"

"Like I said, I've been here awhile. I got one of the bots to dig through *Alvitr's* remains for it. I tried to find Gammarow's too but I fear it was lost at L4," Vladia said. Her face was stoic, but Cornelia could hear sadness creeping into her voice. Yet it was not a sadness to be mocked or ashamed of. It was a sadness filled with respect for those lost.

"I'll have to give up my key eventually but there is no reason for you to," she continued. "I've got other things I'll be carrying with me."

Cornelia guessed she was referring to her robotic arm. That, indeed, was a reminder not easily brushed aside. She felt compelled to say something kind to Vladia. Reassure her or tell her she was sorry. Something. Anything. But Cornelia had never been one for talk like that.

"I think that," Cornelia began, "well, Abel thinks highly of you and he's usually right about people. He's got a talent with people, not like me."

Cornelia wanted to kick herself. Those words, meant to be supportive, sounded so stupid said aloud. Cornelia wished she'd just kept her mouth shut and left. She let out a nervous laugh and pressed on. "What I mean is that if and when the time comes, Abel says he'll follow you and so will I. And Gammarow too."

There, Cornelia released an inner sigh, that should be a good pledge of loyalty. It was the best kind of comfort she could offer her. She had Vladia's back and now she knew it.

Vladia stared blankly at the older woman. "Where?"

The question didn't quite register with Cornelia.

"Follow me where?" The younger woman asked again. She seemed genuinely confused.

Cornelia didn't know how to answer. What was Abel thinking? Did he have this little rebellion of his planned without the one girl he said would lead it? Shit, she cursed at herself.

"You know what, forget I said that. I was just…talkin'," Cornelia said, taking two steps back. "If you see Abel, you tell him I'm looking for him." She had a punch in the face waiting patiently for him.

"You'll have to tell him yourself. He's been avoiding me ever since the last battle," Vladia remarked. She seemed truly bothered, making Cornelia halt her retreat. She hadn't realized Abel was hiding again but she should have guessed this would be the case.

"It's nothing personal, I promise. He's been avoiding almost everyone off and on for years," Cornelia explained. "I think he hadn't realized how close he'd gotten to you until you almost died. That sort of thing, losing someone close, is difficult for him. So his response is to push people away to protect himself from that pain."

"It seems you know him a lot better than I thought I did."

"We grew up in the same facility so we've known each

other a long time."

Vladia nodded but Cornelia's explanation of Abel hadn't helped much she could tell. Cornelia had felt the same thing when Abel had abandoned her after Ceres's death. Even though she'd known it was him not her, she still felt hurt and angry over it for a long time. When he came to her at the bar the other night, Cornelia wanted to hug him she was so happy. Of course she hadn't though.

"Listen," Cornelia began, "I'd like to tell you he'll come back around soon but I honestly don't know. But if you need someone to talk to, you can come to me and I'll lend you an ear." Cornelia couldn't believe she just said that. What was even more surprising was that she meant it.

"Thanks. I'll keep that in mind."

"If I see Abel I'll slap him and say to stop being a selfish asshole," Cornelia said with a smile as she turned to go. "And thanks again for the key."

∞

Vladia sat back down on the cold floor and stared up at *Freya*. Everything felt wrong. If she could just clear her mind she knew she could figure out what to do. But she just couldn't. It sounded so easy but it proved impossible time and time again. Her mind wandered inexplicably no matter how she tried to force it down a particular path of thought. Vladia had never been this unfocused in all her life.

It was the arm that made her feel less human.

It was the promotion that she hadn't earned.

It was Malthus who made both the previous so.

It was Abel who avoided her at all costs.

It was Rehel who reminded her of her other great loss.

She made herself accept all of these things, one by one, determined to carry her new baggage forever without complaint.

Still, even after accepting the inevitable, nothing felt right. She felt paralyzed by something. It wasn't fear though. It was something else just beyond the borders of her understanding; like there was this thing floating just outside her peripheral vision but when she turned to look there was nothing. This was what she sought to uncover. And at this she was utterly failing.

The next assault on Luna was in three days and Vladia felt overwhelmed. She hadn't done more than skim through the L4 incident report, and she hadn't stepped onto her new ship more than once.

The nanos. That was of interest though and she wanted to talk to Tolen about this, but with his new position he was impossible to see at the moment. There was too much to prepare for with only three days left. She'd see him in the battle prep meeting just before the next strike but that would be too late she feared.

She knew Abel would be roaring to blame him for L4 somehow. Despite appearances, she knew he wasn't involved. Sure, it had fetched him a nice promotion, but that wasn't enough to pin this on him. Tolen had been livid about the Valkyries being split up. It seemed clear he'd wanted to keep them all at the Lunar front.

Vladia heard footsteps coming from the corridor. They sounded rushed. Standing up, she made her way behind *Freya's* left leg, veiling her presence from the newcomer.

Abel marched intensely though the door. She'd hoped it was him and planned to corner him, but something in his eyes made her hold back. He looked panicked, yet determined. Vladia expected him to head straight for

Gunnr, but instead he headed to the large weaponry cabinet in the back of the hangar. From her vantage point it was hard to tell what he was doing, but it wasn't hard to guess.

With an arm full of weapons, he sealed the cabinet and headed toward his Valkyrie. There were several storage compartments accessible from both the inside and outside of the ship; with his back to her, Abel opened one on *Gunnr's* back right leg and quickly stowed all the weapons but one. The remaining weapon was compact and Abel easily packed it in his jacket pocket.

He then closed the compartment and opened the adjacent one on the left leg. He scanned the contents, which looked to be condensed food stuffs, and with a nod to himself shut that compartment as well.

Vladia crept towards the exit, then, as if she'd just come in, walked loudly towards Abel.

Abel spun around and didn't at all look relieved it was her. In fact, Vladia thought he looked worse for seeing her. She waved and quickened her pace to greet him.

She'd not mention what she had witnessed. It was clear he was preparing to leave, but why? Asking him would only increase his secrecy, so she'd question Rehel about it as soon as she had the chance. Vladia would bet money on the robot knowing Abel's plans and why.

"I've been looking for you," she began as she finally closed the gap between them.

"Yeah. I've had a lot on my plate lately. How's the arm?" he asked, seeming to relax now that he assumed she had not seen him stealing weapons. He leaned against his ship and crossed his arms over his chest.

"It's okay. Still getting used to it though. The doctors said it'd be a while before I can use it at full capacity so I have to take it easy."

"Well, it's a small price to pay to still be alive. Not all of us were so lucky," he added grimly.

"I'm not complaining," she defended a bit more sharply than she had intended.

"No, I know. Anyway, what did you want to see me about?"

He was cutting to the chase so he could escape her, Vladia decided. Fine. She would make it quick, but not entirely painless.

"As my former partner," she started, adding unneeded stress on the word 'former', "I wanted to give this to you."

Vladia held out her Valkyrie key. Abel made no move to take it from her.

She continued, hand still outstretched, "I can't pilot anything directly anymore. My classification has been changed from human to altered human and you know top brass considers that as no better than a robot when it comes to combat. Honestly, I'm lucky to have a dreadnought. They could have discharged me. Anyway, I wanted someone I could trust to hold onto this for me. You're the only one who came to mind. So take it. Please."

Abel reached out and then hesitated. "No. I can't take it like this."

"What do you mean?"

"I won't let you give this to me. That implies it is mine, not yours. Tell you what. How about I just watch it for you? I'll put it in a safe place until you're ready to use it again," he negotiated with a smile.

"Abel, you know I'll never be allowed to fly *Freya* again."

"I like to keep an open mind about things. You never know how things might turn out, right? Besides, I won't take it under any other conditions."

Vladia supposed it didn't matter one way or another so she shook her head in agreement. Abel took the key and pocketed it.

He didn't act like he was leaving. All this about giving the key back directly implied he would be here to do just that one day. So what was his deal?

"So I was thinking. After this mess with Luna is all over, I'd like to petition a promotion for you. I want you on my ship, but I know you wouldn't come so I was thinking you'd make a nice captain once the squad is rebuilt," Vladia said.

Abel's mood distinctly darkened. Was he recalling the last time he almost made captain? She didn't think so but everything still felt so off. She was having a hard time reading him.

"You know, I'm glad you and I met," he began, completely ignoring her earlier offer. "And I'm glad you trust me enough to hold on to *Freya's* key. You're going to do amazing things one day, and I hope I'll be lucky enough to see them happen."

Vladia was too stunned to respond. This fatalism was never supposed to come from a man like Abel.

This was all wrong.

Abel closed the small distance between them and embraced her gently, making sure he put no pressure on her right arm and shoulder.

It took her a second or two to realize what was happening. She'd not felt tenderness like this since her mother. Not once at her father's estate had either him or Tolen showed her the slightest bit of affection. It was always the same–pushing and pushing to be the best and to gain approval. Yet she never stopped yearning for it.

But what was this? Vladia knew how hard this intimacy must be for him. Was he leaving, was he not leaving? It was just too much.

Vladia pushed him away violently. "What is wrong with you?! Talking about not being around and then this! It's not acceptable, Abel! You can't do this to me!" her heated voice bounced off the hangar walls and reverberated back into her own ears.

Abel stood there and let her scream at him, all the while holding her gaze steady. Vladia looked away. She was too angry and too lost to deal with this.

"You're right," he said, calmly walking past her to the exit. "I'm sorry."

Vladia watched him go. Twice she almost cried out for him to stop. But she didn't. Whatever Abel decided to do it was his decision and she refused to interfere anymore. It would only push him further away. She had her own miseries to deal with and shouldering his would only hurt them both in the end.

∞

Abel rang the buzzer and waited patiently outside Rehel's quarters. The robot answered the door promptly and stepped aside for him to enter.

"I'm all set," Abel said, sliding the picture of him and Rehel to the side so he could take a seat on top of the desk.

"No complications?"

"Almost, but no." Abel didn't feel like elaborating and Rehel always had the decency not to pry. "With the war, no one's going to be looking for or using any small arms so I should be fine. Anyway, I'm gonna contact Dr. Weston soon as I'm in range and see if he can get me some work for a while."

The robot was silent.

Abel smiled. "If I didn't know any better I'd say you were sad."

Rehel ignored his comment. "Are you sure you will be alright?" he asked with as much concern as a robot could.

"No," Abel laughed lightly. "I'd like you to come with me, but I need you here more. Vladia needs you, though I doubt she knows it and, really, that's as it should be. I've outstayed my welcome unfortunately. This next battle will be my only window out."

"I understand."

"So where've they got you stationed for the battle?"

"The *Dragoon*."

"So you'll be with Malthus."

Rehel nodded firmly.

"Well I'll not need to worry about you then," Abel continued.

He picked up the framed picture and held it high, letting the faces look down on him. "Regardless, you're very self-sufficient and you've come a long way."

"Thank you, Abel."

"Could I borrow this?" he asked, setting the picture in his lap. "Just the picture–for the trip? You'll get it back I promise."

"Of course. But now, if I may say so, you are the one who appears sad," Rehel said evenly.

If ever a robot tried to be sarcastic, it was this one, Abel thought and couldn't help but grin. "You got me."

He hopped off the desk and straightened his uniform. Sliding the photograph from its home, he placed the empty frame back on the desk. He stared into the blank rectangle and suddenly felt like his existence had being erased. Maybe that's what he'd been wanting all along.

"Will you see Vladia before you go?"

"Already did," Abel said, reaching into his pocket and pulling out the key Vladia had gave him.

"Here," he handed it to Rehel. "I told Vladia I'd keep it safe for her but I don't know if I can live up to that promise. It'll be far safer with you."

With a nod, Rehel tucked the key in a small pocket on the front of his jacket.

Abel opened the door. "Well. Be seein' ya, Rehel." He hated long, drawn-out goodbyes so he always made his exits quick.

"Be safe, Abel," the robot bid his farewell and the door closed between them.

It isn't goodbye, Abel assured himself. It's only a goodbye if I don't come back. And I'll be coming back. One day.

12

THE BLOODY VAULT

Vladia's heels echoed sharply as she walked the length of the still empty bridge of the *Spartan*. Detached, she stood in front of the, or rather her, commander chair and held a reluctant hand over one of the arm rests. It wasn't that she was in awe or disbelief of her new position; it was the fact that she had not earned it. She was undeserving. She felt like a fraud.

And in her eyes so was Tolen. He hadn't earned his upheaval to higher ranks any more than she had, but she knew he was not bothered by this as she was. He didn't care about the means, only the end result. Many lives had been lost in the last battle and she'd no doubt he had not reflected on a single one, even his own partner she'd be willing to wager. It had all paved the way to his new position as General. Unlike her brother, these deaths weighed heavy on her. Made her feel almost sorry for surviving when others had not.

Vladia ran her hands over her fresh deep green uniform. It was stiff and would be for weeks before it was broken in properly. She suspected the uniforms were purposely made uncomfortable. The collar was always just a bit too high for her liking and the fabric had a roughness that lasted through dozens of washes. She thought it was the military's way of hazing new officers. And it worked. The new uniform's irritation of the body never once let a soldier forget that they were an unproved greenhorn. Of course she didn't need such physical reminders.

On top of that, during battle commanding officers were required to also wear their weighty overcoats as well to display their various honors. The purpose was two-fold: it increased morale for the crew to view their commanding officer's achievements and it increased the officer's desire to attain more awards to pin on their coat. Really, it was just another way to make one uncomfortable.

Bridge officers began trickling in. Vladia, masking her self-loathing and hesitation quickly, took her seat assuredly. Confidence, even if it was just the apparition of it, was one of the most important elements to successfully commanding a crew. If they sensed her true feelings they'd be unable to do their jobs. Insecurity, indecision, wariness, fear: all these were deadly contagious on a ship in battle. She was responsible for all their lives now and she would not let her shortcomings cause her to fail them in her duty.

"Lieutenant Rosen," Vladia called to her lead systems officer, "What's the ETA on system check completion?"

"Fifteen minutes till engine check is complete. Approximately ten minutes on everything else. We'll be finished well before formations begin, Colonel Robespierre."

Vladia nodded. "Very good."

"Colonel, you have a channel request from the *Iron Maiden,*" her lead communications officer, and second in command, said from his post near the front of the bridge.

That was Cornelia's ship. "Thank you, Commander Ramage. Patch it through my private channel," she answered, inserting her ear piece. "This is Colonel Robespierre."

"Vladia!" Cornelia's voice pierced her ears with eagerness. "How you hangin' in there?"

"Just fine, Cornelia. Thanks," Vladia said evenly. She was relieved Cornelia seemed to be her old self again. The awkwardness of their previous encounter had left Vladia unsure about where they stood.

"It's finally sunk in for me. Took standing on the damn bridge to do it."

"Me too."

"Listen, I wanted to thank you again for getting that key for me. I strung it up on a necklace so I could take *Alvitr* with me to battle," Cornelia began in a more serious tone. "I feel like it was all worth it now, you know. I loved being a Valkyrie, just as much as you did, but now I feel like I've been given the chance to really make a big difference. I couldn't do that as a pilot."

Vladia understood the other woman's feelings. And maybe she was right. Maybe they were finally in a position to have a larger impact on this war. They could now make their own calls instead of only following blindly the orders handed down though the chain of command. They could help end this war quickly.

But she still couldn't shake the uneasiness she'd felt for the last two weeks. Vladia was overlooking something important–but what? If only she could–

"Hey, you there?" Cornelia disrupted her thoughts.

"Yeah. Sorry, I was thinking about what you said. I hope you're right. I'd like to make a difference here today."

"Oh yeah. You ever run into Abel?"

"No," Vladia lied. One quick lie was better than the string of lies she'd have to offer up if she wanted to conceal what she'd spied Abel doing in the hangar. And there was no reason to infringe on Cornelia's enthusiasm with something neither could do anything about.

"Well, you'll have your chance after the battle. A solid win should put his sulking ass in better spirits," the other woman assured her.

"Right."

"Well then, I've got to get back to work. Good luck out there!" Cornelia signed off.

"You too," Vladia ended.

With Cornelia's zeal, Vladia had hoped she'd be more at ease. But she was even tenser than before and behind that, the strange fogginess of thought lingered still.

She stood up and walked to the very tip of the bridge. The view screen, which was made up of three panels arranged in a semicircle, was a light grey, matching the interior of the ship so well it appeared to be just another section of walls.

"View screen on," she commanded.

The grey dissolved to reveal a star-studded black sky. Luna was hanging in the distance and from her point of view she could see many of the other dreadnoughts and cruisers as well.

She searched aimlessly for *Gunnr* but spotted no trace of him. With a light sigh, inaudible to her crew of course, Vladia rested her forearm on her holstered blaster, another needless accessory. She wasn't even allowed to draw the damn gun unless they were boarded (unlikely) or if there was a mutiny (even more unlikely).

"Comrades!" Grand Admiral Clovis v. Acadia boomed over the general channel, "As we approach the hour of this decisive battle, let us not forget those we have already lost. I'll not ask you for a moment of silence to honor them. Instead, I ask you to honor them on the battlefield to glory. Let their sacrifice pave our way to a new, stronger, and victorious Earth!"

A cheer erupted over the bridge and resonated from every other ship over the channel as well. Vladia remained composed and let her crew speak for her.

"Now," the Grand Admiral continued, "As you know, Luna's shield is strong. But we've enlisted the aid of every able-bodied ship to take it out. Our smaller crafts, Fighters, Battle Cruisers and what remain of our Valk-yries, will intercept incoming enemy ships as our larger vessels prepare for the main strike. We shall strike only once for there will be no need for more. Coordinates are being relayed to each dreadnought and destroyer as I speak. We will strike all at once and at the exact same location to intensify the damage dealt. I want all systems on minimum, full power to weapons and I will personally countdown to fire once all crafts are ready. Today will be the last day of this insurgency!"

Another round of cheers lasted for a good twenty seconds before the channel was closed.

"Colonel, all systems are a go."

"Very well," Vladia acknowledged, marching back to her commander chair. "Let's get in formation and await further instruction."

Vladia took her seat and a deep breath. Their formation was simple: a triangle with the lead destroyer, in her case the *Dragoon*, at the back point with the *Spartan* and the *Iron Maiden* at the two lead points. Tolen was their group leader which in addition to her and Cornelia's ship was also made up of thirty Battle Cruisers, twenty-five fighters and two Valkyries. Tolen would be focusing on guiding the smaller crafts while the three larger ships prepared for the main event so she wasn't surprised she hadn't heard from him thus far. In fact, she was a bit relieved with his absence. His watching eyes and jagged words would only distract her.

Vladia scanned the nearby ships, again searching for *Gunnr*. She wasn't sure if Abel was in her group or not, but she hoped so. If that was the case, at least then she'd have a legitimate reason to keep a close eye on him during battle.

∞

Abel glided his craft smoothly into formation. His Defender was a guy named Jackson, the former Beta Defender. He was one of the older pilots, grumpy and distant, probably because he knew they'd force him into retirement soon. Abel hadn't spoken more than a handful of words to the man his entire career and not for lack of effort either. He kept his friendly, carefree persona with everyone, but was always shot down by this guy. Despite the circumstances, Abel found it somewhat humorous that he'd been paired with Jackson and now not only would the guy have to speak to him, he'd have to defend him too.

"Jackson," he began, "are you in position?"

"Yeah," was the curt response.

"It's fifteen till we engage. I know we've never spoken much, but I wanted to tell you good luck and thanks for flying with me. I know you're a terrific pilot and I'm glad it's you who's got my back." Abel wasn't patronizing him, though he suspected the old man would take it that way. It was all true; every word of it.

"Whatever. Stop jamming up my channel."

The connection closed abruptly.

It was for the best. Abel had one more item to take care of before the countdown was over and didn't need to waste time bullshitting with his grouchy-ass Defender.

He buzzed Gammarow.

"What's up?" answered a much more welcoming voice than the last one.

"I've a favor to ask," Abel said, getting straight to the point. That was how they operated. Gammarow hated long, emotional speeches and pleas, and Abel was happy to oblige him in that regard. He was a direct man and expected you to be as well, if you wanted to talk to him anyway.

"I don't do favors, buddy." He was also a bit of an ass.

"Things have come up and I may be disappearing for a while," Abel explained, ignoring the last comment.

"Whoa, not so many details! Geez, man, could you be any less specific?"

"That's the point," Abel continued, "I need you to relay a message for me to Cornelia."

"Okay."

"Weston."

"That's it? One word?"

"Yup."

"Right then. Weston."

"Thanks, man."

Abel went to close the channel when Gammarow continued. "So am I not invited?"

He was a lot sharper than he let on, Abel would give him that much. He liked to fight–a lot–and most took his lack of subtlety and discretion for ignorance but that wasn't the case.

"Why do you think you are the one I gave the message to?" Abel retorted with sarcasm he knew his friend would appreciate.

Gammarow laughed so hard it hurt Abel's ears. "Gotcha. We'll be seein' ya soon I'm sure," he signed off.

It was done. His goodbyes had been said in his own way and all preparations were complete. All that was left was for the battle to commence.

∞

Vladia stared into the space before her, now speckled with crafts and debris of various sizes and short bursts of brilliant blasts. The battle had begun and all she did was stand there watching. It didn't feel natural. She wanted to flee the bridge and take the first fighter she could find to dive into the fray. Yet here she must stand.

All the larger ships had to divert available power to weapons to prepare for the blast that her crew had begun calling the War-ending Blaze of Glory. For these large ships, it was not so easy to reroute power. So many things went into to making a ship this size run that it was tricky and dangerous to divert all power to one system. What they had to do was slowly transfer power to weapons, one system at a time, and leave each system at around ten to fifteen percent. This was so that if something were to go terribly wrong they could fix it.

This process would take about twenty minutes, so until then, the smaller crafts must hold off Luna's attack without any assistance from them. It was a lot to ask and many would die before the dreadnoughts and destroyers would report in ready to fire. The one, small, comfort was that it appeared not much more than a quarter of the fleet was cloaked. It seemed Luna had used up a great deal of resources in the last fight. Metamaterial was insanely expensive–too expensive for them to use on all their fighters ever again.

"What's the ETA on completion?" Vladia asked her lead systems operator.

"Nine minutes. Maybe Ten."

She kept telling herself there was no point in rushing. The *Spartan* couldn't fire until all ships checked in and the countdown began.

But she had to do something. "Get me a visual on Valkyrie *Gunnr*," she commanded to no one in particular. She didn't care if Abel was in her group or not.

"Scanning for him now. It might take a moment," a voice from the left hand side of the helm acknowledged.

She couldn't help him anymore, but at the least she could keep her eyes on him.

∞

"Nice shot, Jackson!" Abel yelled as another fighter disappeared from his tail.

"Shut yer mouth and fly right," was the gruff response.

Abel'd been taking it easy, flying more defensively than offensively, and his partner could see it. He needed to keep his damage minimal for his escape. If any of his storage compartments were hit, he wouldn't have enough supplies to make it to his destination.

Abel had to admit, Jackson was doing a damn good job at keeping fighters off him. He'd been worried, very worried actually, since Jackson's partner hadn't made it home from the last battle. But some things can't be helped no matter how good the pilot is.

Diving towards a Luna fighter hot on a Battle Cruiser's tracks, Abel blasted off a round to slow him down.

Once in reach, *Gunnr's* hands were on him and Abel fired point blank at the center hull.

He kicked the carcass away and was greeted with a static warble.

"Jackson?"

No response.

Abel scanned the area and with *Gunnr's* eyes found his partner being pursued by three Luna Fighters.

Jackson wasn't far and Abel made a mad dash for the assailants, firing as he did. He couldn't take three alone, not without a Defender to back him up.

Abel tagged the one closest to Jackson and that seemed to renew the older fighter's spirits as he spun around to meet the last two head on.

He charged the closer of the two and Abel arrived just in time to snag the last fighter, crushing one of its thrusters on contact.

The injured fighter whirled into a wounded 360 spiral, knocking Abel's grip loose as its wing clipped his chest.

Abel winced at the hit, but it wasn't serious enough to endanger his plans.

His prey fled and he didn't bother to chase after him. Instead he turned his attention back to his partner. The other ship was drifting in the distance, a hole blown through the cockpit.

"You alright?"

"Life support's at fifteen. Had to reroute to keep my thrusters," Jackson explained in a transmission still laced with static.

This was the window Abel needed. "Sounds like your comm took some damage too. Fly in for a quick patch up. I'll be fine till you get back."

Jackson grumbled in unhappy agreement and flew towards the nearest dreadnought.

"*Gunnr*. Systems report."

"All systems are at ninety percent or higher. Would you like specific breakdowns?" the computer offered.

"That's okay. As long as we are above ninety we can make it out of here just fine."

With his Defender no longer tailing him, Abel could make his escape. The main assault could be any second and he had to get out of here beforehand.

He had to make it look good though. It had to look like he'd been wounded and was drifting out to deep space. He needed a group of fighters near the edge of the battle. He'd fight lightly for a minute at the most, then with a short burst of thrusters in the right direction, he'd cut all power to one percent and drift. Once out of sensor range he could start back up and be on his way.

He scanned the area and found a dense skirmish between a dozen or so ships near the far edge of the main battle.

Perfect!

"Let's go, *Gunnr*," he commanded as he set his course.

Out of nothingness, shots fired his way, one hitting his left shoulder blaster.

"Shit," Abel muttered. He thought all cloaked vessels had been accounted for.

He didn't have time to be on the defense. He'd have to go all out and end this fast.

He maneuvered evasively while waiting for the short radiation burst to lock on to.

There it was!

Abel fire and missed.

This guy was good.

Abel continued to dart about. Standing still could spell instant death with a cloaked fighter this fast.

But he was running out of time. Abel fired all he had as he spiraled about. If he was lucky he'd nab the ship.

Luck paid off and a fighter burst from the shadows, barreling straight towards him. It was a Forerunner and by the way it moved it was a safe bet the pilot was Captain Gavril.

Abel swore again.

If it was Gavril there'd be no way to out-maneuver him. It'd be just like last time except there was no one to back him up now.

The forerunner slowed suddenly and just for a moment seemed to jerk about uncertainly before plunging straight for him.

It couldn't be Gavril, but either way it was on a collision course. There was only one thing to do. Abel held his ground and fired with all he had.

The Forerunner slowed to avoid most of the blasts, taking a few hits in non-critical areas, but still it pushed forward.

"Abel," *Gunnr's* voice sounded in his head, "Twenty seconds to impact."

Abel ignored the warning.

He'd get this guy. The closer the ship got, the harder it was for it to avoid Abel's shots. But that tactic worked both ways as Abel struggled to dodge as well.

He just needed to hold his position.

"Ten seconds."

The Forerunner was taking more hits now but he was

still coming, showing no sign of altering his course.

"Five seconds."

"Four."

"Come on, God dammit!" Abel screamed as sweat dripped from his forehead into his eyes.

"Three."

"Two."

"One."

∞

"Colonel, I can't find him."

"What do you mean you can't find him?" Vladia demanded, stepping closer to the lead nav officer.

"*Gunnr* is not showing up on any of our sensors."

"Are we out of range?"

"This ship can detect far beyond this battle ground, Colonel," the officer's tone grew solemn.

"He must be docked with another ship for repairs," she decided.

She didn't have time to think about what other conclusions could be drawn. Abel was fine and she had other matters to attend to.

"We're ready, Colonel," her lead systems solider announced.

"Very well, open a channel to the *Doppelganger*."

After a confirming nod from Commander Ramage she proceeded, "Grand Admiral Acadia, this is Colonel Robespierre. The *Spartan* has completed full power reroute and is ready on your mark."

"Acknowledged, Colonel Robespierre," a voice, not the Grand Admiral's, responded. "Countdown will commence once the remaining ships have checked in."

Vladia sighed. She wasn't last, and that was a good thing, but now remained an even more agonizing wait.

Her personal comm buzzed softly in her ear.

"Are you ready, Vladia?"

It was Tolen.

"Yes," she snapped. Of course he'd decide to show his face now, checking in to see if she was handling the stress of it all. "This isn't my first battle, Tolen," she said, hoping her informality disgusted him.

"This is your first war. The bloody vault shall soon shut on Luna, and the screams of nearly a half a million people will fall on our deaf ears. And then, the war will end and everything will return to normal. Almost," he whispered calmly.

"Lovely poetics. Is that all?" Vladia said impatiently. "If so, I'd like to keep the channels clear. The countdown will begin any moment."

"Of course. Good luck." The channel went silent.

What was that really about? she wondered. She'd expected him to be more provoking. She was certain Tolen would mention Abel; he was surely aware of the situation and could easily predict her concern. But he hadn't and that troubled her greatly.

"Comrades!" the Grand Admiral's clamor once again filled her bridge. "All ships have checked in and countdown will commence now. This war ends now."

The crew cheered.

"Ten, nine, eight…" the Grand Admiral began.

Vladia drew in a breath and held it. This was it.

This was the end.

"Three, two, one. Fire!"

The space before her cracked with five dozen bolts of luminous destruction. Vladia had to shield her eyes as the bright burn intensified. Nothing could survive this, she thought.

Even after the blasts stopped, the Lunar surface glowed with a blue-purple haze.

"Colonel..." an officer reported weakly, "The shield is still holding...at sixty percent."

Sullenness pervaded the bridge.

What did this mean? Was this defeat? That was all they had to throw at them. So sure had they been in their victory they didn't have the power to aid their fellow ships.

From the corner of her eye, Vladia spotted a slow movement. It was the *Iron Maiden*. She was changing her course.

"*Iron Maiden* on comm now!" Vladia ordered.

"Cornelia, what are you doing?" she demanded once the channel was open.

"I'm not doing anything. The ship just started moving," Cornelia's voice was steady, but traces of panic lingered in the background. "We've lost control of the helm completely. It's just like L4."

The ships at L4 had lost control after the station exploded; other than the nanobots, she remembered only the vaguest of details about the report. There was something else too. Something Tolen had said to her maybe?

"Leave the channel open, Cornelia. Nav, what's their course looking like?" she asked.

"I've sent out a warning to nearby ships," Cornelia added.

"Colonel! It looks like they're heading for Luna!"

"She's going to crash into the base..." Vladia uttered to herself.

The bloody vault shall soon shut on Luna, and the screams of nearly half of a million people will fall on our deaf ears.

God Dammit, Vladia swore to herself, an iron maiden is a bloody vault.

He had told her! Tolen had laid it out right in front of her and it didn't even register.

"Cornelia evacuate now!"

"We can't," the other woman's voice shook with an uncontrollable dread. It was a dread one would not experience with a swift, unforeseen death. This was the horror of watching death slowly creep towards you. It was the horror of looking death in the eyes and knowing your time would soon expire.

"We can't, Vladia. It's all locked down…"

The terror-filled cries of Cornelia's crew filled Vladia's bridge as the *Iron Maiden* drew closer to the Lunar surface; her own crew was growing uneasy at the sound.

Commander Ramage decisively switched the channel off.

"Keep that damn channel open!" she heard herself scream in an almost unhinged shrill.

"But, Colonel,–" the officer jumped to defend his action.

"I'm your commanding officer and I said to keep it open!"

The crew stared at her blankly, shocked by the outburst.

Vladia didn't care.

"If we don't hear their cries then who will? They deserve that much at least."

The crew seemed to understand now and the channel was reopened.

Sharp wails of desperation filled the bridge once again. Vladia stood firm in the face of her crew's apprehension. They needed to hear this.

"Cornelia, can you hear me?" Vladia's voice wavered. "Cornelia?"

There was no way she could be heard over the frightened crew. But she had to try any way.

"We're here with you, Cornelia."

She felt the tears welling up and made no effort to stop them. The woman warranted more than just her tears, but that was all she could give her.

The *Iron Maiden* sunk slowly into the Lunar surface, destroying much of the base with its impact. The cries of the crew were abruptly buried in static.

Vladia felt her body drop to its knees. She was shaking. Not with grief, but with wrath.

Planting her hands firming on the cool, bridge floor, she forced her body still. Letting the last of her tears fall to the ground, she pushed herself upright.

With a sharp nod to the comm, the channel was closed. Many of her crew bowed their heads in silent respect.

It was just like L4. It all hung together now. Tolen, the nanos, Ceres, L4. Abel had been right. And she could have stopped this if she'd not been so stupidly convinced her brother wouldn't soil his hands so much.

"Colonel. The shield is down. Should we fire?" her lead system officer asked tentatively.

"No." Luna would surrender any moment. There was no need for more death today. Except for one.

"Commander Ramage, this war is over. You have the bridge," Vladia marched away from her post.

"Yes, Colonel," Ramage said with a salute. "But, where are you going?"

There was no need for secrecy. "I'm boarding the *Dragoon*. Don't bother waiting for my return."

13

THE BUTTERFLY AND THE SPIDER

The pounding in her head and chest intensified, as Vladia marched down the *Dragoon's* corridors. The General's Office was close. She'd never been aboard this ship but the design was similar enough to her own that she found her path to be almost instinctive.

She passed a few officers on their way to the bridge for the champagne victory toast; they were too high off their fresh triumph to pay her any mind. Normally, they would be expected to step aside and salute a higher ranked officer. It was best this way. She didn't want her presence to be remarked on. If someone tried to stop her…

There. At the end of the hall. Nice and secluded from the rest of the ship.

Vladia withdrew her weapon, preparing to blast the door down, but as she grew close the door opened expectantly.

Without hesitation, Vladia stepped in and unloaded the rage she'd been cradling, "Tolen!"

The room was dark but he was here.

"Tolen!" she screamed again.

"Welcome, Vladia. You got here quicker than I expected," a voice taunted from the dark.

The walls' panel lights raised just above a dim glow. Vladia's eyes were swift to adjust as she scanned the room. Tolen was standing in front of his desk on the far end of the office, leaning on it casually, arms crossed over his chest.

Without a word, Vladia pointed her blaster at him, aiming for his smirking face.

Tolen smiled. "Really, Vladia? You're going to shoot me?"

"That has yet to be determined."

Tolen shrugged.

"You tell me why."

"Isn't it obvious? To end the war. It was the only way to end it today."

"And L4 too? How did that help do anything but rid you of a squad that in wartime would only preventing you from rising up in the ranks?"

"It was more than that. It was also a test run for today. Now, I am Earth's champion," he confessed readily.

"You're a murderer! All those people on that ship. All those people on that base–"

"All those people on that base would have gladly killed you without hesitation," he interrupted harshly; his smile vanished. "And all those people on that ship would have gladly died for Earth. Otherwise, they wouldn't have been on the battlefield in the first place. I'd wager by ending the war today I saved tens of thousands of lives that would have been obliterated in a war that drug out for months and months, which it seems is how you would have it."

Tolen pushed his body off the desk and took a few

steps closer. "I think you are the murderer, Vladia. After all, it is you who are pointing a gun at me."

Vladia tightened her grip on the blaster. She refused to succumb to his twisted logic. She wouldn't let his words affect her. She would not let him bend her will or provoke her to rash action.

He took another step towards her. "Stop!"

Tolen obeyed cordially.

"What would you have me do, Vladia? Does your self-loathing know no bounds? Should I have sent your ship crashing into the moon?"

"You should have sent your own!" she snapped.

"I'm sure in good time I, too, will die for Earth. But not yet. I have an agenda that must be seen to completion. The plans were set into motion long before you were a Valkyrie."

"With Ceres and that nano laboratory?"

Tolen remained silent.

"Abel was right to be suspicious of you."

"Abel has no clue as to what is going on. He's got good instincts, he's like a blood hound in that regard, but nothing more. I leave nothing to chance so there was never anything for him to find. He could do nothing," Tolen said, his wide grin returned to mock her. "You haven't the power to stop me either."

Vladia fired.

The blast scorched past Tolen's face, missing him by no more than an inch or two. She wasn't trying to hit him–not yet–just scare him.

"I'm pretty sure I can stop you right now," Vladia warned.

Tolen was unmoved. "You've got good aim. But that's not enough."

Again, he stepped closer.

They were still several meters apart and Vladia wanted to keep it that way. "I said stop."

This time he was not so quick to obey. He slowed, but continued despite the threat of her blaster.

"Everything I have done, Vladia, has helped to push you into becoming a better solider. Surely you see that? You've so much potential, and I want you to use it. We must stick together if we want to survive in this world. You and I are not like the others. We weren't raised ordinarily ergo we are not ordinary humans. We are extra-ordinary, you and I."

Tolen was mere inches away from her now, her gun planted firmly against his chest. She knew they weren't like the others. They had been isolated with their father while the other children of Earth were raised together by professionals properly trained by the state. They were atrocities in other's eyes. Abnormalities. That's why they had to hide it.

"This world can never understand the bond of our blood," Tolen continued.

Vladia shook her head fiercely, trying to shake his words from her ears. "None of this matters. Maybe we are extraordinary. Or maybe we're just monsters. But it doesn't excuse what you did. What you've been doing for God knows how long."

"You're right, Vladia. I've done terrible things, but they were necessary, terrible things. I'm not like these military dogs, craving blood and war simply for the sake of it. All I want is a peaceful, unified solar system. I don't like war. So, I ended it. Now I need you to help me rebuild everything. As my sister, my only blood, you're the only one who can do it."

Tolen pulled Vladia close. Wrapping his slender arms around her, he held her gently.

Her gun was still pressed between them, but it was now pointed towards the wall beside them.

Vladia knew she should push him away, like she had Abel. But she couldn't bring herself to do it. She didn't want him to let go of her. Tolen had been right: he was the only one like her. It was a fact that laid heavy on her soul. If she could fix him, if she could save him from sinking further, if he was redeemable then that meant…

"Vladia," he whispered softly in her ear, "This is the end."

A sudden, searing pain shot down her arm. Tolen gripped her right shoulder, digging his fingers into her still tender flesh. Her nerve endings erupted with agony and Vladia couldn't suppress the howl that leapt from her mouth.

She tried to wrench away but he kept her tightly pressed against his body.

"You're far too trusting," Tolen explained, still just above a whisper.

Vladia squeezed the trigger of her blaster, firing it wildly at the wall.

She forced her wrist towards him as much as she could and fired again, grazing his shoulder. If Tolen felt it, he showed no sign of it and only burrowed his fingers deeper into her flesh.

She could no longer see him. Everything was going white.

Her fingers loosened against her will and she heard the clank of the blaster as it hit the floor, then the grind of it against the ground as Tolen kicked it aside.

Vladia felt his abrupt release, then came a powerful

blow to her stomach that sent her flying back against the wall. Blood surged up from her stomach on impact.

"Vladia, I need you to listen to me." Tolen's voice was but an echo in her head and his frame but a dull outline against the foggy white.

"Once upon a time, there was a butterfly and a spider. The butterfly became entangled in the spider's web and when he approached to eat her, the butterfly begged for release. But, the spider explained, 'If I let you go then I shall starve and die. Your life is worth no more than mine and there is no way to save us both.' The spider held no malice and shed no tears as he devoured the helpless butterfly, for it was only in necessity that he killed.

"You came in here with no plan or forethought of what might happen and this is the price you pay, little butterfly," he taunted, kneeling down beside her. "There was nothing you could have done from the beginning. The nanos that hurled Cornelia Arnim's ship towards Luna came from your computer, not mine. I've left a nice copy of the files to be retrieved as evidence."

Gently, Tolen cupped her chin in his palm, lifting her face towards his. "And with your attempted assassination of me, and your recent demotion to altered human, the government will be swift in believing a once fine officer has become dangerously unstable. I know I told you I had those files sealed. The truth is I only had them delayed long enough for this all to come together."

Vladia felt his warm breath caress her cheek as he leaned in closer. "You just can't trust those altered humans; no better than robots, they'll say," he said before backing away.

She struggled to her feet but beyond that she couldn't move. The pain was too great. Her knees began to tremble and against her will she sunk back to the floor.

Footsteps rapidly approached from behind.

"General! The bridge reported shots fired in your office!"

"I'm fine. I managed to defend myself against her. Looks like we've found our culprit," Tolen said.

His voice was clearer now and her vision was coming back slightly. The nanos in her robotic arm were already beginning repairs. This did little for the pain, however.

"What should we do with her, General?" one of the officers asked.

"Bind her and escort her back to the base. I'll arrange for a transport to take her from there."

"Yes, Sir."

Two men scooped her up from the floor and bound her hands together, first at the wrist then at the elbow. Vladia winced at the movement, but the officers showed no concern. She hadn't expected any. They thought her a criminal. If she was in their shoes she'd behave no differently.

She tried to take a step and would have collapsed if not for the men's arms now encircling her waist.

"Carry her out if she can't walk. And send someone down to collect her weapon," Tolen firmly instructed.

One of them picked her up, tossing her roughly over his shoulder.

"Also, I've sent Rehel back to Earth to collect evidence from her quarters," he added, "but I fear he, too, may be involved. Have him apprehended as well."

"Yes, Sir," the officers acknowledged.

Vladia lifted her head as much as her body could bear. Staring back at Tolen, she thought she saw him smile once more before he turned his back on her.

∞

Rehel stepped into Vladia's quarters and proceeded directly to her personal computer. Per his orders, he inserted the data card and began transferring off all files.

It appears that Abel was wrong, Rehel decided. His friend had seemed sure Malthus's wrath would be directed solely at him; no one had even considered Vladia to be in any immediate danger.

Regardless, Malthus forced Abel's hand, accomplishing the goal of getting rid of Abel without having to lay a finger on him. This was proof in Rehel's eyes that at least some of what Abel had been suspecting was true, although there was no factual evidence to convince him of specifics. Malthus put a stop to Abel's snooping and that must be because there was something to be found against him.

Abel stressed Vladia's need to stay out of this from the very beginning. Rehel had thought otherwise, but Abel had certainly been correct in this matter. The order to obtain Vladia's files was unexpected, and with no explanation offered to him he could only guess at what had happened to alter the course of events.

For Malthus to go after Vladia, something major must have changed. In all likelihood, Vladia knew more than she was letting on and had become a threat to Malthus. It was safe to assume the loss of Cornelia's ship was the trigger to this chance of circumstance.

Vladia was sharp and her knowledge of Malthus was unknown. If she had figured something out involving her brother, with her rashness, Rehel wouldn't be surprised if she confronted the man head on. Whatever happened, it happened fast–too fast for Malthus not to have been prepared for it.

Rehel sat down at Vladia's desk. The transfer was extensive and would take some time. There was no telling what information had been planted on this computer and he was tempted to go through the data before turning it over. Yet this would be pointless. The last thing Rehel wanted was to put suspicion on himself as well. He didn't have the option to run away and he could not let himself be dismantled.

This brought up another dilemma Rehel had been trying to work through. The program from Vladia's computer that took control of the *Iron Maiden*–Rehel couldn't figure out how it got here. At first he assumed it must have been transferred remotely, but after close examination of the way the program operated, he decided that was impossible. The program had to be quite complex to begin with, meaning it was large. A remote transfer of a large file would have raised at least one eyebrow surely.

But even working under the assumption that no one noticed a large file transfer, that did not explain its precision in execution. A program could be set up to run at a preset time or after some sort of cue was sent to it.

However, the timing of this was perfect, just moments after the main blast. It was too precise to be coincidental and it was as if someone knew the blast wouldn't be completely effective so they planned to strike just after, as a finishing blow. Furthermore, the main blast could not have been predicated with such accuracy since there were many variables determining the timing of the blast.

This meant someone had to be here, in this very room, monitoring the battle so they could transmit the program to the *Iron Maiden* at the needed time. And there was the puzzle: no one had been in or out of this room except for

Vladia for weeks. Rehel had checked all the security footage on his way here and found nothing. All cameras were operational and there was no sign of tampering with the footage. There were the ventilation system entry points, but they weren't large enough for a human to maneuver through. So who had been here and how did they get in and out unnoticed?

Rehel stood up and walked the length of the room. What was most troubling was himself. He did not want to stay here and transfer files. He wanted to do something to help Vladia. If Abel was here, he'd no doubt have already taken action, but Rehel had orders and he could not break them. For lack of a better phrase, he felt anxious–distracted from the task at hand.

As long as he was given no specific order after this task, he could do as he needed within limits. First, he needed more information. The data transfer would not be complete for another ten minutes so he had time to do some research. Nothing official would be logged yet. If Vladia was still alive she'd be transported back to Earth so that was where he decided to begin.

There were many shuttles scheduled to be received within the next few hours. This wasn't surprising. Most ships would stay in orbit around Luna until a surrender agreement was reached. Although the larger ships had medical facilities, they were limited and the seriously injured needed to get back to Earth via shuttle.

The Kazan United Terran Military Base had thirty hangar bays: seven in each wing and one on the rooftop of the main building and one more in nearby open land owned by the military. The open land hangar was the largest, and only used by dreadnoughts and destroyers so that one could be ruled out completely.

Of the other twenty-eight scattered amongst the four wings of the base, three were being used as storage for ships still in repair and those with no current pilot. The remaining had multiple shuttles scheduled for docking on a fifteen minute rotation. These should be medical transports only. The last hangar, and the most isolated, had only one scheduled landing for the next two hours. That should be the one and it landed in fifteen minutes.

But what could he do about it? He had conflicting assignments. Abel's orders had been to protect Vladia. General Malthus' orders were to transfer Vladia's files immediately. This would incriminate her in some way, yet any order by Malthus outranked Abel's request. Then there was what he considered his original order. The order he could never disregard. All were in conflict with each other. The proper thing to do was to follow the highest ranked order and he should have no issue with this since Malthus' was clearly the highest in command.

Yet he could not.

Rehel yanked the data card from the computer, transfer still incomplete.

As he turned to leave, the door glided open revealing two officers in security attire.

They were armed.

"Robot Rehel?" the one on the left asked.

He nodded in response.

"If you are finished collecting the evidence files you need to come with us."

"I've not quite finished yet. This data card is full and I must obtain another to complete my task," the lie rolled off his tongue with ease. This terrified him to no end, but he knew exactly what was about to happen. They'd come for him. Malthus had his diagnostic report and now he'd use it to get him dismantled. Perhaps that had been the point all along: to have to power to terminate him immediately if needed.

He had to escape.

Rehel made to exit the room, when the officer on the right held up his hand. "I've a spare. Take it and finish up."

Rehel took the card and walked back to the computer. The two officers remained in the doorway, barring his only exit.

"This will only take a few more minutes," Rehel explained.

The officers made no response as expected.

Rehel stared at the computer, trying to think. It was more difficult than usual. His processes were slower than ever, though the human eye wouldn't be able to notice such a small variation. To him it was agonizing; time seemed to pass so slowly.

He had to get out, but he needed to do it without killing them and without them firing at him, causing the alarms to go off. He was faster and stronger and could certainly take them both by force, but the probability of one of them firing a weapon before they were unconscious was around sixty-five percent. He only had one shot and that was too large a probability to bet on.

Rehel suddenly recalled Ceres Forte's unfortunate encounter with the nanobots. This gave him an idea. He'd needed to get as many processes running on Vladia's computer as he could as it was transferring. Then, if he could get some of his nanobots in the system, it would surely short out. His nanos would be furiously trying to upgrade since they weren't accustomed to lower level computers. All of this combined should make at least a little noise and smoke and that's all he needed to distract his captors enough to disarm and immobilize them safely.

The two men at the door struck up a whispered conversation. Now their attention was divided.

Quietly, he started up all the processes he could. On top of the massive file transfer, the computer was already showing signs of strain. Now he had to get creative. He could get the nanos out of his body about as easy as a human could will the blood from their veins.

Cradling his right ring finger in his left hand, he broke the joint at the middle segment. That would get the nanos attention and extra ones would be diverted to address the repairs.

Still holding his wounded digit, he gave it a sharp twist and severed it from his body. He pressed the digit against one of the data slots. Once the nanos detected the underdeveloped computer they would rush to it. It shouldn't be long now.

"You done, yet?" barked one of the officers.

"The computer seems to be having some trouble with the transfer. It's slowed down. I'm afraid this may be some sort of defense mechanism implanted in the computer," Rehel explained, pocketing his injured hand.

"Well, you're a computer, so you can fix that one," the guard ordered.

"Sir, I am not programmed to work on low level computers such as this. You are probably more qualified to repair it than I."

This seemed to stoke the ego of the one on the left and he puffed his chest out. "Well, I did use to tinker with them before the academy. Lemme have a look."

The one guard moved closer while the other remained in the doorway. Rehel backed away graciously, giving the officer access to the key board. The officer set his weapon on the desktop as he took a seat, and then adjusting the setting, projected the view screen to encompass the area above the desk.

"Goddammit," he whispered.

"What's up?" the other officer called.

"It's gotta be a defensive reaction. The thing's running hot as hell. I need to shut her down somehow."

The desk sparked and gave the officer a jolt.

Rehel snatched his weapon from the desk and in one fluid motion hurled it at the other officer, smashing him square in the forehead, then with the same arm struck the last officer on the right temple.

The two men crumbled to the floor.

They wouldn't be out for long though. Using their own clothing, Rehel bound and gagged the unconscious soldiers.

He couldn't believe what he'd done. There was no turning back now and without another thought wasted on the two men, he walked out the door, locking it behind him.

He estimated he had up to twenty-five minutes before anyone would wonder why he had not reported in with his tasks complete. With only thirteen minutes left until Vladia's shuttle arrived, efficiency was essential.

The first thing he had to do was find *Freya*. A quick system scan of the three repair hangar registries gave him the ship's location. Luckily, the ship was in this wing. He could get there in about one minute forty seconds if he ran.

He needed a ship–an armed ship. Abel had given him *Freya's* key, though at the time neither knew the implication this would have. Rehel couldn't be sure he could pilot the thing. He would be breaking some of his most basic coding to do it and it might destroy him in the process. But he had to try.

Rehel slowed just as he reached the hangar bay entrance. It should be relatively empty. He stepped in and scanned for life signs. There were five, most likely technicians. If he only needed the ship he could sneak by them and launch before they knew what happened. But he'd need supplies too. He could do without weapons, but Vladia would need food and there was no getting around that.

He'd have to disable them.

He had access to various fighting forms, though he had of course never used them. Unlike a human, his lack of experience would not hinder him in this instance. The element of surprise was his and these were technicians, not soldiers.

Rehel walked to the center of the hangar. "Technicians, I have a message from Grand Admiral Acadia," he shouted.

Slowly, the men stopped their work to gather around him.

"Don't tell me he's asking us to go up? The work's hard enough down here," one of the younger men grumbled as he wiped droplets of sweat from his brow.

Three men in front of him. Two at his rear.

All unarmed.

"Nothing of the sort. Grand Admiral Acadia asks that you take a short break," Rehel began, again surprised at how easy this lie had escaped his lips.

Confusion played over each face.

"We don't take breaks, robot," a man who looked to be the head technician said, stepping closest to Rehel.

"My apologies. But you will today."

Rehel punched the man directly in the stomach, aiming for the celiac plexus. Before he had even hit the ground, Rehel grabbed the remaining two men in front and slammed their heads together.

Spinning around, he knocked the feet out from under the two behind him.

As their bodies landed, he wrapped one hand around each of their necks, putting pressure on the multiple nerve endings between the jaw and the ear.

In seconds they too went limp.

Rehel stood up and scanned the group. Vitals were stable but they'd be out for at least half an hour.

He wasted no time in dragging the men into the control room out of sight. He didn't have time to bind them, but the need was not pressing.

He made four trips to the supply closet, gathering rations only, and packed both *Freya's* leg compartments with as much as they could hold. There was a med kit on board already so that was taken care of.

Grabbing a pair of flight suits from the equipment rack, he removed his jacket and tugged one on, tucking the other under his arm. Last, he snagged a spare helm then headed to the control room.

One final item.

Inside the control room, he punched in the command to open the hangar for launch. It creaked and the ceiling began separating slowly. Even with the distraction of victory, it wouldn't be long before someone noticed an unscheduled launch and came to investigate.

His clock now ticked a little faster.

Rehel hurried back towards *Freya*.

Where are you running to, little tin man?

The words resonated inside his body. It wasn't so much a voice though. There was no sound. The words were just there, hanging in silence.

He froze in confusion, but as he tried to move he realized it was not him who stopped his actions. Something was holding him in place.

I said, where are you running tin man? Looks like nowhere now.

Rehel ignored it and continued to press closer to the Valkyrie. There were invasive nanobots in his system trying to attack his central-most systems.

He managed a shaky step closer. The strain on his structural core was evident. He tried to take another step, his body violently fighting the opposing force.

That's enough! Down!

Against his will, Rehel sank to his knees. His palms planted on the floor, he stared at the ground.

"Who are you?"

Who? Are you so sure I am a person? Perhaps this is more familiar: "You call Abel by his first name and I want you to do the same for me," it spoke in Vladia's voice. *"Or how about this: "I'll not need to worry about you... you're very self-sufficient and you've come along way,"* it said, switching to Abel's voice.

I can access your memory now. It won't be long before you shut down.

"Negative. It won't be long until you are shut down," Rehel warned.

The moment this cluster of nanos entered his body, the defensive program he'd made after the L4 attack kicked on. It took a minute to get going but already he could feel the invasive nanos losing their hold on him.

It remained silent, but Rehel could feel the rage of the

thing controlling the nanobots as it lost its grip on him.

He pulled himself up from the floor.

The nanos had done some damage, but nothing that his self-repair system couldn't handle.

The biggest mystery, the identity of the thing who'd tried to shut him down, would have to wait. For now, he had to press on with his plan.

Rehel climbed the ladder leading to *Freya's* cockpit and sat down.

It could all end here.

Removing the ignition key from his pocket, he inserted it and let the machine power on.

He checked fuel levels and oxygen first. Both were at full and with Mars' and Earth's current orbit putting them almost at their closest that'd be just enough.

The cerebral connectors humans used would do him no good, therefore he'd have to sync up with *Freya* as if he were running a system scan.

From underneath the main control board, he popped open a slim panel and pulled out a thin green cord. Rehel pulled the cording out as much as it would go. He opened his neck panel then plugged the cord in to the corresponding slot.

"Welcome. Preparing for system scan," *Freya* spoke to him.

"Wait," Rehel commanded. "I am not here to do a system scan."

Freya stopped preparations but said nothing.

"Your pilot, Vladia Robespierre, is in trouble and I need you to let me pilot. Can you sync with me through this connection?" he asked. Even if the ship granted him access, he may not be able to sync with the ship.

"Access Denied. You are not human. You are a machine," *Freya* responded.

"Yes. But this is the only way to aid your pilot. Can you sync with me through this connection?"

"Access Denied. I cannot sync via this connection."

"Will you allow me to pilot you manually?" this would slow him down, but he had six minutes still. He could make it.

After a short pause, *Freya* answered, "Access Granted. Manual Mode enabled."

A small victory. And his systems seemed stable so far.

Rehel strapped in.

Now all he had to do was fly.

∞

She was shown no special treatment. They'd loaded Vladia on a small prisoner of war transport. Two metal bars ran the length of the ship: one center on the floor and the other on the ceiling. Her feet were tethered to the floor bar and her wrist to the one above, forcing her to stand, arms raised above her head, for the entirety of the trip.

She knew what they were doing. It was physical just as much as psychological torture. They wanted to break her just a little more. If she wasn't in such a bind she might've laughed at this textbook method.

Her whole body throbbed from the trauma to her arm, but it was growing fainter by the minute. She couldn't help but feel this had all been planned from the start. He gave her this arm then used it against her. But her saving him in that battle couldn't have been part of his scheme. Tolen hadn't bet on needing saving and his annoyance at that had been clear. Vladia had altered his plans that day, but it seemed he had no trouble adjusting as he had in the past. Tolen had adapted to her reckless, impromptu behavior. It had been her only defense against him and he'd managed to nullify it.

He was in the past now. Tolen had given her up, like a sacrificial lamb, in his pursuit of power. She would not forgive him anymore. She'd defended him and knowingly turned a blind eye so many times. Vladia wanted to keep her Tolen alive–the one she wanted so much to be like. But that Tolen had never even existed; it was just another mask. She must remember this. She must take this anger and use it to her advantage. Newfound strength lay within it. And that was what she needed if she wanted a chance at escape.

But escape wasn't even a real possibility. She knew this. Tolen surely had worked out a response to any action she chose to take. Despite it all, her nature wouldn't allow her to simply give up. She was bound, guarded, injured and unarmed. Not a favorable hand. Still, she had to try.

If she was going to act she had to do it now. Once they landed, there would be no telling how many guns and guards awaited her. What she needed to do was take control of this ship and prevent it from landing.

The two men who had taken her from Tolen's office were escorting her to Earth. They sat in passage chairs, flanking her on either side, each had one visible blaster. The pilot was likely unarmed and the cockpit was closed off from the rest of the shuttle.

She could move her legs five inches in either direction but her arms were completely useless. From her current position she could not reach either man.

She'd have to get one to come to her.

"What's the ETA?" she asked.

No answer came. They weren't even looking her way.

"Not allowed to talk to me, huh?"

Still no response.

Vladia picked the meanest looking of the pair and spat at his feet. "Hey, Asshole, I asked you a question."

The officer stood up, careful not to step in the small pool of germs now festering on the floor. He was a good ten inches taller than her, but the man lowered his face to eye level. He looked kind of stupid but he was a strong guy.

"You say something, prisoner?" he growled. She heard him unsnap his holster and draw his weapon.

"Take it easy, Stan," the other man sounded worried. "We ain't supposed to talk to her so sit down."

Before his anger had a chance to subside, Vladia said, "Maybe you should sit down, Stan. Your ugly face is hurtin' my eyes."

Stan raised his weapon and Vladia slammed her skull into his.

Shots fired at the ceiling as Stan stumbled back and down. Vladia spun around as the guard behind her tried to leap up; she caught the bridge of his nose with her chin and set him right back down.

Neither man was unconscious, just dazed, probably seeing nothing but blur.

Vladia looked above her and saw the blasts had indeed hit the bar holding her arms captive. With a few quick jerks the bar broke and she slid her arm out from around it.

Before either man could fully recover, she bashed them both with the metal binding on her wrists.

Now they were out.

She hastily began rummaging through their pockets until she found the keys to unshackle herself. But she wasn't free yet; the shuttle still moved towards Earth just as if she was still bound up.

She grabbed one of the blasters and quickly adjusted its setting; Vladia would have to take the pilot. She was armed, but had forfeited the element of surprise, so it wouldn't be easy.

She shuffled towards the helm of the shuttle. Pressing the release, the door glided open and Vladia fired at the back of the pilot's chair.

She stepped in and was greeted by a blaster nozzle to the temple.

"Cold-blooded thing, shooting a man in the back." the pilot smirked. "Drop the weapon."

Vladia obeyed.

"It was set to stun," she explained.

"Sure it was," he grinned, kicking the weapon aside.

"We're about to break the atmosphere. Have a seat," he said, motioning to the pilot's chair.

Vladia sat, blaster still at her head.

"It's locked on auto now," he continued. "Even if you'd taken me this shuttle would still have delivered you to Earth."

She tried to think of a way out but with a blaster at her head she was helpless. She eyed the man carefully. His brown eyes were intense and sharp. He wasn't just any pilot, his white and gold uniform told her that much. This man was one of the Grand Admiral's personal guards. He remained standing and steady during the bumpy ride through the atmosphere.

This man would shoot her.

The rumbling of landing gear broke her line of thoughts. She was out of time.

"Get up and move out," he ordered.

They walked past the two still unconscious guards she'd taken down.

"Nice job on those two, by the way. With those skills you could have really made something of yourself."

"I don't suppose you'd believe me if I told you I'd been set up?" she ventured as a last resort.

The man laughed. "Not on your life."

Vladia shrugged and the two walked down the ramp at the tail of the shuttle.

It was night, but cloudless. Twelve armed guards awaited her in a single file line, weapons drawn.

Vladia hesitated. "What's your name?" she asked the man poised to shoot her.

"Commander Victor M. Whitlock, Special Forces Guard. I already know who you are," he responded cordially.

"Well then. Hope to see you again, Commander Whitlock. Under better circumstances, of course," she said taking her first steps toward the dozen guards ready to toss her in the brig until further orders were given.

"Indeed, Colonel Robespierre," he replied with a salute.

Vladia was halfway to her new captors when a barrage of fire came from the sky. Instinctively, Vladia hit the ground.

The blasts continued and then a deafening explosion. She looked back. The shuttle she'd been on was a smoldering pile of fiery debris.

She spotted Commander Whitlock on the ground nearby. He'd been the closest to the shuttle and he was injured but not dead. She was oddly relieved at that.

The other guards scattered in confusion. Some firing, some running for cover.

A massive thud shook the ground around her. Daring

to look up, a giant loomed over her, casting a shadow all around her.

Vladia's eyes adjusted and she realized it was her ship– *Freya*!

The guards, now recovered from their initial shock, fired at her ship and at her. The Valkyrie bent over, shielding her from the blasts.

The cockpit opened and a hand emerged.

"Abel," she cried as she reached out.

But it wasn't Abel.

For a moment everything seemed to stop. The blasts around her slowed and grew quiet. She swore she could hear her own heavy breath. Her outstretched hands locked in time, inches from the one extended to take hers.

Nothing moved.

"Vladia," Rehel instructed, "Take my hand."

The world around her returned with a sudden rush. She grabbed hold of him and the robot lifted her inside.

The cockpit shut as the blasts continued.

"Hold on to something," Rehel warned as the thrusters lifted them off the landing pad.

Vladia watched from the floor as the robot piloted her ship away from the base. He'd saved her. Somehow.

It wasn't until they'd cut through the atmosphere and were surrounded by space, that Vladia realized she was clutching the robot's leg. She let go, embarrassed, but Rehel hadn't noticed.

They didn't appear to be followed. Much of the fleet was still at the battlefield and nothing on Earth at the moment should be fast enough to catch them in *Freya*.

"You seem to know where you're going," Vladia said, aiming for a steady voice and failing.

"We're following Abel. I do not have his exact course,

but I can get close to it."

"He's alive?"

"I assume so, though I cannot verify it. I monitored his actions during battle so I could follow if the need arose. He was attacked just before he vanished. That was not part of the plan." Rehel paused and pulled up a sector map on the main screen. "We will travel to this point, then based on his last known trajectory, we'll plot a course to Mars."

"Okay," she nodded.

Vladia couldn't go back to Earth and from the looks of it neither could Rehel or Abel. These two had a plan obviously, but now was not the time to ask.

She reached up to checked some of *Freya's* gauges, when out of her peripheral a glint of gold caught her eye. Wedged in the zipper of Rehel's flight suit was a small locket.

Vladia freed the trinket and as she cradled the relic in her palm, she felt her face grow hot.

Before she knew it, her arms were around him. She buried her face in his shoulder, fighting hard against the urge to cry.

Rehel let her hold him, all the while continuing to pilot the ship flawlessly.

He'd been here all this time. She had never once let herself belief it could be him. The chances were so small; to even hope would have been foolish. Vladia never wanted to let him go.

She loosened her grip on him enough to face him.

"Listen," Vladia began when she was sure her voice would not waver. "I'm not gonna ask how you did all this. But thanks for doing it. Thanks for coming for me."

Rehel shifted his eyes to meet hers. "A long time ago

you ordered me not to die. You said I was yours and you gave me that order. At that moment, I was your property. The military had not officially seized possession of me and since your mother was dead I was, briefly, part of your inheritance," he explained. "To me, that seemed to be the overriding order. The order above all others."

"But what you did back there. You could have been killed."

"Yes. But I decided that if I couldn't protect you, then I wasn't worth the order you gave me."

Vladia planted a firm kiss on his forehead. Her hands drifted again to the locket resting at his chest.

"You and I are criminals now," Rehel began. "That means we are free of all obligations to Earth. More importantly, this means the right to ownership now belongs solely to you again. I am yours."

Vladia glided back to the floor. "You are only mine if you want to be, Rehel."

"There is no questioning that. Vladia, I am yours."

Nodding in approval, Vladia suddenly felt exhaustion creep upon her.

She tethered herself down behind Rehel and closed her eyes. Her happiness at finding Rehel and being free soon faded, and the only thought that now plagued her uneasy mind was of a single man: Malthus.

14

WHAT MIGHT HAVE BEEN

"Why did you let them go?" a woman's voice resounded in Tolen Malthus's quarters.

Malthus, who'd been laying peacefully on the brink of slumber, now propped himself up on his elbows. "Who says I let them go?"

"I do."

"I suppose I did," he admitted. "But only because my goals were met by either condition."

"What do you mean?" the woman's voice prodded.

Malthus pushed the covers off and sat up. "I needed Vladia out of the picture and she is. Whether she is dead, imprisoned in the catacombs below us, or simply cannot return to Earth doesn't matter to me," he explained.

"I feel like it was a wasted effort. I put my all into setting her up for you. Traveling between systems like that isn't pleasant. And then you just let her go."

Malthus remained dispassionate to the accusations; it was important to be on good terms with her for now. He could mention her failure at eliminating Abel during the battle, or her dismal attempt to stop Rehel from obtaining a Valkyrie. But he refrained from ridicule, as it would only lead to a more lengthy discourse that he had no interest in.

"It was the only way to implicate her completely and you ensured she can't come back. It was certainly not a waste of time," Malthus said. He was also getting rather tired of her popping in whenever she liked. He'd have to limit her access without hurting her feelings.

It was true, though. He could have pursued her and the robot; it was likely he could have caught them too. But that wasn't the reason for any of this. That actually would have been wasted effort.

The point of it all was beyond her understanding. He hadn't counted on her being capable of stopping Rehel from getting to Vladia in the first place. He really just wanted to see what would happen. It was a test, and just like at L4, the results were quite advantageous. Her botched job with Abel also confirmed one more item for him. But that was an issue that need not be dealt with for some time.

"What about the robot? You won't be able to observe any further adaptations," she persisted.

At that, Malthus frowned. It was a shame he had to give Rehel up. In the grand scheme of things, it was an inevitable event that was crucial for the rest of his plan to progress.

"I have all I need from the robot. And be it now or later, his condition will destroy him."

After a heavy sigh, he added, "Now if you don't mind. I, unlike you, still need sleep."

"One more question. Then I'll let you alone, I promise."

"Okay," he resigned as he slipped under the covers. He wondered if this was what it was like to be contracted to a woman. First thing in the morning, he swore, her access would be restricted during the night.

"When will my body be complete? I don't like it in the system, Tolen."

"It will be ready when it is ready. The work is slow and you know why. You are the first and you ought to be more grateful," he said, trying not to be cross with her impatience. "You would have died with your human body if not for my research."

Malthus plucked the middle book from his limited collection in the wall recess beside his bed. He let his fingers trace the indention of the author and title on the cover: *Maria Robespierre, Essays and Research on the Robot Psyche: Progress and Implications*. A banned book; he'd confirmed that this was indeed the only copy left.

He thought back to his childhood when he'd planned to give this to Vladia that time in the library. He'd been kinder as a child and felt a bit sorry for her. Secretly, he'd even hoped they'd become friends. Malthus had no interest in the book back then. How different things might have turned out if he'd decided to give her the book after all.

"I'm sorry," the voice interrupted his reminiscence. "I just get frightened. The longer I'm in here, the more I feel that I won't be human when I finally get out."

"You say that like it's a bad thing."

Malthus tucked the book away and rolled onto his side. "I'm going to sleep. Goodnight, Isobel."

"Goodnight, Tolen."

The End

ABOUT THE AUTHOR

Kimberly S. Daniels currently teaches English Composition and Literature at the University of South Alabama. Her hobbies include writing, reading, more writing, and saving ALL the animals in the world. She lives in Mobile, Alabama with her awesome husband, capricious daughter, two goofy pit bulls, one hyper poodle and a very wicked cat.

www.ingramcontent.com/pod-product-compliance
Lightning Source LLC
LaVergne TN
LVHW091116080826
845145LV00008B/1938

* 9 7 8 0 6 1 5 7 5 1 1 9 1 *